He deepened the kiss,
tasting her in a carnal caress that
inflamed all her senses . . .

Tea and Temptation

"If you're looking for your secretary," a feminine, distinctly American voice drawled behind him, "he's making me a cup of tea."

Denys took a breath, telling himself he had to be mistaken. But when he turned, one glance at the tall, voluptuous redhead standing in the doorway of his office confirmed that his ears had not deceived him. Teal-blue eyes studied him between half-closed lids. The look was one of smoldering sensuality that on any other woman might have been calculated, but for Lola, was as natural as breathing.

How many times, he wondered, had he lain in her bed, his body sated, his mind drowsy, watching her at her dressing table? How many times had he seen her draw gossamer stockings up her shapely legs and dab jasmine scent to the satiny skin at the backs of her knees? Dozens, he guessed. He'd thought those days would never end, but they had ended, and with bone-shattering shock.

The glimmer of anger he'd felt earlier flared up again, burning his insides, making him feel as if he'd just taken a swallow of cheap whiskey. Although that probably wasn't a very apt analogy, for Lola had never been cheap. In fact, she'd probably been the most expensive mistake he'd ever made. And by far the most intoxicating . . .

By Laura Lee Guhrke

No Mistress of Mine
Catch a Falling Heiress
How to Lose a Duke in Ten Days
When the Marquess Met His Match
Trouble at the Wedding
Scandal of the Year
Wedding of the Season
With Seduction in Mind
Secret Desires of a Gentleman
The Wicked Ways of a Duke
And Then He Kissed Her
She's No Princess
The Marriage Bed
His Every Kiss
Guilty Pleasures

Laura Lee Guhrke

No MISTRESS of Mine

An American Heiress in London

AVONBOOKS

An Imprint of HarperCollinsPublishers

NO MISTRESS OF MINE. Copyright © 2016 by Laura Lee Guhrke. All rights reserved. Printed in the United States of America. No part of this book may be used or reproduced in any manner whatsoever without written permission except in the case of brief quotations embodied in critical articles and reviews. For information, address HarperCollins Publishers, 195 Broadway, New York, NY 10007.

First Avon Books mass market printing: September 2016

ISBN 978-0-06233467-1

Avon Trademark Reg. U.S. Pat. Off. and in Other Countries, Marca Registrada, Hecho en U.S.A.
Avon, Avon Books, and the Avon logo are trademarks of HarperCollins Publishers.
HarperCollins® is a registered trademark of HarperCollins Publishers.

16 17 18 19   QGM   10 9 8 7 6 5 4 3 2 1

For Mom, because I love you.
Always and forever.

No
MISTRESS
of Mine

Chapter 1

April, 1892

 "Good God!"

This emphatic oath on the part of Earl Conyers was startling enough to catch the attention of all the members of his family. The earl, as they well knew, was not a man given to profanities, particularly this early in the day.

All of them paused, knives and forks poised, but their attention seemed to go unnoticed. Conyers continued to stare at the letter in his hand and did not explain what news within its pages had caused this sudden inclination to swear at breakfast.

His son, Denys, was the first to break the silence. "Father, what is it? What's happened?"

Conyers looked up, and his expression told Denys the news was every bit as shocking as his outburst had implied.

He waited, but when his father folded up the letter, tucked it back into its envelope, and placed it in the pocket of his jacket with a glance toward the ladies, Denys concluded there was a need for discretion and returned his attention to his breakfast.

"Do you have plans for luncheon?" his mother asked, and when he looked up, he found her watching him with a look he knew quite well. "I'm meeting Georgiana and her mother, so we can discuss the flower show. We'll be dining at Rules, which is close to your offices. Would you care to join us?"

His lips curved in a wry smile. "You're matchmaking, Mama."

"Well, I am your mother." Lady Conyers gave a sniff. "Mothers are allowed to do that."

"Where is that rule written? I should like to look it up."

"Don't be impudent, Denys. And if I were matchmaking, it's not as if I've no cause. I saw you dance with Georgiana at the Montcrieffe ball. Two waltzes," she added with obvious relish.

"True." He gave a heavy sigh of mock suffering. "Given that, I suppose I've no right to complain."

"If you don't want to go, Denys . . ." Her voice trailed off as she looked at him in hopeful inquiry.

He thought of Georgiana, and an agreeable fondness settled over him. "On the contrary," he said. "I should be delighted."

"Oh, I'm so glad!" The moment those words were out of her mouth, she bit her lip and looked away, as if fearing her effusiveness was a step too far. "Georgiana is a dear child."

From her place beside their mother, Denys's sister, Susan, gave an exasperated sigh. "Really, Mother! Georgiana Prescott is hardly a child. She's twenty-eight, the same age I am. Though I daresay she seems older."

"She's more mature, at any rate," Denys put in, giving his irrepressible sister a meaningful glance.

"Either way, she's a dear child to me." Lady Conyers leaned closer to her daughter. "And so are you, pet."

The earl interrupted Susan's groan of reply by setting down his knife and fork. "Forgive me, ladies," he said, rising to his feet, "but I fear I must be off. Denys, might you join me in my study for a spot of business before I go?"

"Of course." He rose, but Susan's voice interrupted before the two men could depart.

"Was the letter very bad news, Papa?"

"No." The reply was terse, and the earl must have sensed it, for his expression softened as he looked at his daughter.

"It's nothing to trouble you with," he said, but even before Susan spoke again, Denys could have told his father that sort of pacification never worked with his sister.

"Don't you want to pat me on the head before you go?" she called after him, as he started for the door.

"He likes patting you on the head," Denys told her as he circled to her side of the table. "So let him."

"But it's silly," she grumbled, tilting her head so he could kiss her cheek. "Why do men always feel impelled to shield women from the slightest hint of reality?"

"Because we love you, that's why." Denys turned to give his mother's cheek a kiss as well. "It's our duty to protect you."

"Rot," Susan pronounced, as he straightened and started for the door. "The truth is, you men like keeping all the important information to yourselves because it makes you feel superior."

He didn't reply, but Susan was not deterred. "We shall ferret out this secret," she called after him. "We always do."

Both men ignored that rather aggravating fact of life and crossed the corridor to the earl's study without a word. Once inside, the door safely closed behind them, Denys was able to reopen the topic. "Now, tell me what's happened."

Lord Conyers moved to sit behind his desk and pulled the envelope from his jacket pocket. He started to hand it across the desk, but then, for no discernible reason, he drew back.

"Father, what the devil is it?" Denys asked. "I'm beginning to find your reticence alarming."

"It's about Henry Latham."

At once, unbidden and unwelcome images of Lola Valentine came into his mind—Lola on stage, in her dressing room, in his bed. Lola in a sheer white peignoir with Henry by her side. He took a breath and forced himself to speak. "What about him?"

"He's dead."

The announcement struck Denys with the impact of a rock thrown at a mirror, and the images of Lola shattered into glittering shards of anger, slicing open a wound he thought had healed long ago. Six years since she'd left him, but suddenly, he felt as raw as if it had all happened yesterday.

"Shocking news, what?"

The matter-of-fact voice of his father brought Denys back to the present, and when he noticed the earl's concerned gaze on him, he tamped down anger and pain. "Very shocking," he agreed. "When did this happen?"

"A month ago."

"A month? Why weren't we informed at once?"

The earl shrugged. "The letter is dated three weeks ago. It was delayed in the post, I imagine."

"May I?" He held out his hand, and after a moment of further hesitation, his father leaned across the desk to place the letter in his outstretched palm.

"Does it say how he died?" Denys asked, slipping the missive out of its envelope.

"Heart attack, so Forbes says. Henry had a dicky heart, apparently."

"Heart?" Denys paused in the act of unfolding the letter, taken aback. Henry had always been such a vital, dynamic personality. The idea of his having a weak heart seemed incongruous somehow.

He looked down at the letter, but he stared at the typewritten lines without reading them. Had she stayed with him all this time? he wondered. All the way to the end?

The wound opened a little more, and Denys reminded himself that Henry and Lola were part of his past, a distasteful business long ago over and done. He refolded the letter, unread, put it back in its envelope, and set it on the desk.

"The question is," he said as he leaned back in his chair, glad to note his voice was quite natural, "what happens now?"

"To the Imperial, you mean?" Looking relieved, his father at once adopted a brisk, practical demeanor that mirrored his own. "What do you think should happen to it?"

Denys paused to consider for a moment before he spoke, just to be sure his opinion was a thoroughly objective one. "We should offer to buy Henry's share," he said at last.

"I agree. But would she accept such an offer?"

Denys couldn't see any reason why Henry's widow wouldn't jump at it if the offer was fair. "Her life is in New York. She wouldn't want to assist with managing it, surely."

"Perhaps not, but thanks to you, the Imperial has become profitable. She might want to keep her half as an investment."

Denys doubted that Gladys Latham would have any more enthusiasm for Henry's theatrical ventures now than she'd had when he was alive. "Or she might jump at the chance to get rid of it."

"True. But if she's not amenable to selling her share, we might consider allowing her to purchase ours."

Denys stared at his father, appalled by the very idea. "Sell our half of the Imperial? Why on earth should we do so?"

Conyers stirred in his chair. "Might be for the best."

"I don't agree."

Conyers gave him a searching glance. "It's a difficult situation. For her. For you. For everyone."

Denys stiffened, knowing his father's true concerns had nothing to do with Gladys Latham. "Henry's death changes nothing, as far as I can see. My unfortunate entanglement with Lola Valentine is long over, Father, and has no bearing on this. I daresay everyone involved will be sensible. The Imperial is one of our most lucrative investments. It makes much more sense to keep it, don't you think?"

"No, I don't. If we can't buy her out, I'll sell her our share. Let her have the whole bloody thing."

His father's terse, peremptory words surprised him. Since handing over the control of their family holdings to him three years ago, Conyers had never overridden him on any decision.

"You seem . . . quite vehement about this, Father."

"Should I not be?"

"Not for any reason I can discern. I thought you trusted me. Have I given you cause to withdraw that trust?"

The earl's shoulders slumped a bit. "No, of course not," he said, and leaned back in his chair with a sigh. "I spoke in haste. However you decide to handle the situation, it is your decision. I . . ." He paused and took a breath. "I trust you."

Denys was relieved and heartened by those words. "You didn't always."

"No, but in my defense, there was a time when you made my trust a difficult thing to give. You were quite wild in your youth, you know."

The reminder pained him, for he was well aware he'd been a rebellious adolescent and a rakish, irresponsible young man. Those less appealing traits of his character had come into full flower on a trip to Paris the summer he was twenty-four.

His only intent had been to visit friends and have a bit of fun. He hadn't intended to go mad.

Nicholas, the Marquess of Trubridge, and Jack, the Earl of Featherstone, had been sharing a town house in Paris and vying for the attentions of Montmartre's most famous cabaret dancer. Fascinated by her, they'd dragged Denys off on his first night in town to see her show at the *Théâtre Latin*, and the moment he'd first set eyes on Lola Valentine, Denys's heart had been lost and his life plunged into chaos.

Lola, in Paris, kicking off men's hats with her toe and winking at him as she passed his table and absconded with his drink. Lola, at the house he'd leased for her in London, standing at the top of the stairs and giving him the radiant smile for which she was famous. Lola, moving beneath him in bed, her dark red hair spread across the pillow and her long, shapely legs wrapped around him.

It had taken a lot of time and effort to straighten out his life after she'd forsaken him for Henry Latham and a career in New York, but he'd managed it, and the careless, stupid mistakes of his youth were well behind him now. With that reminder, Denys brought his attention back to what his father was saying.

". . . sowing your wild oats, with no mind to settle down and be responsible. I had truly come to despair of you. But you've changed, Denys. You've paid off your debts, taken on the duties of your position, and done everything I've asked of you in exemplary fashion. I'm proud of you, my son."

With those words, any vestiges of Lola's memory vanished, and tightness squeezed his chest as he stared back at his father. He was unable to say how much those words meant to him, but thankfully, he didn't have to say anything. His father looked away first, gave a cough, and spoke again.

"Whatever you decide, it will be your decision. You're in charge now. I am merely a gentleman of leisure."

"And you love it," Denys said, smiling.

"I do. I am quite content to leave the tedious business of keeping our fortunes intact to you."

"Speaking of which . . ." Denys glanced at the clock on the wall and stood up, bringing his father to his feet as well. "I'd best be on my way. I have a meeting with Calvin and Bosch at half past nine to sign some contracts, but I have to call at our offices first. All the contract documents should have arrived from our solicitors late yesterday afternoon—"

"Didn't I just tell you these matters are your concern now, not mine?" the earl interrupted, holding up his hands to stop his son's flow of words. "All I intend to do today is go to my club and perhaps a race meeting or two."

The two men departed the study and went their separate ways, but an hour later, as Denys's carriage took him around Trafalgar toward his offices in the Strand, he recalled his father's final words of their conversation, and he couldn't help smiling a little. The earl was bored stiff by matters of business, but Denys thrived on them.

Not that he'd always felt that way. A few years ago, he'd been the sort of fellow who'd spent his quarterly allowance without a thought of where the money came from. The sort who'd found the allure of a beautiful cabaret dancer irresistible.

But his days of being a stage-door johnny were over. Pulled by Nick into a brewery investment three years ago, he'd begun to understand the satisfaction that could come from being a man of business, and the earl, pleased by his son's newfound sense of responsibility, had handed over management of all the family's investments to him.

His carriage turned onto Bedford Street and came to a halt in front of his offices. His driver opened the door for him, but after exiting the vehicle, Denys paused on the sidewalk to study the building across the street, and he felt a fierce wave of pride at the sight of the Imperial's gray granite facing and marble columns.

The Imperial had been a seedy music hall fifteen years ago, when the earl and Henry Latham had first formed a partnership to acquire the place. Henry, already a successful impresario in New York, had been seeking ways to break into dramatic theater in London, and with the earl as a partner, he had succeeded in obtaining the required licenses, finding backers, and garnering a bit of success. But London theater was an exasperating, difficult, competitive business, and the American had eventually grown tired of the project and returned to the States, taking Lola with him and leaving management of the Imperial in his partner's hands.

The earl had happily put his son in charge of the place, along with all the other Conyers's holdings, and Denys was proud of the fact that there was nothing seedy about the Imperial nowadays. Today, it was widely acknowledged as London's finest producer of Shakespearean theater, achieving a level of critical acclaim Henry could only have dreamed of.

Thoughts of Henry inevitably brought thoughts of Lola, and an image of her came to Denys before he could stop it—an image of auburn hair, teal blue eyes, and a body made for sin.

More memories came back to him, memories of how it had all gone wrong. The play he'd financed for her closing in disaster. The house in St. John's Wood standing empty but for the gifts he'd given her and a note that she'd returned to Paris. His refusal to accept her departure, his journey to the cabaret where she was working, his discovery of Henry with her in her dressing room. And her words, the most shattering part of it all.

Henry has made me a better offer.

Denys shook his head, baffled that he could ever have been such a fool. But then, he appreciated with a grimace, he'd been a fool about so many things back in his salad days. Thank God he was not only an older man now but also a wiser one. Beautiful, ambitious chorus girls no longer held any charms for him.

He turned away from the Imperial to study the building across from it. Five floors high, with whitewashed brick, marble pediments, and arched windows of plate glass, the offices of Conyers Investment Group gleamed with prosperity.

The message conveyed by the interior was equally clear. Anyone would know at once that this was a sound and prosperous firm. Its electric lift, telephones, and typewriting machines alluded to modern ideas and the future, but the wide central staircase, the ever-so-slightly-worn carpets, and the comfortable leather furnishings conveyed reliability and longevity, two qualities so necessary to an investment firm.

Denys started up the staircase, nodding to the clerk seated at the desk on the spacious landing as he passed. When he reached the mezzanine, he circled the lobby and ascended another set of stairs, but he'd barely entered his office suite on the top floor before he came to a surprised halt.

His secretary was not at his desk. "Dawson?" he called to the open doorway of his own office beyond, but his sandy-haired young secretary did not reply and did not appear.

With a puzzled frown, Denys pulled out his pocket watch. "Ten past nine," he murmured, closed the watch, and slipped it back into his waistcoat pocket. Dawson was fanatically punctual, always arriving in the office ahead of his employer, a fact that made his absence from his post quite unusual.

Not that it mattered. If Dawson had been called away from his desk, he would no doubt have set out the contracts before departing. Denys glanced over the secretary's desk, but the documents were nowhere to be seen.

He gave an exasperated sigh. "Where is the fellow?"

"If you're looking for your secretary," a feminine, distinctly American voice drawled in answer to his muttered question, "he's making me a cup of tea."

Denys froze in disbelief, for that voice was low, earthy, dipping on the vowels, and somehow able to lend an erotic note to what would otherwise be the rather flat accent of America's Middle West. It could only belong to one woman.

He took a breath, telling himself he had to be mistaken, but when he turned, the tall, voluptuous redhead standing in the doorway of his office proved he'd made no mistake.

Her hair was the same deep, flaming color he remembered, a shade of red most women could only gain from henna dye. Atop those vibrant curls, an enormous con-coction of pink feathers, crimson ribbons, and cream-colored straw was perched at an angle that defied all laws of gravity, and below it was the stunning face he'd hoped never to see again. Her eyes were the same vivid teal blue he remembered, her full lips the same deep pink. In the staid, ascetic atmosphere of his offices, she bloomed with vibrant life, like an exotic cactus flower blooming amid the sand and scrub of the desert.

He took a step closer, scanning her face, but the powder she wore prevented him from seeing the freck-les that dusted her nose and cheeks. It didn't matter, though, for he knew they were there. He ought to. He'd kissed every one of them.

How many times, he wondered, had he lain in her bed at the little house in St. John's Wood, his body sated, his mind drowsy, watching her apply powder to her face, trying to conceal the freckles she despised? How many times had he watched her draw gossamer stockings up her shapely legs and dab jasmine scent to the backs of her knees? Dozens, he guessed. Perhaps hundreds. He'd thought those halcyon days would never end, but they had ended, and with bone-shattering shock.

Looking at her, he thought of the last time he'd seen her, in her Paris dressing room. Everything came back to him as if it had all happened yesterday—the filmy white peignoir she'd been wearing, the opened cham-pagne on the table, her face pale as milk at the sight of him. And Henry on the settee, smiling and triumphant.

The anger he'd felt earlier began to burn inside him,

as if he'd just downed a glass of cheap whisky. Although that wasn't really an apt analogy, for Lola had never been cheap. On the contrary, she'd been the most expensive mistake he'd ever made. And the most intoxicating.

His gaze lowered before he could stop it. She still had the same generous curves he remembered, curves shaped by years of dance, curves that he suspected still owed little to corsets and nothing at all to bust improvers, pads, or bustles.

She was wearing a frock of pale pink silk, and he couldn't help noticing how the color of the dress blended seamlessly into the skin of her throat and jaw. Any other woman, he thought in chagrin, would look maidenly, even innocent, in such a color, but not Lola. Pale pink silk only made Lola look . . . naked.

Denys wasn't usually one to curse, but in some situations, an oath was the only response a sane man could offer.

"Hell," he muttered, but the word seemed wholly inadequate as a vent to his feelings. "Damn," he added, and was still not satisfied. "Damn, and blast, and holy hell!"

She smiled a little. "It's good to see you, too, Denys."

The sound of his name on her lips was like paraffin on hot coals, and all his suppressed anger blazed up, threatening to burn out of control. He pressed a fist to his mouth, working to contain it.

"Aren't you going to say something?" she asked after a few moments. "Beyond a few choice curses, that is?"

He lowered his hand and took a deep breath. "It's odd," he murmured, injecting a level of cool detachment into his voice that he didn't feel in the least, "but I cannot think of anything more I might wish to say to you."

"'Hello' might be a good start," she suggested. "Or you could ask how I've been."

He set his jaw, hardening his anger into resolve. "That question would imply a degree of curiosity I do not possess."

Any trace of a smile vanished from her face with that cold reply. He was being churlish, he knew, a demeanor not at all in keeping with his position or his upbringing, but what had she expected? A warm welcome? Fond recollections of the old days?

She cleared her throat, breaking the silence that had fallen between them. "Denys, I'm sure my call today has caught you by surprise, but—"

"On the contrary. The day you stop being unpredictable is when I shall be caught by surprise. Capriciousness, after all, is part of a mistress's stock-in-trade, isn't it?"

That shot hit the mark, he could tell. A flash of answering anger showed in those extraordinary eyes, reminding him that Lola was not only a redhead, she also possessed the passionate temperament often associated with hair of that shade. "I wouldn't know," she countered with asperity, "since I was never your mistress. I was your lover."

He shrugged, in no frame of mind to debate the

rather blurred distinctions of their past relationship. "And which were you with Henry? His lover, or his mistress? Or were the two of you just good friends?"

She flinched, but if he thought such caustic questions would send her scurrying off, he was mistaken. Instead, she lifted her chin and stood her ground.

"Is there any point in rehashing the past?" she asked. "It's really the future we need to talk about, isn't it?"

"The future?" he echoed, baffled. "What do you mean?"

That question seemed to take her back though he didn't know why it should. "But surely you knew—" She broke off, catching her full lower lip between her teeth, staring at him for a moment before she spoke again. "You haven't heard."

He frowned, feeling suddenly uneasy. "I heard Henry is dead if that's what you mean."

"It isn't . . . quite."

"Is that why you're here? Now that Henry's gone, you want to take up where we left off?" He knew it was absurd even as he said it, and yet he could not imagine any other reason for her presence or her words about the future. "You want me to take care of you?"

"No man takes care of me," she countered with asperity, reminding him of the scrappy, saucy girl he'd met so long ago, a girl who'd kept him at arm's length for over a year and driven him nearly mad before at last becoming his. "I take care of myself. I thought I made that clear six years ago."

"So you did, and yet, Henry seems to have taken care

of you nicely. From what I hear, the show he backed for you is quite the thing in New York. Becoming his mistress paid off handsomely for you."

She opened her mouth to reply, then bit her lip. "Please don't pick a fight with me, Denys. I didn't come all this way for a quarrel nor to see if we could take up where we left off."

Her words brought no relief, for if she wasn't here to reconcile, that meant something else was in the wind. "And yet, you talk of us having a future. What could ever lead you to believe we have one?"

She sighed. "Henry's will."

"His will?" Denys stared at her, and suddenly, it felt as if the earth were opening beneath his feet, as if he were being pulled down into some dark abyss.

"Yes." She opened her handbag of crimson silk and pulled a folded sheet of paper from its interior. She held it up between white-gloved fingers. "He made me your new partner."

Chapter 2

Lola had known calling on Denys with no advance notice would give him a shock, but she'd deemed it a wiser course than to write ahead and request an appointment. This way, he had no chance to refuse to see her.

He could, however, toss her out the window. The grimness of his countenance told her that was a distinct possibility.

"My partner?" he echoed her declaration through clenched teeth. "In what enterprise?"

"The Imperial. Well, technically, I'm your father's partner, but since you manage all his holdings for him—"

"You're mad."

Lola rustled the sheet of paper in her fingers. "This letter to me outlines the exact details of Henry's bequest. The week before I left New York, Mr. Forbes assured me he'd sent a similar missive to your father, along with the news of Henry's death. Obviously, Conyers informed you of the latter, but did he not tell you about the former?"

Denys didn't reply. Instead, he continued to stare at her in stone-faced silence, and watching him, Lola realized all the rehearsing she'd done on the voyage over to ready herself for this meeting hadn't done her a bit of good.

For one thing, he didn't seem aware of the terms of the will. She'd come prepared to face him on the assumption he'd be equally prepared to face her. That, it seemed, was not the case.

Worse, however, was the fact that this man wasn't at all like the Denys she'd known. That man had been easy and carefree, with an irresistible boyish charm and a deep, passionate tenderness. Lola could find little trace of those qualities in the man before her.

This man had Denys's lean cheekbones and square jaw, but there was nothing boyish or carefree to soften them. This man had Denys's brown eyes, but as their gazes met, she could see no hint of tenderness in their dark depths. She'd heard what a shrewd man of business he'd become, and looking at him now, she had no trouble believing it.

The changes had cost him, though, for there were faint creases at the corners of his eyes and across his forehead that hadn't been there before, lines that spoke of responsibilities the Denys she'd known had never been forced to assume. His mouth, once so ready to smile, was now an uncompromising line—though his lack of humor on this occasion might be due to her arrival rather than the burdens of duty.

She'd hurt him, she knew that. She'd taken any affection he felt for her and shredded it. But there'd been no other way to make him see that a girl like her, a girl born beside the cattle yards and slaughterhouses of Kansas City, who'd spent her childhood amid the smells of manure, blood, and rotgut whiskey, who'd started stripping down to her naughties in front of men before she was sixteen, could never make a man like him happy.

Pain pinched her chest, and Lola suddenly couldn't bear the harshness in his face—harshness she knew she had put there. She tore her gaze away.

His body, she noted as she looked down, had changed less than his face. He still had the wide, powerful shoulders and narrow hips of the athlete he'd been, and from what she could see, six years hadn't added an ounce of fat to his physique. If anything, he seemed stronger and more powerful at thirty-two than he'd been at twenty-four.

She'd hoped time would have mellowed any acrimony on his part, but now, she feared that hope had been futile.

Still, there was no going back, and she forced herself to speak again. "I came here today assuming Conyers had received all the information from Mr. Forbes and that he had made you aware how things stand. But I see I was mistaken."

"By God, you've got gall, Lola," he muttered, glaring at her. "I'll give you that. You've got gall."

Resentment was palpable in every line of his face, in the frigid stance of his body, in the very air of the room. But she had no intention of withering in the face of his anger like some tender little hothouse flower, and Lola met his hostile gaze with a level one of her own. "This is a matter of business," she said quietly. "It isn't personal, Denys."

"Well, that relieves my mind," he countered, and despite her intention to remain steadfast, she couldn't help wincing a bit at the sarcasm.

He strode forward, pulled the letter from her fingers, and unfolded it to scan the typewritten lines, but when he looked up, his expression was still implacable.

"Not only the Imperial, but fifty thousand dollars in backing money," he said as he refolded the sheet. "Mistress to heiress in one simple step."

She opened her mouth to deny his contention, but then she closed it again. What would be the point of denial? Her role as Henry's mistress was a fiction of long standing, begun that fateful night in her Paris dressing room six years ago. It was a role both she and Henry had found convenient and one neither of them had ever seen the need to dispel. There was no purpose in telling Denys the truth now, for he would never believe her. Best to let sleeping dogs lie. "Henry was a kind and generous man," she said instead.

"I daresay. But I am curious. How does his family

feel about this particular display of his kindness and generosity?"

"Henry left his wife and children well provided for. The Imperial was only a fraction of his estate."

"Only a fraction?" He held out the letter. "Then I'm sure poor Gladys and the children didn't feel the least bit cheated."

Lola bristled as she snatched the letter from his hand. "His children—who are twenty-three and twenty-six, by the way—didn't give a damn about Henry when he was alive, and neither did Gladys. None of them had the time of day for him unless they wanted more money, of course."

Denys's mouth took on a cynical curve, and his gaze slid downward. "You, I'm sure, were much more devoted."

Hot color rushed into her face. Playing the part of Henry's mistress had been easy in New York, but standing in front of Denys now, there was nothing easy about it. Still, one had to live with one's choices, so Lola took a deep breath and brought the conversation back to the present. "Perhaps instead of talking about Henry, we should talk about what happens next?"

"Next?" He frowned. "I'm not sure I have the pleasure of understanding you."

"I own one-half of the Imperial, and though your father owns the other half, you manage it. That means you and I will be working together—"

"We most certainly will not."

She studied him for a moment, then gestured to the doorway behind her. "Since we see the situation so differently, perhaps we should sit down and discuss it? A mutual understanding might be hammered out."

Not wanting to give him the chance to refuse, she didn't wait for a reply. Turning away, she reentered his office, resumed her seat in the leather chair opposite his desk where she'd been awaiting his arrival, and crossed her fingers that he would follow. After a moment, he did, but his next words provided little encouragement for an amicable interview.

"I fail to see what there is for us to hammer out," he said as he circled his desk to face her.

The opening of the outer door interrupted any reply she might have made, and a moment later, Mr. Dawson came bustling into Denys's office, a laden tray in his hands.

"Here's your tea, Miss Valentine. I hope you like Earl Grey. Oh, good morning, sir," he added as he spied Denys standing behind the desk. Giving his employer a nod, the secretary halted beside Lola's chair and placed the tea tray on the desk in front of her. "I also brought some biscuits for you in case you might be hungry."

"Thank you." In the wake of Denys's hostility, the secretary's friendliness was like a soothing balm, and she gave the young man a grateful smile. "How very thoughtful of you."

"Not at all, not at all." He reached for the teapot and began to pour her tea. "I must say again how exciting it is to meet you in the flesh, Miss Valentine. I saw your one-woman show in New York last year, when I was there with my previous employer, and it was spectacular. I still remember how you kicked off the hat of that man in the front row, tossing it into the air with your toe, though how you managed to land it on your own head, I can't think." He laughed. "I'll wager that chap never forgets to remove his hat in the theater again."

Lola didn't tell him the man with the hat was always in the audience. "I'm glad you enjoyed it."

"I did very much. I hope your presence in London means you intend to do a show here?"

"I'd like to perform here, yes." She looked over at Denys, and his icy countenance confirmed just how difficult a prospect that was going to be. "We'll have to see."

"I do hope you will. I should very much like to see you perform again. Would you care for sugar and milk?"

Lola had no opportunity to reply to that, for Denys interrupted.

"Dawson, stop fawning over Miss Valentine and find me the Calvin and Bosch contracts if you please."

"Of course, my lord." Giving Lola an apologetic smile, Mr. Dawson handed over her tea, then bowed and left the room.

Cup and saucer in hand, Lola settled back in her seat and waited, but Denys did not move to take his own chair. "Denys, do sit down," she said. "Or I'll soon have a crick in my neck."

"This conversation isn't going to last long enough for

that." He leaned forward, flattening his palms on the polished oak top of his desk. "There is no way I shall involve myself, or my father, for that matter, in a partnership with you."

"You are already involved."

"Not for long. Now if you will pardon me," he added before she could ask what he meant, "I have an appointment for which I am already late."

She tilted her head back, and as she studied him, she knew that for now, at least, this discussion was over. If a partnership between them was ever going to work—and she was determined to make it work come hell or high water—she had to begin on as amicable a footing as possible. That meant respecting his schedule.

"Of course." She put the letter back in her handbag and stood up. "When would you like to resume this discussion? I can make an appointment with your secretary, or—"

"I thought I was clear, but evidently not." He paused, and his eyes narrowed, seeming to darken their color from brown to black. "I will accept no appointment with you. I will not be discussing anything with you involving the Imperial or any other matter. Not now, and not in future."

"But Denys, the season is about to begin. Rehearsals for *Othello* begin in two weeks. There are decisions we must make, arrangements for—"

"Of course," he cut her off. "Dawson will give you the names of my solicitors. I'm sure they will be quite happy to keep you abreast of what decisions and arrangements

I am making for the Imperial. You will, I trust, let them know where to send your share of the profits?"

Despite her resolve to be as businesslike as possible, Lola felt her temper flare up a notch. "Now wait just a minute. It's clear you haven't yet been apprised of the situation by Henry's attorney, and I appreciate that this is all coming as quite a shock. But Denys, I have no intention of being shunted off to the side while you make all the decisions for the Imperial and run the show without me. Unlike Henry, I intend to participate fully in this partnership."

A muscle worked along the square line of his jaw. "Not while I breathe air."

"I know you resent me, you probably even hate me. But the fact remains that I am your father's full and equal partner, and I have an equal say in what is done."

"That is another matter you can take up with my so-licitors." Ignoring her sound of frustration, he turned away and exited his office, vanishing from view. "Walk down with me, Mr. Dawson," she heard him say. "I have some things I need you to do while I'm out."

Lola moved to follow, but then she thought the better of it and stopped. She could hardly go chasing him down the corridors and staircases of his own offices, especially when he had his secretary in tow, and he was in no frame of mind to listen to her anyway. It was best to give him some breathing room and allow the reality of their new relationship to sink in.

Despite her decision, she was compelled to say one more thing before he had the chance to depart.

"We're in this together, Denys," she called to him. "This conversation is not over."

"Of course it isn't," he countered at once. "Nothing with you ever seems to be over."

With that parting shot, the outer door slammed, leaving her alone.

How? she wondered as she sank back down into her chair. *How am I ever going to make this work?*

It seemed even more impossible now than it had a month ago, when Henry died.

Lola sighed and leaned back, tiredness washing over her. She'd lost the man who'd been her mentor, her friend, and a better father to her than the man who'd sired her had ever dreamt of being. She'd had to do the last weeks of the winter season with his seat empty every single night, knowing he'd never sit in it again. She'd had to be the one to tell Alice he was gone. And at Mr. Forbes's insistence, she'd had to sit down with Henry's odious relations for the reading of the will.

An image of Mr. Forbes came into her mind, the waxed ends of his enormous mustache bobbing as his dry, legal voice had laid out the terms disposing of Henry's estate—an income to his wife, trusts for each of his children, all the New York businesses and their assets to his son, a dowry to his daughter . . .

Her presence in the lawyer's office had been met with hostile resignation on the part of his family, and it was clear they had already been informed she would be receiving some sort of legacy.

For her part, Lola was in the dark. She couldn't imagine what he might have left her. Not jewelry, surely, or fur coats, or any of the other baubles men gave their mistresses. Alice would have been the one to receive anything like that. Nor could Lola imagine Henry's leaving her some small token for sentiment's sake. Henry had been shrewd, selfish, and razor-sharp, and not the least bit sentimental. He might have left her cash, she supposed, although that seemed odd, too, for she had a tidy nest egg of her own thanks to the success of her one-woman show, a show that had been running for five straight years in Madison Square, a show that had made Henry and his fellow investors a great deal of money.

"Lastly, there is a provision for Miss Valentine."

Lola sat up a little straighter in her chair. She kept her attention on the attorney, meeting his pale blue eyes over the gold-rimmed pince-nez perched on his nose.

"To Miss Valentine, Mr. Latham has bequeathed his 50 percent share of the Imperial Theatre partnership. In addition, she will receive a capital sum of $50,000—"

Shocked gasps interrupted him, but the members of Henry's family weren't the only ones who were shocked. Lola felt as if she'd just been hit by a streetcar.

Half of the Imperial? A partnership between her and Denys's father? That was just plain crazy.

Dazed, Lola stared at Mr. Forbes, trying to assimilate what this might mean, and it took her several moments to realize the members of Henry's family had all turned around in their chairs to stare at her. Slowly, her gaze moved from face to face, and she appreciated that they were mad as hell.

First, there was Carlton, his complexion suffusing with purple at the news that Lola was to receive one of Henry's most profitable investments and a generous amount of cold, hard cash. And Margaret, who had lowered her handkerchief to give her father's supposed mistress a loathing-filled stare from dry, tearless eyes. And Gladys, trembling with rage, her thin lips pressed tight together.

Lola stared back at them, her chin high. These people were Henry's family but hadn't cared a penny about him, and their withering stares didn't wilt her one bit. She watched as Gladys stood up and came toward where she sat apart from the others in a chair by the door, and she tilted her head back as Gladys halted in front of her, keeping her face expressionless as she met the other woman's contemptuous gaze head-on. And when Gladys's hand came up and slapped her hard across the face, Lola didn't even flinch. She wouldn't give Gladys that sort of satisfaction.

She waited until they were gone before she pressed a hand to her stinging cheek. Gladys hadn't known she was slapping the wrong woman, of course, and Lola hadn't had any inclination to enlighten her. Henry would have wanted Alice's reputation protected even after his death. Besides, Lola had never had the luxury of caring what women like Gladys Latham thought of her.

"My apologies, Miss Valentine."

Lola lowered her hand and looked up. "It's quite all right, Mr. Forbes. Someone else's uncivil behavior isn't your fault. Besides," she added, "I can't really blame her. It must be difficult for her to see me here. And Henry, I would imagine, wasn't much of a husband."

The attorney leaned forward in his chair with a confidential air. "Gladys," he said, "wasn't much of a wife."

Lola couldn't help smiling a little at that. "You're a wicked man, Mr. Forbes."

He gestured to the chair closest to him, the one vacated by Henry's widow. "If you can stay a few more minutes, Miss Valentine. I have something else to give you from Mr. Latham."

"Something else?" she echoed as she came forward to take the offered chair. "I can't imagine what. But then, I couldn't imagine his leaving me half the Imperial, either. Earl Conyers and I, partners? Why, that man wouldn't give me a glass of water if I were dying of thirst."

"As to that . . ." The attorney paused to give a little cough. "His lordship does not manage the Imperial himself. My understanding is that Lord Conyers abdicated management of all his investments to his son, Lord Somerton, three years ago."

"Denys runs the Imperial now?" She groaned and leaned forward in her chair. "That makes everything even worse. Oh, Henry," she muttered, rubbing four fingers across her forehead, "what have you done?"

After a moment, she lifted her head. "My question remains. How could he ever imagine that such a partnership could work?"

"As to that, Mr. Latham did not confide in me. But

this may elucidate matters for you." Mr. Forbes lifted a sealed envelope from the desk and held it out to her. "He wanted you to have this after the will was read."

She broke the wax seal, pulled a single sheet from the envelope and unfolded it.

Lola,

Sometimes I'm a little late, but I always keep my promises. Go back to London and knock 'em dead, honey. Prove they were wrong about you. You can do it.

With affection,
Henry

PS — If you turn down this chance because of Denys, I shall come back as a ghost and haunt you.

Tears stung her eyes even as she gave a laugh at the idea of Henry as a ghost. She'd begun to think he'd forgotten the promise he'd made to her that fateful night in Paris.

I'll see that you learn your craft the proper way. And when I think you're ready to give drama another try, I'll find investors to back a serious play for you. I'll even make it Shakespeare. And if you're good, I'll manage your acting career. Maybe we'll even open our own theater in New York, and you can put on your own plays.

She blinked back the tears and read the letter again. This time, however, she found her shock wearing off and the ramifications sinking in. He'd kept his promise, but with one enormous difference. The Imperial was not in New York.

She looked at the attorney in bewilderment. "Henry must've been out of his mind."

"His family may think so," the attorney responded dryly. "But no, Mr. Latham's mental state was perfectly sound."

Lola had always thought so, but this did give her cause to wonder. London was where she'd first tried dramatic acting, where Denys, at his own expense, had financed his first play and gotten her a part. But she hadn't lived up to his faith in her talent. She'd fallen flat on her face and been eviscerated by the audience, the critics, and her peers. Now, Henry wanted her to go back there and try again? Her stomach lurched with fear at the thought.

And what about Denys? The Imperial meant facing him and the choice she'd made years ago. It meant managing a theater with him, for heaven's sake. It would never work, not in a thousand years.

But she was going to do it anyway.

Lola shoved down fear, folded the letter, and put it back in its envelope, then took a deep breath and looked at Henry's attorney. "I don't know much about business, so I don't quite understand what this bequest entails. Could you explain it?"

He had done so, outlining just what being a partner

in the Imperial would mean. But a month later, though Lola had full knowledge of her position, she sat in Denys's London office and wondered if her knowledge did her any good.

The outer door opened, breaking into her reflections as Mr. Dawson reentered the suite.

"Sorry to keep you waiting, Miss Valentine," he said as he appeared in the doorway. "Lord Somerton has instructed me to give you the names of his solicitors and their address. Give me a moment, and I shall write it out for you."

Lola already had the information, but it hardly mattered. Auditions for the upcoming season began in less than a week, and settling this with Denys through his solicitors could take months. Besides, she was pretty sure successful partnerships didn't work through lawyers, and she was determined that this partnership would be a success.

Nonetheless, she didn't deter the secretary. Instead, she drank her tea and considered what her next step should be. After a moment, she set aside her cup, rose to her feet, and exited Denys's office. She crossed to the secretary's desk and halted there, waiting, as he set aside his pen and blotted the inked lines he'd just written.

"I appreciate this so very much," she said, as he stood up and handed her the sheet of paper. "Thank you."

"Is there anything else I can do for you, Miss Valentine?"

"Hmm . . ." Lola paused, pretending to consider

the question. "There is one thing. If it's not too much trouble?"

His expression told her there was very little he would find too troublesome to manage for her. "I'd like to contact someone, and I'm sure you're just the person to tell me how to go about it. I wish to locate Mr. Jacob Roth. You know him, I'm sure?"

"Of course. He is the managing director of the Imperial. Are you acquainted with him?"

She knew the name, of course—everyone in theater did, for he'd been a prestigious actor in his day and a famed director, too, before ever taking over management of the Imperial's acting company. But as for the man himself, Lola didn't know him from Adam. She waved a hand vaguely in the air. "Old days in Paris."

"Indeed? I didn't realize Mr. Roth had ever directed anything in Paris. His offices are at the Imperial," he added before Lola was forced to invent a story of how she'd met the famous director, "though I doubt he would be there now, for the season hasn't begun yet. But you could call there and have his secretary request an appointment for you."

That might give Denys time to get wind of it and circumvent her. "Oh, dear," she said with a sigh, "I do so want to see him, but I'm not sure I want to call at his offices. That seems so formal." She leaned a little closer. "You're such a clever man, Mr. Dawson. I'm sure you can help me think of a better way."

The young man responded to this show of faith in his abilities at once. "You might find him at the Savoy in a few hours. He has lunch there nearly every day, so often that they keep a table reserved just for him."

"Thank you so much," she purred, straightening away from the desk. "You've been so very kind to me."

The young man flushed to the roots of his hair. "Not—not at all. My pleasure, I'm sure. If there is anything else you need . . ."

"If so, I'll come running straight to you." She put the folded sheet with the solicitors' names into her handbag, then pressed one gloved hand to her bosom with a sound of relief. "It's so reassuring for a girl on her own to know she has at least one man on whom she can truly rely."

With that, she left the office, giving the secretary one last grateful smile. She needed all the allies she could get.

As for Denys, if he wanted to ignore her, that was all right for now, since her next course of action was likely to gain his attention more quickly than any wrangling through lawyers could do. It was also sure to make him mad as a hornet, but she couldn't afford to care about that. Thanks to Henry, she had a second chance to realize her most cherished dream.

Becoming a real actress meant she could give up strutting around a stage in provocative clothing, showing off her legs and shimmying her bosom. She'd never have to sing another suggestive song, or kick off another hat, or bend over and wiggle her hips at another man in the crowd. She had the chance to earn the respect of her peers, the respect granted to serious actors, respect that performers like Lola Valentine never got.

And she owned half the theater, a position that gave her a measure of artistic and financial control. After years of answering to investors who chose what she wore and how she performed, she would finally have a say. Never again would she have to dine with men who did nothing but ogle her breasts, dismiss her ideas, and tell Henry he was a lucky man. Her ideas would finally be heard if she could get Denys to listen to them. Some could come to fruition if Denys could be persuaded to go along.

Somehow, she had to get him on her side, persuade him to teach her everything there was to learn about theater management, and work with her instead of against her. How she was going to manage that particular miracle, she wasn't quite sure, and as she went down the stairs, Lola could only cross her fingers that she'd figure out a way.

Chapter 3

 Denys's meeting with Calvin and Bosch about forming an Argentine railway company proved a success, and the contracts were signed within an hour, but afterward, he could remember nothing about the meeting. He'd been in a daze the entire time, stunned by the return of a woman he'd never expected to see again.

The images of Lola that he'd thought safely buried in the past now refused to leave his mind, and against those images, her words of this morning seemed not only ludicrous but impossible.

I'm your new partner.

What the hell had Henry been thinking?

Denys paused on the sidewalk. There were moments like this, he realized as he glanced up and down the crowded street looking for a cab, when he found Henry Latham absolutely baffling, despite having known the man most of his life.

The American impresario had taken London by storm from the moment of his arrival. Due to Lord and Lady Conyers's adoration of the theater, Henry had been a fixture of Denys's youth. A driving force within the artistic coterie that had been so much a part of Denys's childhood, Henry had been a familiar face at dinner, a mandatory addition to any party his parents gave, and a highly valued acquaintance. Denys had been the one to introduce Henry to Lola, never dreaming what would result.

Henry's taking Lola away from him hadn't affected the partnership between Henry and his father. On the contrary, the earl had regarded Henry's act of spiriting Lola off to New York as a great favor and a blessed relief. And by the time Denys had taken over all the family business ventures, he had put the whole ghastly business behind him. With Henry in New York, content to work with Denys via the impersonal method of written correspondence, managing the Imperial hadn't been any more difficult than managing any of the other family holdings.

Being in partnership with Lola was an entirely different kettle of fish. What she'd done to him was all water under the bridge now, of course, and he was over it, but for all that, the terms of Henry's will were no less incomprehensible.

What reason could the other man have had for doing this? And how could he think a partnership between Denys and Lola could ever work? Oil and water were more likely to mix.

It's a difficult situation. For her. For you. For everyone.

His morning conversation with his father came back to him, and the little oddities about it began to make sense as he realized he and the earl had been talking about two different women. He had not actually read the letter from Mr. Forbes, he remembered, and he'd assumed Gladys Latham had inherited the Imperial from her husband. The earl, however, having read the letter, had known Lola to be the beneficiary, hence his worried study of his son across the desk, his delicate inquiries as to Denys's intentions and state of mind, and the surprising suggestion that it might be best to sell their share of their most profitable investment.

It was understandable the earl would be concerned. Lola had visited upon Denys a sort of insanity—a passion beyond all reason, ignited the first time she'd looked at him from the stage and given him the wide, radiant smile for which she was famous. It had been a passion so wild and ungovernable that he'd been impervious to the pleas of his family, deaf to the scandalized whispers of society, and utterly blind to the true character of his inamorata.

Until she'd left him.

It still made Denys grimace when he thought of the

money he'd spent, the fights he'd engaged in, the friends he'd almost lost, and the fool he'd made of himself over a bit of skirt who in the end had proved as faithless as the wind. Looking back, he knew there was only one explanation. He had been mad.

He was now sane.

With that reminder, the stunned haze that had been enveloping him all morning dissipated, like a fog lifting off the moors. Though he and the earl had been speaking of two different women, they had agreed on a course of action, and he saw no reason not to carry it through. That required a call upon the family solicitors.

A hansom crawled past, and Denys hailed it. After the driver had navigated the traffic that always seemed to clog Trafalgar Square, Denys was deposited at the offices of Burrowes, Abercrombie, and Moss in Regent Street. Despite his lack of an appointment, Mr. Burrowes was able to receive him and quite willing to allow him use of their telephone. A call to White's and a brief discussion with his father verified his conclusions about their earlier conversation, and after offering his father a few reassurances of how he intended to proceed, Denys rang off and spent the remainder of the morning ensconced in Mr. Burrowes's office.

Lola, he learned, had not yet called upon the solicitor, but Denys had no doubt she would, and he intended to stay one step ahead of her. After informing Mr. Burrowes of Henry's death and the terms of his will, Denys then asked how the partnership could be dissolved. Informed that it would require the consent of both parties, the disbanding of the acting company, and the permanent closure of the theater, Denys inquired if he could buy his partner out instead. Upon receiving an affirmative answer, he pulled out his watch. "I've an hour before my next engagement," he said, and tucked the watch back into his pocket. "Might we draft terms right now?"

"Of course." Burrowes pulled out a sheet of notepaper, took up his pen, and opened his inkwell. "Let's begin with the purchase amount. How much do you wish to offer?"

Denys considered a moment, then dictated terms he felt Lola might accept. He must have been generous in his estimate, for Mr. Burrowes raised an eyebrow; but wisely, he made no comment.

When the terms were outlined, Burrowes assured him a draft would be on his desk first thing Monday. Satisfied, Denys left the solicitor's office, hailed a taxi, and journeyed to Rules, where he discovered that Georgiana and their mothers had arrived before him and were already seated at one of the restaurant's red-upholstered booths.

Lady Georgiana Prescott, the only daughter of the Marquess of Belsham, could trace her lineage back to William the Conqueror, but her image—pale skin, chiseled cheekbones, noble brow, and aquiline nose—might just as easily have been seen on the temples of ancient Greece. Her dark hair was swept back from her face in perfect waves and caught up beneath the brim of a small, elegant hat, with nary a stray tendril daring to escape.

He and Georgiana had known each other most of their lives. Not that there had been an understanding, precisely, between their families, but it had never been a secret that both sides had always wanted them to make a match of it. Had he not gone to Paris that fateful summer so long ago, the ambition of their families might very well have been fulfilled.

His passion for Lola Valentine had been not only a shock to both sets of parents but also a keen disappointment. And though Georgiana had never spoken a single word about his three years of insanity—she was far too well-bred for that—Denys suspected their parents weren't the only ones he'd let down by taking up with a cabaret dancer.

During the past few months, however, he and Georgiana had begun to reestablish the quiet fondness of their childhood, and Denys wasn't as inclined to rebel against the expectations surrounding them as he'd once been. In fact, he'd begun to consider fulfilling them instead. He didn't know her opinion on the matter, for Georgiana wasn't one to display her emotions, and their rapprochement had not proceeded far enough for him to inquire, but for the first time, he felt as if something more than friendship between them might be on the horizon.

As if sensing his gaze, she looked up and spied him by the doors. Realizing he was just standing there like a chump, he started forward at once, making his way toward the table where she sat beside her mother and opposite his own.

She didn't smile as he approached, for she had a slight overbite to her teeth, and being of such a fastidious nature, she was painfully self-conscious about it. But she did tilt back her head to watch him with those grave gray eyes of hers as he came toward them, and despite her serious expression, he thought she was glad he'd agreed to join their party.

"Is this seat taken?" he asked, placing a hand on the back of the chair beside his mother.

That did earn him a smile, a little one that curved her closed lips. "I believe it is now. And I'm gratified that you decided to join us at last."

"At last?" he echoed in surprise. "Am I late?"

She glanced down at the brooch watch pinned to her gray-and-white-striped walking coat. "Ten minutes, I'm afraid. We'd quite despaired of you."

He thought he'd left Burrowes's office with plenty of time to spare, but when he glanced at her lapel, he was forced to admit that Georgiana, as usual, was right. "Sorry," he apologized as he pulled out his chair to sit down. "I had no idea it would take so long to arrive here from Regent Street. Good day, Lady Belsham," he added to the marchioness. "Mama."

"Regent Street?" Georgiana echoed, as he sat down. "Is that where you've been? No wonder you're late. The traffic is beastly around Trafalgar. I always allot extra time."

A declaration that from Georgiana didn't surprise him in the least. She was never unpunctual. "Shall we order?" he asked, and looked down at the menu card before him.

"I fear we must," Georgiana replied. "We have shopping to do, then calls to make, and tea." She tapped her brooch watch briskly. "Time is getting on."

If there was a hint of rebuke in that, he couldn't see it reflected in her face. Her expression as she looked down at her menu card was smooth and impassive as ever, and he decided he'd been mistaken. He signaled for the waiter.

"So," he said, settling back in his seat once their order had been placed, "how are you ladies getting on with your plans for the flower show?"

"Rather well, for we have at last found a suitable venue," Georgiana replied. "At least," she added, looking at the woman opposite, "I think it will suit. Lady Conyers, the hospital fund is your committee's responsibility. What do you think of my idea?"

"Oh, my dear, I am relieved." His mother gave a deep sigh, pressing a hand to her bosom. "And so glad I enlisted your aid. I confess, when you first told me your idea, I was not enthused. But now that we have toured the grounds, I am able to see your vision, and I believe you are quite right. Lady Belsham, what is your opinion?"

The Marchioness of Belsham, an older, perhaps more rigid version of her daughter, gave a nod of agreement. "The greatest obstacle, of course, might have been Lord Bute."

"Lord Bute?" Denys echoed in surprise. "Where is this flower show to be?"

Georgiana was the one to enlighten him. "Regent's Park, in the garden at St. John's Lodge, which is owned, as I'm sure you know, by Lord Bute, who has agreed to allow the event to be held there. I do hope the venue proves a success, Lady Conyers."

"Of course it will," his mother answered warmly, and turned to Denys. "Georgiana's choice in such matters is impeccable."

Georgiana waved aside the compliment with the tactful complacency of one who seldom had occasion to be wrong. "The important thing is the funds raised, and if it works as we hope, this show will bring a great deal of money to the London hospitals." She lifted her long, graceful hands and crossed her fingers. "Unless it rains."

Denys studied her for a moment, trying to imagine that particular possibility, and failed utterly. Anything Georgiana involved herself in always proved a success. If she rode in a point to point, she won. If she hunted, she brought down more grouse than her father. And if she deemed an outdoor venue appropriate for a flower show, Denys couldn't see even the traitorous English weather defying her. "It won't rain," he told her. "It wouldn't dare."

She smiled at that. "There will be tents, of course. But everything will go so much better if the day is fine." She turned to his mother. "An Afternoon-at-

Home is next, I think. We should arrange it at once, before Mama and I return to Kent."

"Kent?" Denys echoed in surprise. "I thought you were to be in town for the entire season."

"We are, but we still have so much to finish at home before we settle into the house in Cavendish Square. We only came up to town to assist your mother."

He wondered if he might be the reason for Georgiana's willingness to help with a charity that wasn't her own, but he dismissed the thought. Georgiana loved charity work. "There's the Bring and Buy for the church tower," she went on, proving his point. "And the Sale of Work for orphans, and, of course, the village school. We simply must find a new teacher."

"It seems I won't be seeing you for ages," he remarked, and as he spoke, he felt rather relieved. Lola and Georgiana were two distinct parts of his life: the past and—possibly—the future. He deemed it best they not collide in the present.

"We shall only be away for two weeks," she assured him, and turned to her mother. "But don't you think, Mama, that an Afternoon-at-Home is the perfect paving of the way for Lady Conyers's flower show?"

"I do," Lady Belsham replied at once. "We shall be able to inform all our friends of the hospitals' dire need for funds."

"Just so," her daughter replied. "And yet, we must also provide an atmosphere of infinite leisure in which our friends are completely at ease. There must be the right mix of people, as well as good food and plenty of excellent champagne."

"Thus priming them perfectly to pull out their bank books," Denys added in amusement.

Georgiana gave him a look of reproof. "I wouldn't put it quite so bluntly as that."

Of course not, for Georgiana was never blunt. Subtlety and restraint were in every inch of her. He continued to study her as they dined, while they discussed his mother's flower show, and it struck him—not for the first time—what a perfect wife she would make. She was well-bred, intelligent, loyal—

But not the least bit exciting.

The moment that pesky little thought crossed his mind, he quashed it by reminding himself he was done with excitement. To fulfill his duty to his name and title, he needed to marry, and in that regard, Georgiana was as close to ideal as a man could find. He could think of no reason not to marry her.

A ringing endorsement.

"Denys?"

"Hmm?" He came out of these contemplations to find the object of them looking at him inquiringly. "Sorry. I was woolgathering, I'm afraid. What did you say?"

She gestured to his plate. "I asked if you were finished. We really must be on our way if we're to do any shopping today."

"Of course." He set aside his napkin and hailed the waiter, and minutes later, he was assisting the ladies into a taxi.

"Are you certain you won't come with us?" Georgiana asked him through the window.

"Shopping in Mount Street?" He made a great show of looking appalled. "I'd rather work."

"A gentleman shouldn't work at all," she said, frowning a little. "Especially during the season. Surely you can take time away from that beastly office? We could forgo our shopping," she offered, and glanced at her companions. "Couldn't we?"

Despite the eager assent of their mothers, Denys had to refuse. "I am flattered by the sacrifice, ladies," he said, smiling, "but I'm afraid I have far too much on my plate today. *Othello* is coming up at the Imperial, you know, and it's the first play of the season. There's a great deal to do."

It bothered him, somehow, mentioning the Imperial to Georgiana, and he was glad he'd moved forward so quickly with the strategy he and the earl had discussed that morning. The sooner Lola Valentine was out of his life again, the better.

He waited until the cab had turned the corner, then he turned and started up Maiden Lane in the opposite direction, heading toward his offices. He turned onto the Strand, and as he passed the Savoy Hotel, it occurred to him that it might be wise to inform Jacob of the Imperial's change in ownership, however temporary that change might be. If he was lucky, he'd find the director still in the restaurant, lingering over his dessert.

Careful to avoid the broughams, hansom cabs, and other vehicles circling the Savoy's U-shaped courtyard, he entered the hotel and crossed the lavish foyer to the dining room.

"Lord Somerton," the maître d'hôtel greeted him as he paused inside the door. "This is an honor. May I show you to a table?"

"I'm looking for Mr. Roth. Is he still here?"

"He is, my lord, but . . ."

The other man paused, a curious reticence suddenly entering his heretofore unctuous manner, and Denys looked at him in some surprise. "Is something wrong, monsieur?" he asked, as a dull red flush crept into the maître d'hôtel's cheeks.

"My apologies, my lord. I had not been informed you would be joining Monsieur Roth for luncheon today."

"I shouldn't think you had," Denys answered. "He doesn't know I'm here, but I daresay he won't mind if I join him."

The maître d'hôtel, accustomed to giving way to the aristocracy, capitulated. "Of course," he said, and began leading Denys between the crowded tables toward the far corner of the room. "I ask your lordship's pardon, for I did not mean to be impertinent. It is only that Mr. Roth is not alone today. He is having luncheon with a lady, you see."

"A lady?" Even as he spoke, Denys felt a sinking feeling in his guts, and when he followed the footman, he was not surprised to find Lola sitting with the director of his next play, looking far too intimately acquainted with the fellow for his peace of mind.

She smiled at the director, the same heart-stopping

smile that had enthralled not only him, but also most of his friends, Henry Latham, and audiences from Paris's cabarets to New York's Madison Square. Denys knew how much havoc that smile could create, and he cursed the fateful night in Paris when Nick and Jack had first dragged him to the *Théâtre Latin*.

Chapter 4

 Lola knew the crucial moment was at hand. Mr. Roth's stomach was full, his second glass of wine and his dessert had been consumed, and his gaze was warmly admiring. It was time to make her move.

"Mr. Roth, I understand the Imperial's first play of the season is to be *Othello*?"

"Yes, indeed. I myself shall be directing."

"Really?" She gave him her best look of amazement. "Why, how wonderful. You see . . ." She paused, leaning forward in a confiding manner. "I have always wanted to act in drama—"

"I don't know why," a wry voice cut in. "You always seem to have plenty of drama in your private life."

Damn. Lola caught back a groan. She'd known, of course, that once he learned she didn't intend to sit idly by, he wouldn't either, but she had hoped it would take him longer than a mere three hours to discover what she was up to.

Still, she was a partner now, and by finding her here, he knew she intended to act like one. "Lord Somerton," she said, pasting on a smile and tilting her head back to look him in the eye. "How lovely to see you again so soon. What are you doing here?"

One dark brow lifted. "I might ask you the same question."

She shrugged and took a sip of wine. "Is it so surprising? I'm staying at the Savoy."

"And dining with my managing director, I see. How fortuitous."

"Wasn't it, though?" she agreed, choosing to ignore his implication of her opportunism. "Here I was, having my lunch, when who should I find being seated at a table right by my own?" She paused, gesturing to the man opposite. "None other than Jacob Roth, London's most lauded theatrical director."

Denys, however, was no fool. He smiled at her. "Bribed the waiter, did you?"

She laughed as if that were a joke, and, fortunately, Mr. Roth did the same.

"Really, Somerton," the director reproved, "you do Miss Valentine little credit. I doubt she would have to resort to bribery to have her way with any man. One of her smiles," he added with a little nod to her, "would be more than enough persuasion to give her whatever she wanted."

Lola could only hope he meant that.

"And in any case," Roth added, "it was I who initiated conversation, breaking all rules of etiquette, I am sure. It was my idea that we dine together."

"It's amazing," Denys murmured, "how often someone else's idea also happens to be just what Miss Valentine wants."

Lola widened her smile. "Only because I'm openminded enough to consider the ideas of others," she said sweetly.

"Either way," Roth put in, "having her join me for luncheon has been a pleasure though I am quite saddened by the news of Henry Latham's death." He shook his head. "A great loss to theater, on both sides of the Atlantic."

"A great loss indeed," Denys agreed. "But did Miss Valentine tell you of her own good fortune? She's taken Henry's place as my partner in the Imperial."

His voice sound so genial and so insincere, she grimaced.

Roth, luckily, didn't seem to notice. His expression lightened once more. "Yes, so she has informed me. I envy you, my friend. Most business partners are not so charming as yours." He gestured to the table. "Will you join us?"

His presence would ruin everything, and Lola spoke up at once. "Oh, but I'm sure his lordship is far too busy—"

"I'd love to join *you*, my friend," he interrupted, and Lola did not miss his emphasis on the pronoun. "But first . . ." He paused, and when he looked at her, Lola felt her dismay deepening into frustration, for she knew she was about to be called on the carpet and dismissed, as if she were a recalcitrant child. "I hope you will excuse us both for a few moments? I need to speak with Miss Valentine privately about certain details involving our . . . partnership."

She decided she was in no hurry to be called on the carpet. Instead of rising to her feet, she gestured to her plate. "But I haven't finished my lunch."

"Yes, you have." Still smiling, he bent down close to her ear, and when he spoke, his voice was low enough to prevent the man across from her from hearing his words. "Roth only appreciates a scene if it's on stage, and if you don't come with me right now, there will be a scene, I promise you."

Lola knew that Denys hated embarrassing public scenes, too, but she couldn't afford to assume he was bluffing. She needed Jacob Roth on her side, and she wouldn't gain that by embarrassing him in the dining room of the Savoy.

"I'm so sorry," she told him. "It seems the business Lord Somerton wishes to discuss with me is urgent and cannot wait. If you will pardon us?"

As she rose to her feet, the director did also, setting aside his napkin with a little bow. "Of course."

"Jacob, I've already dined," Denys said, "but would you be so good as to order coffee? I shall rejoin you in a few moments, and we can talk."

Lola didn't miss the glance exchanged by the two men, nor Denys's exclusion of her from any further conversation. She, no doubt, would be the primary topic of discussion between them later, but there was little she could do about it, so she followed Denys out of the dining room, across the opulent foyer, and down the corridor to the elevators. One carriage was available, its doors open, a liveried attendant waiting. Denys cupped a hand beneath her elbow and stepped inside the elevator, pulling her with him.

"Now," he said, propelling her to the back of the elevator and out of the way as the boy closed the wood-paneled doors and the wrought-iron gate, "tell me what you think you're doing."

"Having lunch?" she suggested with an air of bright good cheer.

"You mean you were cozying up to my director, though how you found out he would be dining here defies explanation."

That made her smile. "I have my methods."

"I daresay. And by waylaying Roth in this shameless fashion, what do you hope to gain? Information? Support?"

"Both, actually, but my main goal was to gain advice on how best to deal with my partner."

"I can tell you how to do that. Go away."

A little cough broke in before she could reply, and both of them glanced toward the attendant, who was gazing at them in polite inquiry, his hand poised atop the brass orb of the elevator mechanism.

When she didn't supply the requisite information, Denys turned toward her with a sound of impatience. "Where's your room?"

"Why, Lord Somerton, what an improper question," she murmured, unable to resist needling him. "I'm not sure I should answer you. The Savoy isn't really that sort of hotel, you know."

"Your room?" he repeated in a hard voice.

"You've become so staid." She glanced at the boy, who was staring at the floor, pink as a peony, and she took pity on him. "Sixth floor," she said.

The young man gave her a grateful glance, then pulled out the handle, turned the crank, and sent the elevator into motion.

"You didn't used to be this way, you know," she went on, returning her attention to Denys as they were carried upward. "You've changed."

"Yes, I have," he agreed at once. "I've grown up."

"Oh, is that what you call it?"

"I do. What would you call it?"

She studied him for a moment, thinking how to describe the changes in him. Her mind flashed back to their days in Paris and London half a dozen years ago, and the affable, carefree young man she'd fallen in love with. "Sad," she said at last.

He made a sound of derision at that description, but though he seemed to want to argue the point, he didn't do so. Instead, he turned away, staring straight ahead, and they traveled the remaining floors in silence.

When the elevator deposited them at the sixth floor, she removed her room key from her handbag as Denys handed the attendant a tip, but when she started down the corridor toward her room, he didn't move to follow her, and she stopped. "Aren't you coming?"

"No. We can say what we need to say right here. It's private enough, I daresay." He cast a pointed glance over his shoulder at the attendant, who gave a start and immediately pulled the doors closed, vanishing from view.

"Don't worry," she said in some amusement as Denys returned his attention to her. "I doubt an elevator boy has the power to ruin your reputation."

"It was decided," he said stolidly, "that we would settle the matter of this ridiculous partnership through solicitors."

"That's what you decided." She dropped the key into her bag and closed it with a snap. "I decided something different."

"What do you hope to accomplish by accosting Jacob while he is enjoying his lunch?"

"He didn't seem to mind my company. An unfathomable concept to you, I know, but true nonetheless. As for the rest, solicitors are always so slow, and I didn't feel it was wise to dither. Auditions for the season's acting company are on Monday."

"A fact that has nothing to do with you."

She sighed, noting the hard set of his jaw. "Look, I realize this is all still quite a shock to you, but does railing against facts accomplish anything? If you intend to continue this intransigence, our partnership shall be fraught with strife."

"All the more reason not to continue with it, then." He spread his hands in a self-evident gesture. "How much?"

She blinked at the abrupt question. "How much what?"

"I want to make an offer for your share of the Imperial. I'll be generous, I promise you. Name your terms."

She was shaking her head in refusal before he'd even finished speaking. "I'm not selling."

"I should advise you to reconsider. Given our history, we can't possibly work together."

"Ah, but we don't have to work together," she said sweetly. "All you have to do is let me know where to send your share of the profits."

He didn't seem amused by having his own words thrown back at him, for his expression became even grimmer than before. "This notion that you and I could ever work together is mad."

"I thought so myself at first, but after thinking it over, I changed my mind. I believe it can work if we both give it a chance."

"I don't want to give it a chance. So, how much money will it take to end it?"

She closed her eyes, remembering how his father had once asked her a similar question.

How much money will make you go away?

She opened her eyes and gave the same answer. "I won't take your money."

"Taking all receipts and expenses into consideration," he went on, and she wondered if, like his father, he was going to pull out his checkbook and start writing a check. "The theater has, at best, a profit margin of five thousand pounds per annum. So twenty thousand pounds is a fair offer, wouldn't you agree?"

"More than fair," she acknowledged, "but irrelevant."

"It would be a sure thing, Lola. Theater, on the other hand, is always uncertain. The public's tastes are fickle and arbitrary. Over half of all theatrical productions lose money."

"Nonetheless—"

"The Imperial doesn't use outside financial backers."

"Thank God," she muttered, thinking of Henry's investors.

"As a partner," he went on doggedly, "you would be expected to contribute capital anytime a show fails."

"Which is why Henry left me cash along with my interest in the theater," she reminded him. "And I have cash of my own."

"A few flops, and your money will be gone."

"Since the Imperial has made money every year you've been managing it, I'm not particularly worried."

"You seem well informed about our financial condition."

"I am," she countered at once. "Would you expect any less of a partner?"

"Despite your faith in my abilities, I have backed plays that lose money. You," he added with a pointed glance, "ought to know that better than anyone."

This reminder of *A Doll's House*, of how badly she'd failed in her first attempt at acting and how much money he'd lost as a result of her failure, made her cheeks flush with heat, but she refused to be intimidated by that. "Yes, Denys," she agreed with as much dignity as she could muster. "I do know."

"Theater is a capricious business. What I'm offering you is a sure thing. Combined with what Henry left you, it would put an enormous fortune at your disposal, enabling you to live in luxury, with no risk to your future. Or you could marry. You would certainly have a sizable dowry to offer."

His assumption that snaring a good marriage prospect and living a life of luxury were what she cared about flicked her on the raw. "If security and luxury and marriage were the only things that mattered to me, I'd have married you."

He stiffened, telling her she'd just stepped onto thin ice, but when he spoke, his voice was politely stiff. "Quite so."

"Hell," she said, regretting her impetuous retort. "I didn't mean—"

"It doesn't matter," he cut her off. "What if we make it twenty-five thousand? Thirty," he added, when she continued to shake her head.

The ease with which he raised the amount of his offer told her he was prepared to go even higher, but no matter the amount, it remained irrelevant. "Stop, Denys. Please stop. This isn't about money or what money can buy. It's about my dream."

He stared at her, horror dawning in his face. "Oh, God," he groaned, raking a hand through his hair. "I remember the two of us having this exact same conversation about six years ago."

"Yes, and *A Doll's House* did not change my mind. Despite that failure, I still want to become a respected dramatic actress."

"I don't know whether to admire your tenacity or question your sanity."

"Henry's legacy gives me a chance to do what I've always wanted to do."

"I fail to see what your aspirations to act have to do with the Imperial or with me." He folded his arms, looking grimmer than ever. "Perhaps you'd better explain that part."

The hallway of the Savoy was not where she'd have chosen to discuss it. On the other hand, he was standing still and listening to her. She might not get a better chance than this.

"Henry believed in me. He never doubted that I could act."

"Good on him. But as far as I know, he never financed an actual play for you, did he?"

"He would have done. Eventually," she added, feeling defensive all of a sudden. "But he never got the chance."

"Or he never intended to do so because he had already learned from my mistake, and he was just jollying you along all this time so he could make money off you. Either way," he went on before she could take issue with his assessment of Henry's motives, "the fact remains that he didn't renew your acting career himself. He chose to foist you on me."

"I'm not being foisted on you! I'm your *partner*. I'm prepared to assume all the responsibilities that come with that position."

"Ah, but owning a theater wasn't your dream. Your dream was about acting."

"The two things are not mutually exclusive, as you well know. Many actors own or manage their own theaters. Sir Henry Irving, for example, manages and acts at the Lyceum. He directs, too."

"Sir Henry Irving has the bona fides to back up that sort of hubris."

"I have bona fides, too, Denys. I have accomplishments. My one-woman show has been a hit for five seasons running."

"Which is still musical revue. *A Doll's House* aside, you have no real acting experience."

"That's not true. I'm acting every moment I'm on stage."

"It's not the same thing, and you know it. So, what is expected of me, then? Because you're my partner, I am now required to put you in my plays?"

"Our plays," she corrected. "And hiring the season's acting company is not your decision, or mine. It's the manager's. And choosing who in the company is cast in each play is up to each play's director. You relinquished control of all that when you took over for your father."

"As I said earlier, you are well-informed. And since Jacob Roth is my theater manager, as well as the director of our first play of the season, you are here to butter him up."

"I wasn't buttering him up! All right," she amended, as he gave her a skeptical look, "maybe I was, but so what?"

"You think a few smiles over lunch will gain you a place in the company? Or did you offer him something more?"

Lola bristled. "I am not even going to dignify that with an answer."

"You needn't pretend it's an alien concept to you," he shot back, his voice tight. "But Jacob won't play that game. He'd never put a woman who can't act in one of his plays just because he wants to sleep with her."

"I didn't become your lover because of your contacts in theater, and I never used our relationship as leverage for my ambition to act. Never. *A Doll's House* might have been a failure, and my poor performance might have been the reason why, but I never asked you to finance that play for me."

"That's true," he admitted, but the bitterness in his voice told her there was no victory for her in the admission. "Putting you in that play was my folly and mine alone. It was also one of the most painful performances I've ever witnessed."

Lola sucked in a sharp breath, surprised by how much it hurt to hear him say that even though she knew it was true. "That was a long time ago."

"Not so long that I've forgotten what happened. Do I need to remind you how all the critics shredded you into spills? How we had to close the play after only a one-week run? How your fellow actors blamed you for bringing the entire play down?"

"All right, you've made your point," she muttered, hating that years of hard work and proved success could not seem to erase her biggest, most spectacular failure. "But it was the first dramatic role I'd ever done, and I'd had no training. Since then—"

"The Imperial is a Shakespearean theater," he cut in. "Have you any experience in Shakespeare? Any at all?"

She thought of all the time she'd spent studying, all the mornings when, still bone-tired from the previous night's show, she'd gotten out of bed to attend acting classes, to study with tutors, practicing roles such as Juliet, Lady Macbeth, and Desdemona, reciting passages from *Hamlet* or *The Tempest*, until now, she knew the lines of Shakespeare's greatest heroines by heart. "I have training in Shakespeare, including *Othello*. I know the role of Desdemona backward and forward—"

"In other words," he cut in incisively, folding his arms, "you're a dedicated amateur."

"I am not an amateur! I have vast experience on stage and a proved record of successful performing. And I've spent all my spare time training for dramatic acting.

Henry hired tutors, I went to classes. He even worked with me himself. He taught me so much—"

"Yes," Denys cut in, his voice icy. "I daresay he did."

Frustration welled up within her, for though Denys was the only man who'd ever backed her in something that didn't involve using her body in a provocative way, she knew damn well he hadn't done it because he thought she had talent.

"Considering our prior relationship," she said coolly, "I don't think you have room to take the high ground on what Henry did for me, do you?"

He stiffened, demonstrating she'd made her point. "Either way, *A Doll's House* was a huge mistake, and I never make the same mistake twice."

She took a deep breath, reminding herself they were supposed to be on the same side. "Denys, I realize you lost a lot of money—"

"Sod the money. My involvement with you cost me something far more important than money. It cost me the respect of my family, something it's taken me years to earn back."

"Having spent over a decade strutting around a stage, displaying my body for men to look at, I think I know a little something about lost respect, too," she shot back.

He pressed his lips together and looked away, shaking his head, and she didn't know if he was trying to deny her point, or if he was just so exasperated with her that he didn't know what to reply. "Denys, your relationship with your family isn't at risk. They can hardly blame you for any of this. Besides, it's Roth, not you, who makes the final decision about which actors are hired for the season, and your family knows that."

"And you think that lets me off the hook and makes everything all right?" His gaze swerved to her again. "The moment London society finds out about this partnership, they'll think we've rekindled our affair, Roth be damned."

"I realize you've always cared what people think far more than I ever have, but being that you're a man, this situation won't hurt your reputation."

"You think not? If you're in one of my plays, I'll be the laughingstock of London for being twice a fool over you."

"You're only twice a fool if I fail. If I do well, you're clever. Nothing succeeds like success."

"Forgive me if I'm not willing to take that risk a second time," he said dryly.

"So what will you do? Attempt to block me? Tell Roth not to let me audition? Why not just trust our manager to make the right decision? I'm willing to accept it either way," she went on without waiting for an answer. "I didn't come into this expecting a place in the acting company just because I'm a partner. I'm happy to audition like any other performer. I just want the chance to prove myself."

Something flashed in his dark eyes, something dangerous. "Why the hell should I give it to you?" he demanded, his voice low and tight. "When you have no record of success in acting to back you up? When I don't know if you can tell the difference between Shakespeare and Sheridan? When you lied to me and betrayed me and were unfaithful to me with another man, why should I ever give you a chance at anything again?"

Lola stared at him helplessly, not knowing how to answer that. She thought of how she'd ended their affair, and she wished there had been some other way to do it, for the only way that could truly set him free had also made him despise her.

"Denys, I wasn't unfaithful—"

"Don't," he cut her off before she could even attempt an explanation. "Spare me any claims of innocence, or offer me excuses about what happened with Henry and why."

"If you don't want me to defend myself, then stop throwing what happened in my teeth."

He glared at her for a long moment, then he gave a deep sigh. "The question isn't what happened in the past, or why. The question is what I'm supposed to do with you now."

"What you can do is work with me, not against me."

"Did Henry really believe I'd go along with this?" Though his flash of anger had faded, his scorn and bafflement were obvious. "I realize you probably persuaded him to do it, but—"

"I did no such thing!"

"But how could either of you think that I would accept this?"

"I know you won't believe me, but I did not put Henry up to this. How he arranged his will was as great a surprise to me as it was to you. As for what he was thinking, I believe that he thought—that is, he hoped you would be fair, Denys. And give me a fair chance."

That struck a nerve, she could tell. His head went back, his nostrils flared, and a muscle worked at the corner of his jaw. "You want that, do you?" he asked, his eyes glittering hard. When he spoke again, she was sure he intended to tell her to go to hell. "You want a chance to fall on your face again? Very well. I'll give it to you."

"You will?" Her relief was so great, her knees wobbled, and she had to flatten one hand against the wall beside her to steady herself. "Thank you, Denys."

"If Roth agrees, you'll have one chance to prove yourself." He held up his index finger. "One. If your audition convinces him to give you a place in the company, I won't object. But," he added before she could feel any relief, "if you take a step out of place, if you do anything to fuel speculation that we are romantically involved, or if you put my reputation or the Imperial in jeopardy in any way, this partnership will be over. I'll destroy the Imperial before I let you make a fool of me a second time. Is that understood?"

"Of course," she said with dignity.

"Good." He turned to press the electric bell that called for the elevator. "You can pick up the audition sides for Bianca at the Imperial tomorrow."

"Bianca?" She gave him a rueful look. "No doubt you chose Bianca because it's the smallest female part in the play."

He didn't deny it. "Look on the bright side. If you do earn a place in the company, Bianca will provide the perfect opportunity for you to hone your acting skills."

"My skills are honed. What do you think I've been doing the past six years? Eating chocolates and sitting on my behind?"

"I doubt it," he countered at once, leaning back, his gaze sliding down. "Your *behind* looks exactly the same if my memory can be relied upon."

Lola felt a jolt of shock at those words, but when he straightened and his gaze met hers, she couldn't see any hint of the desire that used to be in his eyes when he looked at her. Those days were long past.

Looking at him now, knowing that, she felt a pang of nostalgia, but she pushed it away. She opened her mouth to offer a flippant reply, but the elevator arrived before she had the chance, rumbling to a halt in front of them.

"Auditions start at nine o'clock on Thursday," he told her, as the attendant pulled back the door panels, and he stepped into the carriage. "I'll ask Roth to add your name to the list. Unless," he added as he turned to face her again, "the idea of having only a bit part has caused you to change your mind and give up?"

She made a scoffing sound. "As if I'd let you rid yourself of me that easily."

"I suppose not." He stepped back for the attendant to close the doors and latch the gate. "I'm not that lucky," he muttered, as the doors closed between them.

Chapter 5

Denys didn't like the idea of anyone's being publicly embarrassed, and though to his mind, Lola's flailing her way through Shakespeare and being eviscerated for it by Jacob Roth would be no more than she deserved, he took no enjoyment in the prospect.

He could still remember watching in horror from his seat at the Adelphi as she had flung herself far too fervently into her part in Ibsen's play. Every snicker from the audience at her overwrought gestures, every grimace of her fellow actors at her stilted dialogue and raw technique had made him wince on her behalf.

Witnessing another performance as ghastly as the one he'd seen so long ago was not a prospect any man with a conscience could anticipate with pleasure. He might have avoided it, of course, for his presence at auditions wasn't strictly necessary. But since taking over the Imperial, he'd always made a practice of observing the season's first auditions, giving his opinion if asked for it, and he had no intention of abandoning that practice just because Lola was auditioning.

Still, Thursday morning, when her name was called and she came out on stage, he couldn't help feeling a hint of dread. Her approach to the front of the stage was tentative, almost timid, and as she paused beside the actor assigned to read with her and faced the seats, she looked like a deer ready to bolt for the woods. Despite the heat of the stage's gaslights, her face was pale, and as she lifted the audition sides in her hands, he could see the sheets of paper tremble in her grip.

She cleared her throat. "I have been asked—"

Her voice cracked, and she stopped. The sides rustled as she clenched them tighter in her fingers, and though her lips parted, she didn't speak. Instead, she stared wordlessly out at the seats. Despite his wish that she just go away, Denys felt a hot, painful embarrassment on her behalf, echoing back to that fateful opening night at the Adelphi, and for some stupid reason, he felt impelled to come to her aid.

"Is something wrong, Miss Valentine?" he asked, putting a deliberate hint of mockery into his voice. "You're not nervous, are you?"

That did the trick. A flush of color came into those pale cheeks, revealing a hint of the temperamental, passionate woman he recognized, and he cursed himself for goading her. If he'd resisted that impulse, her propensity to be tongue-tied just might have been enough to do her in.

"I am perfectly well, my lord, thank you," she answered, her voice steadier than before. She once again lifted the sheaf of papers in her hands. "I have been asked to read for Bianca."

"Very well." Reminding himself it was best to have this over with as quickly as possible, he once again settled back in his seat. "Why don't you begin with your entrance in Act Five, Scene One?"

"Act Five?" She stared at him, clearly surprised by this unexpected scene choice. And she wasn't the only one.

"Usurping my job, Denys?" Jacob asked beside him, and when he turned toward the director, he observed the other man studying him in some amusement. "Taking a rather strong interest in the proceedings, aren't you?" he murmured.

"In this case, it's warranted, don't you think?" Denys countered, his voice equally low, but adamant. "I lost a lot of money the last time this woman was in a play I backed."

"Perfectly understandable of you to take an interest then," Jacob replied, seeming not the least bit fooled. "But I am curious, my friend. Why Act Five? Bianca has only a few lines. That's hardly sufficient to show the girl's ability."

"On the contrary," Denys replied, his voice equally low, "Bianca sees that Cassio is injured and may be dying, and she's accused of injuring him, so this is a very dramatic moment, the perfect place for Miss Valentine to demonstrate her skills."

Jacob's mouth quirked. "And if she's terrible, we

won't have to sit through very much before we send her packing."

"Well, yes, that, too."

Chuckling, Jacob sat back, spreading his hands in a gesture of surrender. "Carry on, my friend. In this case, I am content to observe."

Denys returned his attention to the stage. "Jimmy?" he called to the reader. "Are you ready?"

The young man nodded and held up his script. "Yes, my lord."

"Excellent. You may begin, Miss Valentine. That is," he added, watching her flip through her sides to locate the appropriate page, "if you can find Act Five?"

She paused to look at him, and her eyes narrowed a fraction. "I don't need to find it," she said, and dropped the clipped sheaf of papers to the floor behind her. "I was merely keeping busy until you had finished your discussions with Mr. Roth. If *you* are finally ready, I'm happy to begin."

She turned away without waiting for an answer and walked to the wing of stage right, then turned and faced Jimmy. " 'What is the matter, ho?' " she recited as she started toward him. " 'Who is't that cried?' "

She made no effort to mask her American accent, but even Denys had to admit her cant was decent. Many talented actors, even in British theater, found Shakespeare's dialogue a trial.

As if spying Cassio's injured body on the ground, she gave a cry and sank to her knees, a show of abandon quite unnecessary for a first audition. Denys tensed, bracing himself for more of the overdone histrionics she had displayed in *A Doll's House*, but to his surprise, she didn't live up to that expectation. Instead, her distress over the injuries of her lover was restrained, and—as much as he hated to admit it—believable. A few moments later, accused of being the one who had injured Cassio, her denial was convincing enough that he began to think perhaps she actually had learned something about acting while in New York.

For heaven's sake, Denys, what do you think I've been doing the past six years? Eating chocolates and sitting on my behind?

Drawn by that provocative question, Denys's gaze roamed over her form. Memories enabled him to see beneath the plain blue skirt and white shirtwaist to the splendid body beneath, and images came into his mind before he could stop them—full, round breasts and lushly curved hips, pale, luminous skin and long, exquisite legs, dark red hair spilling across ivory sheets and deep green emeralds glittering around her throat, emeralds he had insisted on buying her.

He began to burn, memories pulling him down, down into that dark, sweet place where lust and love and obsession had once melded together to enslave his soul, where nothing in the world had mattered to him but having her. He'd been ready to sacrifice everything dear to him, to turn his back on everyone else he loved, in order to keep her.

And then, she had left him.

Denys dragged himself out of the past, and it was

like thrashing in the water to come up for air—an exercise that only twenty-four hours after her reappearance in his life already felt exhausting.

He blinked, staring at the stage, focusing on the present, telling himself that her audition wasn't all that impressive, that several of the other actresses here would be better suited. By her last lines of the scene, he had almost convinced himself she'd been little more than adequate.

" 'Fie,' " Jimmy said, " 'fie upon thee, strumpet!' "

Lola's frame stiffened, and her chin went up. Something in the air shifted, like the crackle of static electricity, and then, with a suddenness that took his breath away, all the courage previously hidden beneath Bianca's jealous nature was at the fore, clear as daylight.

" 'I am no strumpet,' " she declared. Turning her head to look straight at him, she said her last line of the play. " 'But of life as honest as you that thus abuse me.' "

He knew that for Lola, the words were a lie, but in her role as Bianca, the declaration rang out true, vehement, and convincing. Her face, as always, was breathtakingly beautiful, but at this moment, it also showed Bianca's inherent courage.

My God, he thought, startled, sitting up a bit straighter in his seat. *What if she really can act?*

Even as that thought passed through his head, he tried to dismiss it. There wasn't any meat to the role she was reading for. And Jacob had been right to point out that Act Five wasn't much of a basis on which to judge her talent.

"Well, well," Jacob murmured beside him, laughing a little. "Your plan seems to be backfiring, my friend. I think a more demanding test of Miss Valentine's skill is required."

Without waiting for an answer, Jacob turned toward the stage. "Thank you, Miss Valentine," he said, breaking the silence. "If Lord Somerton has no objection, I'd like to see more."

Denys stirred, but hell, what could he say? He was supposed to be an observer, and nothing more. This, he appreciated darkly, was what a man got for being *fair*.

At the confirmation that she'd passed first muster, she pressed a hand to her chest and gave a little laugh of relief. "Of course," she said. "What shall I read next?"

"Why not continue right where we left off? Read Act Five, Scene Two."

Denys jerked upright, dismayed, but Lola spoke before he could object. "Scene Two?" she echoed, sounding bewildered. "But Bianca has no lines in Scene Two."

"Just so," Jacob said, and in his voice there was a hint of amusement Denys could only think was at his expense. "I want you to read for Desdemona."

Her lips parted in astonishment, and despite his usual rule, Denys felt compelled to intervene. "Jacob, what are you doing?" he muttered. "I thought we decided weeks ago that Arabella Danvers would play Desdemona. We've already offered her the part and a place in the company."

"You think about box office receipts too much, my

friend," Jacob chided him. "But never fear. Arabella will play Desdemona. Still," he added, raising his voice so that Lola could hear what else he had to say, "I haven't decided who shall be understudy. I want to determine if Miss Valentine has the necessary skill to take on that role should it become necessary."

"She doesn't," Denys muttered, whether for his own benefit or Jacob's, he wasn't quite sure. Either way, the director only chuckled and waved a hand encouragingly in Lola's direction.

Lola, however, didn't see his gesture, for she was staring at Denys, waiting, as if expecting him to override his director's decision, but he had no intention of doing so. Giving her plenty of rope was his only option at this point.

"You seem hesitant, Miss Valentine," he called to her. "Desdemona is a demanding role, of course, particularly for someone of your limited experience. It would be understandable if you don't feel you're ready for it."

Her chin lifted at once. "I am prepared to take on any role, my lord."

"Then let's begin," Jacob said, putting an end to any more baiting on Denys's part. "Jimmy, you may start with Othello's bit about cruel tears."

Jimmy complied, drawing Lola's attention, but Denys's gaze, however, remained fixed on her, and he watched with a hint of dread as she began. Desdemona was one of the most overdone roles in the Shakespearean repertoire, and Lola, as he well knew, had always tended to overdo it. But as she played out the scene, there was no sign of the girl whose performance six years ago had been shredded by every theater critic in London. She displayed none of the awkwardness or overdone theatrics he remembered. Her American accent didn't seem to matter. Nor did the lack of props, scenery, and costumes. At this moment, not even Denys could doubt that she was Desdemona, the wronged innocent.

Lola, as he well knew, wasn't innocent, and she certainly wasn't the wronged party in their past, but in this situation, their past should not matter, only her ability. And as he watched her prove him wrong in that regard, he began to feel a hint of desperation.

She's always been trouble, he reminded himself. *From the moment you met her.*

That was irrelevant, and he knew it, and Denys began to fear he'd be saddled with Lola, and all the havoc that came with her, for a long time to come.

She sank to the floorboards, heedless of the hard, unforgiving surface, and Denys watched with a mixture of artistic admiration and personal dismay as she demonstrated the murder of her character.

She reached for the sides behind her prone body, but not, he realized at once, because she needed to read from them. Instead, she slid the sheets of paper over her face, a representation of the pillow Othello had used to suffocate his wife. With her face hidden, the twitching of her body against the floorboards seemed such a convincing display of Desdemona's death throes that it didn't matter that Jimmy was still on his feet. It was easy to envision Othello kneeling over her, committing the act of murder.

"My God," Jacob said beside him.

Denys knew the director well enough to appreciate that those two muttered words were an expression of artistic appreciation, and they deepened the dismay he felt.

Her body stilled. There was a moment of silence, then Jimmy seemed to realize this was his cue and began reading the next lines of the play. Denys, however, kept his gaze on her, waiting with bated breath, knowing what was to come. At last, she moved, demonstrating that Desdemona was not yet dead, and when the improvised murder weapon slid away from her face, he leaned forward in his seat, straining to hear her last lines.

" 'Commend me to my kind lord,' " she said, her voice soft but pitched to carry perfectly to the very last row of the theater. " 'O, farewell.' "

She missed her best line, he thought, but then, her head lolled toward the seats, her eyes looked straight into his, and he realized he'd been mistaken.

" 'A guiltless death I die,' " she rasped, and the words hit him with the impact of a blow to the chest.

She hadn't forgotten anything. She'd deliberately put Desdemona's best line at the last, so that she could be looking at him, rather than at her fellow actor, when she made the heroine's protestation of innocence her own.

He watched as her face relaxed, and her eyes closed, and in the moment of Desdemona's death, she looked so lovely and so without guilt that he suddenly wanted to believe that last night in Paris had all been some horrible mistake.

But his rational mind knew no mistake was possible. Lola, wearing the sheer, intimate clothing a woman only donned for a lover, moving to sit beside Henry on the settee, her words in the face of his marriage proposal so clear and uncompromising that there had been no room for doubt.

Sorry, but Henry has made me a better offer.

A glimmer of the pain he'd felt that night, pain so long suppressed that he'd almost forgotten it, came roaring back with sudden force, violent enough that he jerked in his seat.

He wanted to tell her to go to hell and take Henry's absurd notions of partnership with her. He wanted to say that, partner or not, he would never, ever, allow her to gain a part in any play he produced.

But it was too late for that.

He thought you would be fair.

Henry, it seemed, had known him better than he knew himself. Lola had been good today, damn it all, too good to be dismissed when the only reason for it would be that she'd wronged him years ago.

"Well, Denys," Jacob murmured beside him, sounding far too pleased with himself. "I'm not sure Miss Valentine performed quite as you expected."

Denys refused to be drawn. "Thank you, Miss Valentine," he called to her as he gave the man beside him an impatient glance. "You may wait backstage with the others. Next, please?"

He beckoned to the rather reedy-looking young man waiting at the edge of the stage, but he wasn't able to avoid offering an opinion of Lola's audition quite as easily as he'd hoped.

"Denys?" Jacob prompted, when he said nothing. "Say something, man. What did you think of Miss Valentine's performance?"

Denys sighed, grim resignation settling over him.

"I think," he muttered, studying the seductive sway of Lola's hips as she walked off the stage, "my life just became much more complicated."

Chapter 6

Lola hadn't been required to formally audition for a part in years, and as she lingered in the reception room backstage with her fellow actors, waiting to hear the final casting call, it came home to her just how nerve-racking the process was.

The success of her show in New York had ended the need for auditions, and the only readings she'd done had been for tutors or for Henry in the sitting room of her New York apartment, and any assessments they gave of her work, while keenly critical, had always been offered with suggestions how to improve.

Reading for Jacob Roth, with Denys beside him and dozens of curious peers watching from the wings, was a whole different matter, and she didn't have a clue as to the caliber of her audition.

Thankfully, she hadn't forgotten her lines or tripped

over her skirt, or stuttered over Shakespeare's tricky dialogue. But now, surrounded by actors probably far more experienced than she, those facts did not seem very reassuring.

Voices swirled around her, engaged in the usual self-deprecating conversation punctuated by nervous laughter, as actors greeted each other and speculated about their chances, but Lola did not attempt to join in.

After her disastrous performance in *A Doll's House*, spiteful things had been said behind her back, lurid accounts of her affair with Denys had hit the scandal sheets, and within days, London's theater coterie was treating her like a plague contagion, sure she was only in the play because it had been financed by her lover. And why shouldn't they have thought it? It was the truth.

Don't worry, Denys had said. *I'll take care of you.*

He'd meant to console and reassure her, but Lola could still remember lying in bed with him at the house he'd leased for her in St. John's Wood, those words echoing through her brain and a sick feeling knotting her guts as she realized just what she had become.

I'll take care of you.

She'd never wanted that, but that was where she'd ended up, becoming a kept woman without even realizing it. Little by little, with every gift he'd given her that she couldn't bear to give back and every offer to help her that she couldn't seem to refuse, with every touch of his hand and kiss of his mouth, she'd belonged a bit less to herself and a bit more to him. And with her acting career over before it had really begun, she'd lain in his arms that last afternoon in London and wondered if being a kept woman was the inevitable path for a girl like her.

She had fought so hard to avoid that fate. Men had been pursuing her from the time she was old enough for a corset, and though her mother had gone back to her high-society set in Baltimore long before then, leaving Lola and her father far behind, Lola hadn't needed a mother to explain the facts of life, not about men. Somehow, she'd always known that the sort of pursuit most men had in mind didn't involve a church, a vow, and love everlasting.

Before Denys, she'd given in only once, back in New York the winter she was seventeen, and the result of her very brief, very stupid liaison with handsome man-about-town Robert Delacourt had been a hard, humiliating confirmation of the first lesson every girl on the boards had to learn: stage-door johnnies don't marry dancing girls.

After Robert, she'd taken what little cash she had and moved to Paris, where she'd been quite happy to keep the stage-door johnnies at arm's length. It had been easy as pie to refuse the dinners, the champagne, and the jewels, for she knew all those gifts came at a price.

But then, Denys had come along, with his affable charm, his dark good looks, and—most of all—his deep, genuine tenderness. Tenderness was something she'd had little of in her life, and her parched soul had taken it in the way a wilting plant took up water, and eighteen months later, she had somehow become what she'd promised herself she would never be: a kept woman.

She had also become a danger to Denys's future. Earl Conyers had called at the house in St. John's Wood, waved his checkbook in her face, and suggested with thinly veiled contempt that she should leave London before he was forced to disinherit his son.

She'd torn up the draft of a thousand pounds Conyers had written and thrown the shreds in his face, but she'd also known she could not allow Denys to keep supporting her. She'd returned to Paris, secured a position at yet another Montmartre establishment, and tried to accept the brutal reality that she'd be singing and dancing in the cabarets until her looks went and her legs gave out and the smoke of men's cigars destroyed her voice.

And then Henry had come, arriving at her dressing-room door with champagne—not, he'd assured her at once, as any sort of romantic overture, but in celebration. Denys, he explained, was coming from England to make her an offer of marriage.

She could still remember what she'd felt in that moment—the burst of keen, clear joy at the prospect of marrying Denys, and the cold, harsh reality that had at once overshadowed it.

"So you're here to congratulate me?" she'd asked, shoving down girlish idiocies. "That's a bit premature, isn't it?"

"Most women would be chomping at the bit to marry

a lord. You don't seem quite so eager." He gave her a shrewd glance she feared saw far too much. "But then, you're an unusual woman."

"What is your real reason for coming here?"

Henry smiled, the knowing smile of a man of the world. "I'm here to give you an alternative to saying yes."

"What makes you think I'd want an alternative?"

"Call it a guess. You've always impressed me as a sensible girl, tough, practical, and hardheaded."

"I'm flattered."

"Conyers knows I'm here. He also knows Denys's intention to make an honest woman of you. They had quite the epic battle about it yesterday. It was especially lurid, I understand, since Conyers had just discovered how Denys financed *A Doll's House*."

Lola frowned, uncomprehending. "What do you mean?"

"Don't you know? He mortgaged his estate, Arcady, the one his father bequeathed to him when he came of age."

Oh, Denys, she thought, heartsick, *what have you done?*

"Needless to say," Henry went on, "the earl doesn't much fancy the idea of you as his daughter-in-law."

"So you're here to try bribing me on his behalf?" She made a sound of derision. "When will he accept that I won't take his money to give Denys up?"

"He already has, which is why I'm not here to offer it. And forgive me for pointing out the obvious, but it seems that you already have given Denys up. Otherwise . . ." He glanced around the dressing room. "You wouldn't be working here."

She didn't much like being so transparent to a man she barely knew, but she gave a nonchalant shrug. "When I left London, I didn't know a ring was in the offing."

"If you had known, would you have stayed?"

"I don't know," she said truthfully.

"And if you were to marry Denys, could you make him happy?"

She felt cold suddenly, fear brushing over her the same way the chill winds of autumn brushed aside the languid, sultry days of summer. She didn't reply to Henry's question, but she didn't have to. They both knew the answer.

Viscount Somerton, the son and heir of Earl Conyers, being happily married to a cabaret dancer was a glorious and impossible fantasy, akin to a sailor marrying a mermaid, or a butcher from Kansas City marrying a society girl from Baltimore by mail-order proxy. The chance of happiness for such unions was precisely nil. And yet . . . and yet . . .

Yearning welled up within her.

"I have to change," she said, and started to close the door, but Henry flattened a palm against the door to stop her.

"May I wait?"

A man didn't come into a girl's dressing room, especially with champagne, unless he was an intimate acquaintance or she wanted him to become one. On the other hand, Henry Latham was a powerful man in theater circles, not one to be snubbed lightly.

"I'm not here to seduce you," he said as she hesitated, "or to throw Conyers's money in your face. I have an entirely different sort of offer to make. We can talk about it while you change."

She wanted out of her costume. She was tired and sweaty, and her ribs ached, as they always did after dancing in a tight corset. Abruptly, she turned away. "Do as you like."

Leaving him in the doorway, she crossed the room and stepped behind the dressing screen. Henry's voice floated to her over the top as she slipped out of her dancing shoes.

"Shall I tell you what I have in mind?"

She was skeptical, but it never did any harm to listen. "Sure," she answered, bending down to untie her garters and roll off the flesh-colored stockings that had helped make Lola Valentine so wickedly notorious. "Why not?"

"I want you to come with me to New York. As I said, this isn't a romantic offer. I think you have enormous talent, and I can make you a star."

She laughed, a cynical sound forged from years on the boards. How many times had men said those exact words to her? Still, Henry Latham at least had the bona fides to make such a claim credible. "Don't you live in London?" she asked as she unhooked the bodice of her costume and slid the dress down. It landed in a pouf at her feet.

"Yes, but I've decided to return home. Come with me, and I'll give you your own show and make you famous. And I'll pay you a generous percentage, far more than you're getting here."

Lola peeked around the side of the dressing screen. "I'm not sure I want to go back to New York. I've . . . danced there already."

"What do you want?"

She ducked back behind the screen and hung her dress on one of the pegs on the wall and didn't answer.

"You don't have to tell me," he said, as she began loosening her corset laces. "I can guess. You want to be an actress."

Lola paused, her arms falling to her sides.

"You want to thrill audiences, hold them spellbound. You want to hear them gasp and sigh, and you want to know they'll be talking about you long after show is over and the lights are out. You want what all performers want. You want to be loved."

Was he mocking her? She couldn't tell. "That's not it," she answered as she unhooked her corset busk. "I already have all that. Men love watching Lola Valentine strut around, kicking off hats with her foot and singing bawdy songs." She could hear the tinge of bitterness in her voice as she spoke. "Men love seeing Lola pout her lips and show off her legs and shimmy her bosom. They adore Lola. Were you in the audience tonight? Three curtain calls. Lola's famous here in Montmartre. Or, maybe I should say she's notorious."

"Ah, now we're getting the truth," he murmured.

"You want to act because you want to be taken seriously. You want respect."

She gave a harsh laugh. "Well, if that's what I want, I'm doomed to disappointment."

"Not necessarily."

"Did you read the reviews for *A Doll's House*?" she asked as she hung her corset over the top of the screen and began stripping out of her sweaty underclothes. "According to the *Times*, my performance was 'reminiscent of a drunken butterfly, brilliantly colorful, but also awkward, graceless, and infinitely pathetic.'"

"You don't have to quote your reviews, honey. I read them. I also saw the play." He paused. "Denys thought you could act."

"Denys is . . ." She paused and swallowed painfully. "Blinded by passion."

"I'm not, and I agree with him."

The words were like lighting a match to a stick of dynamite. "Don't," she ordered fiercely, peeking around the screen again to glare at him through narrowed eyes. "Don't butter me up, Mr. Latham, and tell me what you think I want to hear. It won't get me to come to New York with you."

"What about training? Would that persuade you?"

"Training?" Intrigued, she started to step out from behind the screen but stopped just in time, remembering she was naked. "What do you mean? What kind of training?"

"Truly good acting isn't something where you just step out onto a stage and start giving brilliant performances. It takes rigorous training. It takes practice and criticism and direction. You, I assume, haven't had much of that."

"I haven't had any of that. Well, not until I started rehearsals for *A Doll's House*."

"So I'll train you. I'll pay for lessons. You can perform for me, and I'll critique you, offer direction. I was quite an actor in my day, you know. I'll see you learn your craft the right way. And when I think you're ready to give drama another try, I'll back a serious play for you. I'll even make it Shakespeare. As far as serious acting goes, he's the top of the tree. And if you're good, I'll back your career. Maybe we'll even open our own theater in New York, and you can put on your own plays."

"This is all really nice of you." She paused, tilting her head as she looked at him. "And what do you get?"

"At least three years of Lola Valentine performing her one-woman show in Madison Square."

Her eyes narrowed with suspicion. "And that's all?"

"I don't want to sleep with you, honey," he said bluntly. "I'm getting too old for girls like you. I've got a mistress already, one my own age who suits me just fine. I met her here, but she lives in New York. That's why I'm going back."

Lola ducked back behind the screen, excitement rising inside her like fireworks. To learn the craft, to do it properly, to perform Shakespeare. To be more than just a great pair of legs and a sultry voice. To be respected for her work rather than ogled for her body.

She wanted that. Lola took a deep breath. She wanted it so badly, she ached. And yet . . .

What about Denys?

Agonized, Lola stifled a groan and lifted her head to stare at the garments on hooks before her: the austere dress of plum velvet she preferred to wear for supper after shows, the spangled silver dance costume she'd don tomorrow night, the delicate, luxurious peignoir of white silk chiffon that she liked to wear here in her dressing room while applying and removing her cosmetics. These gowns were the tight compartments of her dancer's life. But she couldn't dance forever. Eight years, maybe ten, and her body would start to give out. What would happen to her then? If she didn't take Latham up on his offer, what other choices would she have?

Denys, a little voice whispered. *If you married him, he'd take care of you.*

But at what cost? He'd already alienated his family because of her. Hell, he'd mortgaged his estate. And those were nothing compared to the sacrifices he'd have to make if he married her.

His family would never accept the match. The earl was the only one who had ever met her, but she was aware that all of them loathed her to the core and thought her a gold-digging tramp. If Denys married her, Conyers would surely follow through with his threat and disown his son.

Society wouldn't accept the marriage, either. They'd freeze her out, and, eventually, Denys as well. His titled friends, pressured by their families, would turn on him, too. Nick, Jack, James, Stuart—they all liked her well enough when she was kicking up her legs and making them laugh, but surely not as Denys's wife. Losing their friendship, losing his family, being ostracized and disgraced—these sacrifices would break him apart.

She wanted a secure future for herself, yes, but not by sacrificing Denys's happiness. And he could never be happy with her—not as his wife, his countess, his help-mate for life. When his passion cooled, as it inevitably would, what sort of marriage would they have?

And what about herself? As much as she wanted to act, becoming Viscountess Somerton, the future Countess of Conyers, was a part she just wasn't good enough to play. Not every waking moment for the rest of her life. A girl like her, married to a lord? It was ridiculous.

A tear slid down her cheek, and she squeezed her eyes shut. A sailor's falling in love with a mermaid might make for a blissful fairy tale, but she knew, better than anyone, what happened when the fairy tale was over.

Her mind flashed back to the days of her childhood, with her mother gone, and her father, head in his hands, soaked in whiskey and sobbing like a child. It had taken him ten years of hard drinking to finally end his pain in the most permanent way possible.

She thought of her burlesque days in New York, when she'd taken the train down to Maryland and stood on the front steps of one of Baltimore's most opulent houses, and a butler with haughty eyes had told her

Mrs. Angus Hutchison had no daughter and had never had a daughter.

Behind her, the dressing-room door opened. "Lola?" Denys's voice floated to her above the other sounds that came through the doorway—raucous piano, teeming voices, drunken laughter. "Lola, are you in here, or—"

His voice broke off, and she knew he'd just seen Henry.

Dismay jolted her as she realized what he would think, but then, a much more dismal realization struck her. She knew what he'd think, yes, but wasn't that better?

She grabbed the peignoir and slipped it on before she could change her mind. Bracing herself to give the most convincing performance of her life, she stepped out from behind the screen. "Denys!" she gasped as if in horrified shock. "What are you doing here?"

His dark gaze lowered to the flimsy garment that covered her naked body, then moved to the champagne Henry had placed on her dressing table. "You—"

He broke off, and in the silence, she could see shock giving way to wariness and caution. "You left London."

"The play closed." She shrugged as if it was a matter of no consequence. "I had to find work."

"Without even seeing me to say good-bye?"

"It seemed the best way."

His gaze locked with hers. "Best for whom?"

Her courage began to flag, but she didn't look away. "I told you, I had to find work, and no one in London seemed willing to hire me. So, I came back here. The *Jardin de Paris* was happy to offer me a place."

"You didn't have to do this. I told you . . ." He paused,

his gaze sliding to Henry, then back again. "I'll take care of you."

She didn't reply, and he took a step toward her, but then he stopped. "Henry," he said, his gaze not leaving her face, "leave us, please."

"That won't be necessary," she said before Henry could comply, and she knew she had to end this quickly, or she'd lose her nerve, and—God help them both—let him talk her into a different future. "I'd like Henry to stay."

He set his jaw. "Why?"

"We've become . . . friends." She sauntered over to where Henry sat on the settee and sank down beside him, watching Denys as an appreciation of all the implications dawned in his eyes. Pain followed—his pain—slicing into her like a knife, and she knew she had to get this over with before it annihilated her.

"I heard you're thinking we might get married." She laughed, a brittle sound that made him grimace. And although it took every scrap of willpower she had, and cost her more than anything she'd ever done on stage, she held his gaze. "I'm flattered, but Henry has made me a better offer."

"A better offer?" He shook his head, refusing to believe, and she knew she had to hammer the point home.

"Yes. He's going back to America and taking me with him. He's giving me my own show in New York."

Denys's jaw tightened. "I see."

He took a step back, and she felt as if her heart were ripping in half. "Yes," he said, nodding, "I see."

She could see, too—she could see him hurting, hardening, any love he might have for her withering right before her eyes. But it was better for him to hate her now, when he wasn't stuck with her for life, when he could still find someone else, someone who wouldn't be an embarrassment to him and a stain to his family name, someone suitable who understood his life and could share it. Better for him to look at her with loathing now than with regret and blame a few years from now. Better to end this affair before there was a marriage that could not be undone and children who would suffer for their mistake. But as his eyes raked over her, what was better didn't seem much comfort.

"I'm glad we understand each other," she said, and caught the quiver in her voice. She forced herself to steady it, to speak with quiet finality. "Good-bye, Denys."

The silence was smothering. Her chest ached, and she couldn't breathe, and she knew that if he stood there much longer, she was going to break down. But just when she thought she couldn't take it anymore, he turned his back and walked out, slamming the door behind him.

"So," Henry said beside her in the silence. "I guess that means you've decided to accept my offer."

She was tough, she reminded herself. She was hard-headed and practical, and she'd done the right thing. "I guess I have," she said, and burst into tears.

Henry had given her a handkerchief, a stiff drink, and a fresh start. With his backing and support, she'd taken Lola Valentine to Madison Square, and within a year, she'd climbed to the top of New York music-hall theater. With the training he'd promised, she slowly learned the craft and the discipline of serious acting, and Henry's encouragement had given her hope that one day she'd be able to perform drama again. But now?

What am I doing here? she wondered wildly as she glanced at the actors all around her. She was in partnership with a man who had every reason to hate her and would like nothing but to see the back of her. He'd never let her be part of this company. And, she thought, taking another look at the people around her, why should he?

These were serious actors with established bona fides who performed Shakespearean drama and Greek tragedy, while she was known for a risqué song-and-dance routine. The only acting role on her resume had lasted a week. Most of these people had years of experience reciting the lines of Hamlet and Clytemnestra, while her most famous soliloquy was a bawdy rendition of *You Should Go to France and See the Ladies Dance*.

Self-doubt seized her like a fist, clenching and twisting her guts. Everyone already thought she'd slept her way to success, and being partners with Denys was only going to reinforce that. Even if she proved she could act, it'd take forever for people to respect her for it. And what if she didn't prove herself? What then?

"Lola? Lola Valentine?"

She looked up to find a woman of about her own age standing by her seat, a woman whose round, china-doll face she recognized at once from her Paris days. "Kitty Carr," she cried, jumping to her feet with a laugh of disbelief. "My goodness!"

Kitty's big brown eyes crinkled at the corners as she offered an answering smile. "What's it been? Seven years, now?"

"Since the *Théâtre Latin*? Closer to eight, I'm afraid."

"Seven or eight, it's long enough that I could hardly believe it when I saw you walk out on that stage."

"You were watching?"

"Back row." She bent to place the large, slim valise of black leather she was carrying on the floor beside her. "I had no idea you were in London."

"I could say the same about you."

"Well, I am a London girl," Kitty reminded her. "A year after you left Paris, I decided to do the same. I tried to look you up, but you'd already gone to New York. When did you return?"

"Just a few days ago." Lola gestured invitingly to the empty space beside her. "Are you auditioning, too?" she asked, as both of them sank down on the bench seat.

Kitty shook her head, tucking a loose lock of her straight blond hair behind one ear. "No. I'm here to see Mr. Roth about the backdrops for the play. I paint scenery nowadays."

"You gave up the stage?"

"I did. It proved too much for my constitution."

Lola pressed a hand to her stomach. "Right now, I know just what you mean."

"You've no cause to worry. You did well."

"Do you really think so?"

Kitty groaned, shaking her head as if in exasperation as she turned toward her and propped one shoulder against the wall behind them. "You've become a real actor, I can tell, what with all this blatant fishing for compliments."

"I'm not! But this is my first Shakespeare audition."

"Ever?" When Lola nodded, Kitty's answering glance held complete understanding. "A bit intimidating, what?"

"More than a bit."

"Well, if it's any consolation to hear praise from an old friend, I think you were head and shoulders above the rest."

As gratifying as it was to hear that, it did little to ease her apprehensions.

"Where are you staying?"

Lola drew a deep breath, grateful for the distraction of Kitty's conversation. "The Savoy. At least for now."

"Heavens, I knew you'd become quite the thing in New York, but really, Lola! Staying at the Savoy?" Kitty stuck her pert nose impudently up in the air. "My word and la-di-da. I'm not sure you ought to be seen with the likes of me."

"Oh, stop!" Lola protested, laughing. "I'm only there because it's the most respectable hotel in the theater district, and I'm raising quite a few eyebrows by being there with only a maid. The staff thinks I'm quite depraved, I'm sure, and the maître d'hôtel looks down his nose whenever I go in the restaurant. I fear any moment, I'll be deemed a shameless hussy and booted out because I'm giving the hotel a bad name. I'd welcome an alternative, but you know how London is."

Kitty abandoned her impudent air and offered a sigh of commiseration in its place. "I know, I know, London's awful. And it's the season just now, which means even a garret comes dear. Only by a stroke of pure luck did I find rooms."

"You're living out? But what about your family?" She frowned in an effort of memory. "Don't you have an aunt here?"

"Vile woman." Kitty shuddered. "The sort who always has to remind you she did you a favor by taking you in. About a year ago, I decided I couldn't stick it, so now I share a flat with another painter, Eloisa Montgomery, at a lodging house in Little Russell Street. A very respectable place, and just for women. No riffraff lounging about, and the omnibuses go right by. All meals in or not, as you like, and tea as well."

Lola opened her mouth, but before she could ask if Kitty and her friend might be willing to rent her the use of the flat's settee until she found lodgings of her own, the entire room went suddenly silent, and when she turned her head, she spied Denys standing in the doorway.

As he came in, anyone sitting immediately stood up, and anyone standing came to full attention, all rather as a well-trained regiment might do when the commanding officer arrived. Lola followed suit, though standing on ceremony with Denys seemed rather an alien concept to her.

I'll take care of you.

That tender, well-intentioned reassurance of long ago shimmered through her consciousness like a whisper across the silent room. As if he'd heard it, too, Denys turned his head and looked at her, but there was nothing tender in his expression, and nothing the least bit encouraging. Lola's stomach gave another nervous lurch.

"Ladies and gentlemen," he said, and looked away, glancing over the crowd as he moved out of the doorway to make room for Jacob Roth to enter. "We appreciate the time all of you have taken to audition today. We would like the following people to be here two weeks from today at nine o'clock for the table read of *Othello*. Rehearsals will begin the following Monday. As for the rest of you, thank you very much for coming, and we encourage you to try out again next season." Pausing, he lifted a clipboard in his hand and began to read a list of names. "Breckenridge, John. Fulbright, Edward. Ross, Elizabeth. Lovell, William . . ."

Lola closed her eyes. This was it, everything she'd been training for.

"Whitman, George. Cowell, Blackie . . ."

It might not happen. She was still a partner, of course, but that seemed little consolation right now.

"Saunders, Jamie. Breville, Henry. Maclean, Hugh."

Suddenly, Denys stopped reading names, and Lola felt the silence like a boxer might feel a knockout blow.

Her name had not been called. Evidently, despite all Henry's instruction and training, she still wasn't ready.

The admission was a bitter one, but what else was there to do but accept it? She bit down on her lip against the stinging disappointment and forced her eyes open, only to find Denys looking straight at her.

"And lastly," he said with a sigh, "Valentine, Lola."

Surprise and relief came over her in a rush, and she didn't know whether to jump for joy or throw up. Dizzy, she sank down on the bench, doubling over until her forehead hit her knees and sucking in great gasps of air.

Kitty leaned down beside her. "Told you so," she murmured, then straightened away and reached for her valise. "I'll call on you at the Savoy. What about tomorrow evening? We'll have supper and a long visit."

Without lifting her head, Lola nodded. "That sounds lovely," she said, her voice muffled by her skirts.

"Right. I'll be off, then." With a congratulatory pat on the back, Kitty departed, but Lola remained where she was, breathing deep and trying to assimilate the fact that she finally had the chance she'd worked so hard for.

Voices—some buoyant, some dejected—eddied and faded as the actors began to depart. Lola waited until the room was silent before she sat up, but when she did, she discovered she was not the only one who had remained behind. Denys was still standing by the door.

"You seem surprised," he said, watching her.

"Not surprised." She rose to her feet. "Stupefied is more like it."

That made him smile a little. "So is Roth. You impressed him, and that's no easy task."

"And you?" she couldn't help asking. "Were you impressed?"

He stirred, as if the question made him uneasy. "You said your lines at the end in the wrong order."

She waved that aside. "But do you think I'm any good?"

"Does it matter what I think?"

She held his gaze steadily. "Whether you believe it or not, your opinion has always mattered to me, Denys."

"If that's true, you've demonstrated it rather poorly in the past. Still," he added before she could reply, "you did well today. Very well."

She caught the surprise in his voice. "You didn't think I would," she said, watching his face. "Did you?"

"No," he admitted, and looked away. "I did not."

She studied his profile, knowing full well what his thinking had been. "You let me audition, but you were sure I'd fail. What did you think? That losing one part would send me off with my tail tucked in defeat?"

"Something like that," he muttered, and looked at her again, his expression rueful. "I should have known better. Defeat is a circumstance you don't seem to accept."

She grinned. "Not for long, anyway. I'm to play Bianca, then?"

"Yes. And you'll understudy Desdemona, too. If you think you can manage both?"

"You watch me." She laughed, jubilant, exhilarated, and so, so relieved. "Thank you, Denys."

"Thank Roth. He wanted you. He was quite adamant about it."

"Well, we both know how you feel about me, so the two of you must have had quite a row on the topic."

"On the contrary, we were in complete agreement. You rather stole the show."

"Oh." Lola stared at him, and in his countenance she saw—or thought she saw—a trace of the Denys she used to know, but it was gone before she could be sure. "So," she said, forcing herself to speak. "Who did you choose to play the lead?"

"Arabella Danvers."

"Ugh." Lola groaned, seizing on that diversion like a lifeline. "You must be joking."

"I never joke about business."

Lola frowned, not quite convinced. She'd been jumpy as a cat on a hot sidewalk this morning, true enough, but if Arabella had auditioned, she was sure she'd have noticed. That woman was the sort who, when she arrived anywhere, made sure everyone noticed. "But Arabella didn't audition today, did she?"

"Mrs. Danvers needs no audition. I offered her the part without one."

Lola made a wry face at him. "So exceptions to the rules can be made for her but not for your partner."

"She's played Shakespeare. You haven't. And she's one of London's most successful and popular actresses. You're not."

"Ouch." Lola grimaced. "You don't have to rub it in," she grumbled. "And Arabella may be popular with audiences, but not with anyone else. You must know her reputation? It's legendary. She's temperamental, difficult—"

"A case of the pot and the kettle if ever there was one."

"I'm serious, Denys. If you take on Arabella, you and Roth will be regretting it in a week."

He clearly did not appreciate her opinion on the subject. "Disparaging Arabella isn't going to gain you the lead, so stop angling for it."

"I'm not! I'm just warning you what you're in for. I believe Arabella would stab her own grandmother if she thought it would get her anything."

"I doubt Jacob and I are in any danger. We don't have to like her to appreciate her popularity or her talent."

"Talent?" Lola couldn't help offering a derisive snort. "If you say so."

"You've hardly room to talk," he pointed out dryly. "And given your animosity for her, I am wondering if you should be her understudy."

"That's not your decision, remember?" She gave him a look of triumph. "It's Roth's, and I think he likes me. And I won't make any trouble, I promise. After all, the peace of our partnership is at stake."

"You're too good."

That rejoinder impelled Lola to stick out her tongue at him, but it was a wasted effort, for he had already turned away.

"Rehearsals begin at nine o'clock in the morning, and they run six days a week, Monday through Saturday," he said as he walked toward the door. "Bring your lunch with you, and don't ever be late. Jacob hates to be kept waiting, and trust me, you don't want to lose his goodwill. And Lola?"

He paused in the doorway to look at her over his shoulder. "When the play opens, don't even think of sending Arabella a telegram from a dying aunt."

She stuck up her chin, adopting a dignified air. "I would never do such a thing."

He expressed the trust he had in that assurance with a brief, skeptical, "Uh-huh," as he began to pull the door shut.

Lola, however, wasn't about to let him escape before she got in the last word. "I wouldn't," she insisted. "Arabella doesn't have an aunt."

The door closed, but not before she heard his shout of laughter.

Lola stared at the closed door, astonished. She'd made him laugh. Maybe he didn't hate her as much as she'd feared. Maybe they really could work together. She grinned. Maybe there was hope for this crazy partnership after all.

Chapter 7

"Ah . . . room service for supper." Kitty set down her fork, dropped her napkin onto the tray in her lap, and leaned back against the sofa of Lola's suite with a contented sigh. "What a treat."

"But didn't you say your lodging house serves meals in?" Lola asked, beckoning her maid to take the supper trays as she poured more champagne. "Is the cook no good?"

"It isn't that." Kitty stretched an arm toward her on the sofa to accept the refilled glass from her outstretched hand. "But Mrs. Morris's cook doesn't serve champagne, Lobster Newburg, braised ptarmigan, and *gateau au chocolat*!"

"I suppose not." As she returned the champagne to the ice bucket on the cart beside her, Lola noted that the serving trays were now almost completely devoid of food. "We did eat an awful lot, didn't we?"

"Too much." Her friend grimaced, pressing a hand to her ribs. "When I suggested yesterday that we have supper together, you should have warned me you intended to order half the menu. I'd have left my corset at home."

"Well, at least you don't have to worry about fitting into costumes anymore. Remember at the *Théâtre-Latin* how Madame Dupuy used to line us up in our corsets and give us the once-over before each show?"

"Oh, yes! What a terror she was. She'd look you over, and if you'd gained an ounce, she knew it. She'd slip her measuring tape around you, and if you weren't laced tight enough, she relaced you then and there, tighter than you needed to be just to drive the point home. It's a wonder some of us didn't pass out on stage. Those were mad days, weren't they?"

Her own champagne flute in hand, Lola faced her friend, propping her back against the arm of the sofa. "You sound as if you miss those days."

"Sometimes I do." Kitty faced her, mirroring Lola's position at the other end of the sofa. "When I came home from Paris, I danced at the Gaiety for a bit. Now, I'm over there sometimes, arranging sets or painting scenery, and if I see the girls kicking up their legs in rehearsal, I feel quite a pang."

"So why did you give it up?"

Kitty made a face, her doll-like nose wrinkling up a bit. "The usual reason."

Lola understood at once. "A man?"

"His people didn't think I was good enough for him, so we decided . . ." She paused, pain crossing her face, and she swallowed hard before she went on. "He decided we wouldn't suit. He jilted me."

"I'm so sorry."

"At least, coming from you, it's not meaningless sympathy. You know what it's like to be seen as not good enough for the man you love."

Lola decided they needed a different topic of conversation. "You didn't go back to dancing?"

"Heavens, no. I'm twenty-nine, a bit long in the tooth for the cancan. I tried my hand at acting once—I joined a repertory company, but I couldn't stick it. I got through one week before I quit. Unlike you, I'm not brave enough for real acting."

"Brave?" Lola couldn't help a laugh. "Crazy is more like it. Last time I tried this, I was a colossal failure."

"Which is why I say you're brave. In your place, I'd have stayed in New York, used my inheritance as a dowry, found myself some nice, respectable chap to marry, and given up the stage for good. I'd certainly never have come back here and tried again. But perhaps . . ." Her friend paused and took a sip of champagne, giving Lola a wide-eyed stare over the rim of her glass. "Perhaps acting wasn't your only reason for returning to London?"

Lola stiffened. "I don't know what you mean."

"Oh, Lola, really!" Her friend laughed, not the least bit put off by her attempt at hauteur. "This is Kitty you're talking to. We shared a dressing room in our Paris days, remember? Do you think I've forgotten how often Somerton called on you there with champagne and chocolates?"

"That was a long time ago, as we've just been discussing. And," she added, wrinkling up her nose in rueful fashion, "Denys liked me much more in those days than he does now."

"It seemed a mutual feeling to me, luvvy. Oh, how you used to sigh and swoon over him."

Pride compelled her to object to that description. "I have never swooned over a man in my life. Not even Denys."

"Tell it to the marines! I remember how he used to wait outside our dressing room while you dithered over which dress to wear or whether a gentleman like him would think you too forward if you dabbed perfume behind your ears. And when he asked you to move to London to be with him, you were over the moon!"

"I have never swooned," Lola reiterated. "And I don't sigh, and I don't dither. And even if I was as silly as all that once upon a time, I'm certainly not that way now."

"No? I saw you looking at him while you said your lines yesterday." She paused to set aside her champagne, then she lifted her hand to press the back of it against her forehead. "'Commend me to my kind lord,'" she quoted with melodramatic fervor as she fell back, draping herself artistically over the arm of the sofa, her glass held high. "'A guiltless death I die.'"

Kitty sat up, laughing, but Lola felt no inclination to

laugh with her. "I have not come back to London to rekindle a romance with Denys!"

"Haven't you?" Her friend studied her face for a moment, then sighed, looking let down. "You mean it really is about acting?"

"Partly. Denys and I are also business partners."

Kitty cocked an eyebrow. "I beg your pardon?"

She proceeded to explain, and though the other woman listened with rapt attention, Lola's explanations didn't seem to impress her.

"Business partners, hmm?" She gave a wink. "Well, that's a start, I suppose."

"Really, Kitty, you're impossible!" She made a sound of impatience, sitting upright on the sofa. "Have you really forgotten what Madame used to say? 'The lords, they love to chase the dancing girls, *n'est-ce pas*? But—'"

" 'They don't ever marry them,' " her friend finished with mock solemnity.

The idiom wasn't quite true in her case, but Lola wasn't above using it to veer Kitty off this topic. "Well, there you are, then."

"It's time one of our lot beat the odds, I say. Why shouldn't it be you? You know better than most that a girl has to have big dreams if she's to accomplish anything."

"I have no objection to big dreams," Lola assured her. "Just impossible ones."

"Is it so impossible? He loved you once. Why shouldn't he fall in love with you again?"

Lola stared at her in dismay. "It's not like that. We

are *business* partners. That's going to be hard enough to manage without bringing any crazy ideas of romance into it."

"I don't see how you can think *not* to bring romance into it. You two have a history."

"There's no reason why we can't just be indifferent acquaintances."

Kitty stared at her askance. "You and Somerton?"

"Yes," she said, even as she mentally crossed her fingers. "Platonic, indifferent acquaintances."

"You two have been many things, Lola, but indifferent has never been one of them."

Lola's mind went tumbling back into the past before she could stop it—the torture of keeping him at arm's length in Paris, the bliss of their meetings at the house in St. John's Wood. His mouth on hers and his body on hers and the frantic, wild euphoria of afternoons in bed together. Warmth flooded through her, pooling in her midsection, flooding her cheeks, tingling up and down her spine.

"Acquaintances, hmm?"

Kitty's amused voice was like a splash of icy water.

"Yes," she said, scowling. "And if you keep making fun of the idea, I fear our friendship is not long for this world."

"Sorry." The amusement vanished from her friend's face at once, replaced by a somber expression. "All teasing aside, I'm not sure a man and a woman can ever work together. Romance, I should think, would always get in the way."

"That's not true. I know plenty of people who've had love affairs, broken up, and worked together quite amicably afterward. It happens in theater all the time, and you know it."

"Well, yes, for a play here and there, maybe. But you're talking about a lifetime of being in business together. And besides," she added before Lola could argue, "even if you and Somerton do establish a platonic relationship, very few other people will believe that's what it is."

"I don't care what people believe."

"Somerton does."

Lola grimaced at that unarguable fact. "I know," she acknowledged with a sigh. "But I don't see what either of us can do about it. Over time, people will just have to accept there's nothing of that sort between us."

"And his sweetheart? Do you think she'll accept it?"

Lola blinked, taken aback, though she knew she shouldn't be. "Denys has a sweetheart?"

"That's the rumor."

"Who—" She paused, her voice gone and her throat dry, and she felt the need for a swallow of champagne. She gulped down the entire contents of her glass before she could voice the inevitable question. "Who is she?" she managed at last, and she was absurdly proud of the indifference in her voice.

If Kitty wasn't deceived, at least she didn't tease about it. "Lady Georgiana Prescott. Daughter of a marquess. Very highbrow and elegant, if the scandal rags are to be believed."

Lady Georgiana. Of course. How fitting, how right that he should return his attentions to his childhood love, the woman his parents had always wanted for him, the perfect sort of woman to marry an earl's son. Even as that thought passed through Lola's mind, however, she felt a bit bleak.

"Well, there you have it then," she said, striving to sound brisk and matter-of-fact. "When he becomes engaged to Lady Georgiana, it will show everyone there's nothing between us."

"You are underestimating the depths to which people's minds can sink. Most people will assume Somerton is having his cake and eating it, too. After all"—Kitty swirled her champagne, her eyes meeting Lola's over the rim of her glass—"he always did find you quite a scrumptious slice of cake."

"Denys would never do what you're suggesting! He's far too honorable. And," she added before her friend could say something cynical about the baser aspects of the masculine nature, "I wouldn't let it happen. Why would I?"

"Why?" Kitty tilted her head as if pondering the question. "Hmm . . . let's see. He's good-looking, rich, a viscount, a future earl, and a very nice fellow who once had quite a passion for you. Yes, why, indeed?"

"I ended our affair," she reminded her friend hotly. "I left him for another man."

Kitty shrugged, running one finger idly around the rim of her glass. "You wouldn't be the first woman who'd broken things off with a chap and taken up with another only to realize she'd made a mistake."

"I did not make a mistake! I left him for a man who knew what I was, who would never expect me to become something I could never be. We are both better off, and Denys would agree."

"I'm sure he would."

Her friend's mild agreement only impelled Lola to hammer the point home. "Lady Georgiana will make him a much more suitable wife than I ever would have. And," she added as Kitty opened her mouth again, "I'd never become entangled with another woman's sweetheart! How could you think I would?"

"Sorry, sorry." Kitty held up a placating hand. "I'm not impugning your character. But I am concerned for you. Are you certain you and Somerton can work together?"

"We have to. It's the only sensible thing to do."

"Very sensible," Kitty agreed gravely, but Lola caught a distinct hint of amusement in that reply. Before she could decide, however, the other woman spoke again. "What are you doing three weeks from tomorrow? There's a flower show that day in Regent's Park. It's for charity—London hospitals, army widows, or some such. I bought two tickets, thinking my flat mate and I would go, but she can't, I'm told. Care to take her place?"

"I'd love to, but I'm not sure I'll be free. Rehearsals run on Saturdays, too."

"Only until noon at the Imperial, and the flower show isn't until three o'clock. You'll be done in plenty of time. Say you'll come. You ought to see something of London since it's the season, and you can't work all the time. Unless, of course, you're using work to keep your mind off a particular man?"

"Stop it, Kitty."

"I know, I know. It shall be all business between you two from now on," her friend went on blithely, "and he's going to marry Lady Georgiana, and all's well that ends well."

As Lola envisioned a lifetime of being Denys's platonic, indifferent acquaintance while he married the elegant, well-bred, and oh-so-suitable Lady Georgiana, she found the picture a bit . . . depressing. "Yes," she said. "All's well that ends well."

"Then why," Kitty murmured, "do you suddenly look like a dying duck in a thunderstorm?"

"Don't be ridiculous." Lola pasted on an indifferent expression and reached for the champagne, reminding herself that there was no point in worrying about the future. She had more than enough to worry about in the present.

"YOU'VE DONE WHAT?"

The question was a roar so loud that even Denys, who was prepared for just this sort of reaction from the earl, couldn't help but grimace. Conyers's fist slammed down on the dining table so hard that the silver rattled, the footman jumped, and Monckton, the ideal personification of the unflappable English butler, nearly dropped the port decanter.

"I allowed Miss Valentine to audition for *Othello*, and Jacob cast her as Bianca."

Hearing it for the second time didn't seem to make any difference. His father continued to stare at him across the dining table, and though the smoke of his after-dinner cigar hung thick in the air between the two men, it couldn't mask the baffled fury of his expression. "Are you mad?"

There were times in Denys's life when his involvement with Lola had made him go rather off the rails, but this time, he knew he did not have that excuse. All he had was the truth.

"She was good, Father. She was very, very good. I realize," he added, as the earl made a scoffing sound, "you may not think me a fair judge in that regard, but Jacob couldn't be accused of any such bias. He wanted her for the part."

"I'd have thought Jacob to be possessed of more sense than that. Am I the only man on God's earth that woman hasn't been able to captivate?"

"He called her performance sublime."

"I don't believe it for a moment. That dancing girl? You and Jacob are both daft. And besides," he added before Denys could get a word in, "Bianca's a small part. Nothing to it. Surely, any number of women who auditioned would have done just as well."

"For Bianca, perhaps you're right." He paused, knowing he was about to step onto some very thin ice. "But not to understudy Desdemona."

"Lola Valentine as Desdemona?" His father stared at him, looking as appalled as Denys had anticipated. "Good God."

"She's not playing Desdemona," he hastened to point out. "She's merely understudying the role."

"Even so . . ." The earl's voice trailed off, and he swallowed hard before speaking again. "You cannot be serious about this."

"I'm afraid I am. Though I take little pleasure in the fact, Lola Valentine's reading of Desdemona was the best of the day, and one of the finest either Jacob or I had ever seen. If you had been there, you would have agreed."

"I doubt it. Why the devil did you allow her an audition in the first place?"

"She requested one. I deemed it wise to accommodate her."

The earl's sound of outrage interrupted him. "Devil take it, I wish I could understand, but I can't. I simply can't." He paused to down the last of his port, then went on, "What is it about that woman that impels you to abandon every scrap of good sense you possess?"

The question was one the earl had asked quite often during Denys's misspent youth, but in this case it was hardly warranted. "Like it or not, she is our partner, Father," he pointed out. "To some extent, we have to cooperate with her."

"I don't see why."

"Then it's clear you don't recall the bylaws of the partnership agreement. She is within her rights to oppose me on any decision I make. An audition seemed a small price to pay for her cooperation. I didn't think she'd actually earn a part. But she defied my expectations."

"That woman defies many things, including decency," Conyers muttered, waving Monckton forward to pour him another port.

Denys chose to ignore that. They'd had that particular argument about Lola often enough in the past. "By allowing Jacob to cast her in the play, with two roles for which to prepare, she'll have no time and little cause to make trouble. And acting's always been her ambition. In a small way, we're allowing her to satisfy it. Where's the harm in that?"

"The plan was to get rid of her, not pacify her!"

"I made her an offer. She refused." He spread his arms in a gesture of inevitability. "What would you have had me do?"

"Isn't it obvious?" The earl rubbed a hand irritably around the back of his neck. "Keep raising the offer until she agreed."

"You might give me some credit, Father. I raised my offer as high as thirty thousand pounds, but she refused to sell. No amount, she said, would be enough. I believe she meant it."

"In which circumstance, you were supposed to offer to sell our share to her."

He shook his head. "That wasn't possible."

"And why not?"

He stirred in his chair. "I have no intention of surrendering our share of a profitable business, one that I built. When you and Henry bought the Imperial, it was barely scraping by, but now, it's one of London's most prestigious theaters. I made it what it is today, and I'll be damned if I'll surrender what I accomplished because Henry did something mad."

"So this is about your pride?"

Denys met his father's angry gaze with a cool, determined one of his own. "You could say that, yes."

His father sighed, seeming to back down a bit. "I suppose I see your point. But why let Jacob give her a place in the company or a part in the play? You could have persuaded him to refuse her. Being cut to ribbons by Jacob Roth would have made her more amenable to selling, I daresay."

"I doubt it. Besides, it's never good policy to ask people to lie, and shredding her performance would have been a lie. I wouldn't have dreamt of asking Jacob to do so. It would not be right. It would not be—" He paused, grimacing. "Fair."

"Yes, yes, I suppose it sounds unethical when you put it like that." The earl leaned back in his chair, eying his son unhappily. "God, Denys, I hope you know what you're doing. That woman is your nemesis."

"That's a bit of an exaggeration, don't you think?"

"Is it? I don't need to remind you of how deeply she got her hooks into you, surely? Of how much you went into debt? Of how often you flitted off to France and neglected your estate—an estate I gave you upon your coming of age, one you mortgaged—"

"You don't need to remind me of my past follies," he cut in. "I've changed, Father, a fact you remarked on just yesterday. If you've revised your opinion in light of this—"

"I haven't done anything of the kind," Conyers interrupted, pushing that concern aside with a wave of his hands.

"Then why rehash the past?"

"Because you're my son, damn it all, and I love you. And," he rushed on before either of them could be embarrassed by such a frank declaration, "I have a duty to see that you don't repeat past mistakes. Even now, I cannot help but fear that woman's influence upon you."

Denys knew his father was speaking from deep and genuine affection, and he had to swallow hard before he could reply. "You needn't worry. Miss Valentine may have a part in the play, but I shan't be directing her. In fact, I can't see having much to do with her at all. She's Jacob's headache now, not mine."

"That woman isn't just a headache. She's a nightmare."

"Only until one wakes up."

"And have you?" Conyers gave him a searching glance. "Have you woken up? Had I asked you that yesterday, I would have been sure of your answer, but this day has given me cause to doubt."

Those words cut deep. His passion for Lola had

almost ruined his life and his future and torn apart his family. It was quite understandable for his parent to be concerned, but Denys had no intention of going down that road again.

"In assuaging your doubts, Father, I must allow the past few years to speak for me. As I said, Miss Valentine is no longer my concern. Jacob is the director, and he shall be the one who has to manage her. I am quite happy to let him. In fact," he added as he set aside his glass and stood up, "I doubt I shall even see her again until opening night."

Chapter 8

Denys might have assured his father he wouldn't be seeing Lola again until *Othello* opened, but it took only twelve hours for her to prove him wrong. He'd been at his desk a mere forty minutes the following morning before Dawson was opening his office door to announce, "Miss Valentine to see you, sir."

"What the devil?" He looked up, but he had no chance to instruct Dawson to tell her he was unavailable. The secretary had already stepped aside, allowing Lola to walk right in.

"Good morning," she greeted him as she came toward his desk, the frothy concoction of aquamarine silk and cream-colored lace she wore rustling as she walked. "Thank you for seeing me."

"I didn't seem to have a say in the matter," he muttered as he stood up, wishing he'd thought to tell his secretary that Lola Valentine was not to set foot in his office again without his permission.

Vowing to make that clear to his secretary at the first opportunity, he turned his attention to Lola, but Dawson spoke before he could inform her that he was too busy for a conversation.

"May I bring you some refreshment, Miss Valentine?"

"Miss Valentine won't be staying long enough for that," he answered before she could reply. "You may go Dawson."

He regretted the dismissal the moment he uttered it, for when the secretary departed, he closed the door behind him, and suddenly, the room seemed far too intimate.

"I didn't know if you would be in," she said, "but I thought I'd take a chance. I'm sorry if I'm disturbing you."

"You're not," he said, his assurance as much for his own benefit as hers. Surprise visit or no, he had no intention of allowing himself to be disturbed by her in any way.

That resolution had barely crossed his mind before she moved closer to his desk, and the delicate scent of jasmine was a forcible reminder of sultry afternoons in bed with her. Valiantly, he ignored it.

"What do you want, Lola?"

The question was curt, his tone barely cordial, but if she noticed, she gave no sign. "Nothing earth-shattering. I simply wanted to inquire when we shall be convening our first partners' meeting."

So much for thinking she'd be satisfied with a part in the play and would leave him in peace. "I'm not sure I know what you mean," he hedged. "There is no need for a meeting at this time."

"No need?"

"The annual partnership meeting convenes in January. It's always been a formality, of course, for Henry never felt compelled to attend. But if you wish to do so, that is your prerogative."

"I do, yes, but that's almost nine months away. I should think a change of partners warrants a meeting now, don't you agree?"

He didn't, but she gave him no chance to say so. "As long it's not during rehearsals," she went on, "I'm happy with any date and time within the next week or two that would be convenient for you."

He feared no time would ever be convenient. Lola, alas, was not a convenient sort of woman. "Whatever you wish to discuss, let's discuss it now." He gestured to the chair opposite, and when she accepted the offered seat, he resumed his own. "Best to have it over and be done, I suppose."

"It's not a matter of having it 'over,' as you put it," she said as she settled her skirts around her. "We need to discuss how we'll operate under our new partnership. Set up our ground rules, so to speak."

"Ground rules?"

"Yes. I should like to review the first-quarter financial statements. The box office receipts, expenditures, production costs, all that sort of thing."

"Certainly. I am happy to forward them to you. Inform Dawson where you wish them to be delivered—to the Savoy, or to the office of your solicitors—and you can peruse them at your leisure. Now, if that is all . . ."

He started to stand up, but Lola did not take the hint, and he sank back into his chair. "Obviously, it's not," he muttered.

"I think reviewing the company's financial condition is something that we ought to do together."

He stiffened. "That is neither necessary nor appropriate."

"Denys, we each own fifty percent. Neither of us has a controlling interest, so it's important that we learn to discuss and decide things for the Imperial together."

"Henry never found it necessary to involve himself in the running of the Imperial. Why should you?"

"Because I want to be involved. Henry didn't, partly because he was three thousand miles away and partly because he had many other projects that required his attention."

"You're pretty occupied yourself these days. Or isn't being in the play and understudying the lead enough to keep you busy?"

"I'm not doing this to keep busy. I am your *partner*, and unlike Henry, I have no desire to be a silent one. I appreciate that this isn't easy for you, and I'm sorry about that, but it can't be helped."

"Just what is it you hope to accomplish here, Lola?"

"Theater is my life, Denys. I want to participate in all facets of it."

"Why?" he demanded. "Why can't performing be enough to satisfy you?"

"Why can't managing your estate be enough to satisfy you?" She didn't wait for an answer. "Because you love the challenges that being a man of business provide you, that's why. I'm not any different."

"You can hardly be a man of business, Lola. Because you're not a man."

"Which gives me all the more reason to want a say in what we do here." She smiled a little, seeming to perceive his utter bafflement. "I can see that makes no sense to you. But why should it? You're a man."

"If you're trying to tell me you've become a suffragist—"

"Heavens, no. I wouldn't mind being allowed to vote, for I think it's ridiculous that women can't. But I'm not going to go marching in the streets or chain myself to railings. I do, however, want to be taken seriously in what I do."

"So why not content yourself with acting? Good actresses are taken seriously."

"Yes, as long as they do the plays their producers and investors and agents decide they should do." She leaned forward in her chair. "Henry would have dinner with investors, and sometimes, he would take me along."

Denys did not want to hear about her and Henry, and he stirred restlessly in his chair, but she didn't take the hint. "Henry," she went on, "always gave me the chance to talk to those men, tell them my ideas, but if any of those ideas were different from what I was already doing, the answer was always no. Those men were happy to back my show, but only if it was a Lola Valentine show, with plenty of cleavage showing, and lots of bawdy songs and jokes. If I wanted to put a dramatic sketch in there, or I wanted to sing a ballad? Forget it. Do you know how tired I got of kicking off the man's hat, Denys? But I always had to put that bit in the show. I was never, ever allowed to take it out."

"Because that's what the audience had come to see."

"Yes, but it was *my* show," she said, laughing a little, pressing a hand to her chest. "I'd created it, all of it was my vision. And yet, not one of those investors could ever trust that my next creative idea would be as appealing to the audience as one I'd already come up with. I had become the victim of my own success. No one wanted me to do anything else."

"There are business reasons for those sorts of boundaries. You and I stepped outside those boundaries when I financed *A Doll's House*, and look what happened."

"Which is why I want to be part of deciding where those boundaries are. It's not just about wanting to perform, Denys. It's about so much more than that. If I want to play Lady Macbeth, I don't want to sit by powerless while someone else decides what costumes I'll wear, and what sets I stand on, and which director I'll work with. I want to be a part of making those decisions."

"You want a great deal."

"Yes," she said simply. "I do. But I am willing to work for it. And I know I have a lot to learn."

"And I'm supposed to teach you, is that it?"

"I think we can teach each other. The Imperial is a

Shakespearean theater, and that's a limited repertoire, so the only way to keep things fresh is to innovate within each production, and I have plenty of ideas on that score."

"Keep things fresh?" He stirred, impatient. "This is England. That's not the way we do it."

"Maybe it should be."

He shook his head, for it was clear she didn't have a clue what British audiences would accept, but before he could point that out, she went on, "I realize what I'm asking for is going to be difficult for you—for both of us—especially at first, but this is the best chance I'll ever have to be in control of my own career and express my creative ideas, to show my vision of what good drama could be. I need to be involved. The alternative is to sit passively by while you—or some other producer at some other theater company—makes those the decisions for me. I won't do that, Denys. Not when I have the chance to do more. I can't."

Of course she couldn't do it. His gaze slid down to her full, rouged lips, along her slender throat, and over the curves of her generous bosom. Lola, he remembered full well, had never been passive.

Desire shimmered through him before he could stop it, and furious with himself, he jerked his gaze back up to her face. "Considering our past—"

"Can't we forget the past?"

Given that he had asked his father to do that very thing the night before, he couldn't very well refuse to do so himself, but when Lola leaned closer, the scent

of jasmine floated to him across the desk, a potent reminder of all that had once been between them, and the
desire in his body began to deepen and spread.

"We are business partners," she went on, as he tried
to force back the desire overtaking him. "Can't we get
along? Respect each other's strengths? Work amicably
as colleagues?"

"Colleagues?" He lurched to his feet with such force
that the movement sent his mahogany office chair rolling backward across the floorboards. It hit the credenza
behind him with a bang.

The sound made her wince, but she didn't stand up,
and he knew he had to be brutally forthright, or she'd
never leave him in peace.

"I can see I need to make you aware of exactly where
you stand and what you may and may not expect from
this partnership." He leaned forward, flattening his
palms on his desk. "When Henry and my father bought
the Imperial, it was a shabby, second-rate theater that
on a good night was never more than half-full. I built it
into what it is now, and I accomplished that on my own.
I didn't need Henry to work with me, and I certainly
don't need you. And I will not risk what I've built,
taint my reputation, and bank on your notions of good
drama when you have no knowledge whatsoever of the
business implications. You have ideas? Well and good.
Present them to Jacob. I'm sure he'll consider them,
and if they have merit, he'll bring them to me."

She opened her mouth, but he didn't give her time to
offer a reply.

"As to the rest, you have every right to copies of the financial statements, and I will forward them to you each month, just as I did for Henry. In addition, I am perfectly willing to allow you to examine the premises and audit the accounts whenever you wish, and I can bring in one of my clerks to provide any clarification you may require and to answer any questions you may have. If you prefer, you may involve an accounting clerk of your own choosing, or have the accounts examined by your solicitors. That is all I intend to offer you. By the terms of Henry's will, we are—at least for the present—forced to be partners, but we shall never be colleagues. I hope I have been clear enough?"

"I'm afraid you have." She rose slowly to her feet. "But that doesn't change my intentions. You have every right to mistrust me, and the only way I can overcome that is with time. I also know you resent me, but you don't have to like me in order to work with me, and despite your enmity, I intend to keep trying to make this partnership function even if you keep refusing to cooperate with me." She paused, but she didn't move to leave, and as the moments went by, the silence became unbearable.

"Is that all?" he asked, trying to be cold when all he could feel was heat—the heat of anger, resentment, and desire were like fire inside him.

"There's one more thing I want to say." She paused. "I know I hurt you, Denys, and I'm sorry about that."

"Are you?" His gaze raked over her, and he didn't believe her for a second. "If you could go back, would you make a different choice?"

She squared her shoulders. "No."

"Then don't be a hypocrite. Don't apologize for things you don't regret."

There was a tap on the door, then it opened, and Mr. Dawson appeared in the doorway, a sheaf of papers in his hands. "Begging your pardon, my lord, but Mr. Swann just delivered the application forms from yesterday's auditions."

Denys didn't know whether to be exasperated or relieved by the interruption. There was plenty more he'd have liked to say to Lola, but it was probably best if he left it there. "Bring them in, Mr. Dawson. Miss Valentine," he added with a pointed glance at her, "was just leaving."

"That's just it, sir. Miss Valentine is the reason I interrupted you. Her form is incomplete." He held up the application in question, and when Denys beckoned him forward, he crossed to his employer's side and put the sheet in Denys's hand. "You see?" he added, indicating the blank space on the application. "Since she is here, I thought she could provide the missing information?"

"Thank you, Dawson. I will take care of it."

The secretary gave a nod and departed, once again closing the door behind him.

"I can't imagine what I left out," Lola said, circling his desk and pausing beside him to study the sheet of paper in his hand. "I thought I'd been most thorough in my application."

He pointed to the appropriate place on the form, and as she leaned closer, he instinctively turned his head, inhaling the luscious scent that clung to her hair. But that was too much provocation for his already heated body, and he jerked his head back again at once, hastening into speech. "You did not give the name and address of your agent in London."

"Oh, that." She straightened, but the infinitesimal amount of distance the move put between them wasn't nearly enough to contain the traitorous feelings in his body. He had to get her out of here.

"Perhaps," he said, feeling a bit desperate, "you could give Dawson that information on your way out?"

She waved one hand in the air, dismissing that suggestion. "It's not necessary."

"But it is. To draw up your contract, our solicitors require that your agent be specified in the terms."

"And if an actor doesn't have an agent? What then?"

"You don't have an agent?" He stared at her askance. "Why on earth not?"

"Henry handled all of that for me. Since he died, I haven't looked . . ." She paused and her mouth tightened at the corners. "I don't see the need for an agent now. That's all."

This reminder of Henry was sufficient to keep the traitorous sensations in his body from wholly overtaking him. "Lola, this won't do. You need an agent."

"Why?" Unexpectedly, she smiled at him. "Do you intend to take advantage of me, Denys?"

The room was far too warm, and he felt an almost irrepressible desire to loosen his tie. He suppressed it. "Don't flirt with me," he reproved in as cool a voice as he could muster. "It's a deflection, Lola, one you use whenever you don't like the direction of a conversation. What I don't understand is the reason you're prevaricating."

Caught out, she gave a sigh, but she didn't explain.

"Is Henry the reason for this aversion to having an agent? Do you . . ." He paused, but after a moment, he forced himself to go on. "I'm sure you miss him, but you're not doing yourself or his memory any good by procrastinating about finding someone else to represent your interests."

"I'm not procrastinating," she protested. "In my current situation, I just don't see the need for an agent. Someone who'll charge me an outrageous percentage to arrange a contract between me and my own partner? Seems quite silly to me."

"Just because I'm giving you a fair situation, it doesn't mean others will. You need an agent. To find you work, to negotiate your contracts—"

"I already have work. As to negotiating my contract, I think you and I can muddle along without bringing a third party into it."

"You're far too trusting."

"I'm not trusting at all, but I know you, and I know how scrupulously honest you are. You could no more cheat me than you could betray your country."

He found this evidence of how well she understood his character rather galling. "And what if you don't retain your place in the company next season?"

"I'll worry about that when it happens."

"What if you wish to obtain work elsewhere?"

"A competitor?" Her scoff made short shrift of that possibility. "As I said, I want to work with my partner in my company, not somewhere else. Besides," she added with a smile, "I intend to see that we only hire those directors who appreciate my brilliant dramatic skills."

His opinion about that must have shown on his face, for her smile faded, and she sighed. "That was a joke, Denys."

He didn't feel like laughing. "If *Othello* proves a flop," he went on doggedly, "you may wish to pursue a place with some other company—"

"It isn't going to flop." Her eyes opened wide. "With Arabella Danvers, London's most famous and popular Shakespearean actress, in a leading role, how could it ever be a flop?"

Despite everything, that almost made him smile. Impudent minx, he thought, to toss his rationale for hiring Arabella back in his face. "Mrs. Danvers's involvement, as valuable as it is, is no guarantee of success. You know as well as I do there's no predicting how these things will go."

"We can safely make one prediction, at least," she said, flashing him a grin. "On opening night, they'll be packed to the rafters just to see if Lola Valentine proves as spectacular a failure this time as she was last time."

He caught the pain behind those words. "Which is why it's best if you find an agent now," he pointed out even as he wondered why he should care.

"To hedge my bets, you mean?" She sobered, looking at him. "I'll do my best not to let you down a second time."

"That's not what I meant. I only meant that a failed play could color your entire season, making it harder for you to find work next year if you do go elsewhere. An agent would make the process easier."

"I doubt it." She wrinkled up her nose with a rueful smile. "You've obviously forgotten I had an agent during *A Doll's House*. When the play closed, he was no help whatsoever. He suggested I consider abandoning acting altogether. He said it didn't really matter, anyway, since I already had another, much more lucrative career."

"Dancing?"

"No." Her smile faltered as her gaze locked with his. "You."

Denys sucked in his breath, feeling that reminder of their former relationship like a knife between his ribs. He yanked open the left-hand drawer of his desk, shuffled through the cards docketed there, and pulled out three. "Here," he said, holding them out to her.

"What are these?" she asked as she took them, but after one glance at the card on top, she shook her head. "Denys, I told you—"

"I don't care what you told me. These men are well-regarded agents, tenacious at negotiation, and scrupulously ethical. Jamison might suit you best since he represents the widest variety of clients, but none of these men will try to shove you into musical revue or dance if those aren't what you want. They'll fight for you, they won't cheat you or abandon you, and they certainly won't make unsavory insinuations about your private life. Go interview them and pick one. Or find one on your own. Either way," he added, hoping he would at last be able to bring this meeting to an end, "I won't sign contracts with you until you have an agent."

She bristled at that. "You're being very autocratic about my career."

"If you don't like it, you are free to find work elsewhere." It was his turn to smile. "The Gaiety would probably hire you."

Her displeasure seemed to vanish as quickly as it had come, and even before she smiled again, he knew she was changing tactics. When she spoke, her words came as no great surprise.

"Let's compromise. That's what partners do together, isn't it?"

He thought again of afternoons in bed with her, but this time, he managed to keep his gaze on her face. "What sort of compromise did you have in mind?"

She held up the cards. "I'll find an agent if you'll agree to a partners' meeting."

He gave a laugh. She was so outrageous, he couldn't help it, even now, with erotic images in his mind and desire seething in his body. "So to get something you want, you're offering to do something that benefits you?"

She bit her lip, looking at him over the cards in mock apology. "I suppose that's one way of looking at it."

"And if I agree to this, what's in it for me?"

"What do you want?"

That provocative question was like a gust of wind on burning coals. His amusement vanished, and his arousal flared into outright lust, providing irrefutable proof—as if he needed any—that being partners with Lola was an impossible undertaking.

"Nothing," he answered, hating that even now, even after everything that had happened, he could still be aroused by her against his will. "There is nothing I want from you except for you to stay out of my way."

"And I can't accept that. So the only alternative is tear the Imperial apart. Is that what you want?"

He hated that it came to that sort of Hobson's choice. Hated that he was trapped in something from which the only escape route was annihilation. "If it would rid me of you," he answered, "then yes."

"If that were true, you'd never have agreed to let me audition for a part in the first place. You'd have shown me the door and told me to sue you in the courts."

"A choice I'm questioning more and more with each moment you stand here," he muttered, glaring at her. "Business partners don't have to like each other, but they do have to trust each other, and my trust is something I will never give you again."

She flinched, but she didn't move to leave. "Never is a long time, Denys, and I intend to earn your trust. And I know you're seething with resentment, which is understandable, but that's a hard thing to keep up, day after day, year after year."

The mention of years was a reminder of just how trapped he was. "Be damned to you. What you're suggesting is impossible."

"I don't see why."

"Don't you?" Provoked beyond bearing and frustrated as hell by a desire that still seemed unconquerable, he wrapped an arm around her waist. The application form fluttered to the floor as he pulled her hard against him.

"What are you doing?" she gasped.

"You want to know why this won't work, Lola?" Desire thrumming through his body, he cupped her cheek, his thumb pressing beneath her jaw to tilt her head back. Her skin was as soft as he remembered, the fragrance of her hair as intoxicating as ever, and even as he told himself he was making a fatal mistake, Denys bent his head. "This is why," he said, and kissed her.

Chapter 9

 The moment his lips touched hers, pleasure pierced Lola like an arrow, pleasure so keen and so sharp that she cried out against his mouth.

He responded at once, his arms tightening around her as he pulled her even closer, and her mind tumbled back into the past, to summer afternoons in St. John's Wood, to scents of bay rum and jasmine, to hot, frantic lovemaking and its languid, luscious aftermath, to a time and a place where sensation and bliss were the only things that mattered, where they had tried to burn away the social difference between a viscount and a cabaret dancer.

Denys, she thought, and the pleasure deepened and spread until it was in every part of her body, bringing a yearning she hadn't allowed herself to feel in years.

Her lips parted, and he deepened the kiss, tasting her

tongue with his own in a carnal caress that inflamed all her senses. Her handbag hit the floor with a thud, and she wrapped her arms around his neck.

He made a rough sound against her mouth, and his embrace loosened, but he did not push her away. Instead, his hands slid down, gliding along her ribs to her hips. His palms felt like fire, seeming to burn through all the layers of her clothing as he pulled her closer.

Somewhere in the back of her mind, she knew she should stop this, for it could ruin everything she'd come here to do, but she feared it was already too late. The sandpapery texture of his cheek, the taste of his mouth, the hard feel of his body, were so achingly familiar, and when his grip tightened and he lifted her onto her toes, bringing her hips flush against his, she couldn't summon the will to push him away.

She'd thought enough time had gone by. She'd thought both of them would be over this by now. Denys's kiss, his caress, his lovemaking, those afternoons together—she'd worked so hard to make all of those things nothing but a distant memory. She thought she'd succeeded. Yet now, with his body against hers and arousal flooding through her, it was as if not a single day had passed.

Without warning, he broke the kiss. His hands tightened on her hips, then he shoved her away and took a long step back, his hands falling to his sides.

Lola stared at him, wordless, her senses reeling and her lips still burning. She ought, she supposed, to say something—something offhand so they could both get their bearings and pretend this hadn't happened. But for the life of her, she couldn't think of a thing. She pressed her fingers to her mouth and said nothing.

It was Denys's voice that broke the silence. "God," he said, his voice ragged, "if this doesn't prove the point, nothing will."

She frowned, striving to think. "What point?"

He took a deep breath and another step back, rubbing his hands over his face. "The one I've been trying to make since you arrived here."

Those words hit her like a splash of ice water, snuffing out all the fire raging through her in an instant, leaving her as spitting mad as a wet cat. "You kissed me to prove a point?"

"No, I didn't. Although it's a damn fine way to make the case, and I wish I'd thought of it." He glared at her, seeming as angry as she, though why he thought he had any grounds to be angry was beyond her. "But when you're anywhere in the vicinity, my capacity to think, even of devious plots to drive you away, deserts me utterly."

"So what just happened is my fault?" Lola glared back at him, outraged that he was painting her as some sort of wicked seductress. "Of course it is. I was standing here, after all, and a man can't be expected to conduct himself in honorable fashion when a notorious dancer with a ruined reputation is standing in front of him. That's too much to ask of any man, even a *gentleman* such as you."

That shot hit the mark, she could tell, for a hint of

what might have been regret crossed his face. But if she thought he'd offer an apology, she was mistaken. "As I said before, I didn't do it to prove a point, but the point is made just the same. A partnership between us just can't work."

"Oh, no." She shook her head. "Oh, no, no, no. If you think your conduct this morning—deliberate or not—will enable you to wriggle out of your obligations here, you are mistaken."

"Obligations?"

Her anger hardened into resolve. "I'm calling a partners' meeting. According to the Imperial's bylaws, I have that right, and I'm exercising it. I will make the arrangements with your secretary."

"Make whatever arrangements you like, but I have no intention of attending any such meeting."

"Do as you please." She bent and picked up her handbag from the floor. "If you are absent, I will make whatever business decisions I deem necessary. You will be apprised in the minutes of what I have decided. I think I shall begin by deciding next year's playbill."

"A pointless exercise. Without my consent, you can't carry out such a decision, or any other, for that matter."

"Neither can you."

His eyes narrowed to slits. "If you think you can stonewall me, Lola, you are sadly mistaken."

"Call it what you will, but we are still equal partners—"

"Are we, indeed?" he cut in before she could finish. "In a legal sense, I suppose you're right. But in a partnership of true equality, each partner brings something of benefit to the whole. What do you bring that I don't already have?"

"Plenty. I have ideas—"

"Every actor worth his salt has ideas. Every actress has notions of how to play her part and what costume she wants to wear. But that doesn't make her a valuable business partner. For that, Lola, you're going to need more. Do you have connections I've no access to? Influence in London theater circles I don't possess? Experience in production? Theater management? Do you have any business acumen at all? Hell, for all these ideas you claim to have, can you contribute even one idea that would increase the Imperial's profits? Or," he added, his dark eyes hard as granite, "is your greatest talent merely that of sleeping with the right man at the right time?"

"Oh," she breathed, outraged. Clearly, he was attempting to intimidate her, but it was not going to work. "First of all," she said through clenched teeth, "I've only slept with two men in my entire life, and one of them was you, so perhaps instead of pointing out my supposed deficiencies, you ought to take a good, hard look at your own. Hypocrisy being a prime example, as your lack of gentlemanly conduct has just demonstrated."

She paused just long enough to suck in a breath before going on. "Second, as much as you deny it, the fact remains that legally, I am your full and equal partner, and though it's obvious I can't expect your trust or your forgiveness or your personal respect, I damn well expect you to accord me the consideration, equality, and respect my *position* demands. We make decisions together, Denys, or we don't make them at all."

She turned and walked out, and she took great satisfaction in slamming the door behind her. Not a very ladylike thing to do, of course, but then, she'd never been a lady anyway.

DENYS STARED AT the closed door, resentment and arousal seething through him in equal measure. During the past half dozen years, he'd seldom had cause to feel both those emotions at the same time, but now that Lola was back in his life, he had the feeling this tumultuous state was one he would find himself in quite often.

Perhaps instead of pointing out my supposed deficiencies, you ought to take a hard look at your own.

He grimaced, painfully aware he was in no position to deny those words. Throwing an accusation of immoral conduct in her face had been hypocritical, not to mention unthinkably boorish, and she'd had every right to call him out for it.

I've only slept with two men in my entire life, and one of them was you.

He frowned, uneasiness supplanting his anger. The other man was Henry, of course, and yet, even as he thought it, he felt a stab of doubt. The idea of Lola as a virgin when they'd become lovers didn't square with what he remembered. Granted, she'd had less experience than he would have expected from a girl of her profession, but he'd never have thought her a virgin.

Which, if she'd been telling the truth just now, meant that she and Henry hadn't been lovers, and that was ridiculous.

Wasn't it?

Denys muttered an oath. God, was he really trying to find a way to justify her actions and believe in her again?

He was. God help him, he was. And he knew why. Despite everything that had happened, and everything she'd done, he still wanted her, wanted her enough that he'd hauled her into his arms and kissed her without a thought of restraint, control, or consequences. Hell, in those few moments, he hadn't been thinking at all.

He pressed his hands to his skull, grinding his teeth in frustration, wondering what on earth was wrong with him that he wasn't over this by now. He wasn't in love with her anymore, and he certainly didn't trust her, but he wanted her as much as he ever had, and he didn't know what he could do, short of hurling himself off a cliff, to stop wanting her. If a shredded bank account, a broken heart, and six years hadn't cured him of this mad, insatiable passion for her, what would?

Feeling the need to move, Denys lowered his hands, circled his desk, and began to pace his office, but if he thought that would cool his blood and help him regain a semblance of sanity, he was mistaken. As he approached the window, he glanced down at the street below, just in time to see the object of all his tumultuous thoughts step out onto the sidewalk.

The sight of her stopped him in his tracks. As she paused at the corner for the traffic to clear, he told himself to look away. But though his mind gave the command, his traitorous body refused to comply. He didn't move, and all the desire he kept trying to suppress flared up again, every bit as strong and hot as it had ever been.

Nothing's changed, he thought darkly, his hand coming up as if to touch her, his fingertips pressing against the window glass as frustration and desire clawed at him. *Eight and a half years since I first met her, and nothing's changed.*

She leaned out over the curb to look for a break in the traffic, a move that emphasized the lush curve of her hips, and Denys turned away from the window with an oath. To feel all this again after half a dozen years of peace and sanity was aggravating as hell. To know his control and his will could slip away any moment she was near him was just too galling to bear.

No man could be expected to endure this sort of situation. There had to be a way out of this, by God, and he was going to find it, for he had no intention of wrecking his life a second time because of her.

LOLA STRODE AWAY from Denys's office mad as a hornet, so mad that she paid no attention to where she was going except that it was away from him. She couldn't even remember now what reply she'd offered to his infuriating remark, but whatever she'd said didn't matter, for no words would have been sufficient to express her fury. She ought to have hurled an inkstand at him instead.

Or is your true talent merely that of sleeping with the right man at the right time?

Of all the hypocritical, ruthless, downright unfair remarks—

But not wholly unwarranted.

She stopped on the sidewalk, so abruptly that she was nearly run down by the man walking behind her. He dodged, just managing to avoid a collision, and went around her, while she stood motionless on the sidewalk and faced the brutal fact that though Denys's accusation wasn't technically true, it was a reasonable conclusion. She had no right to be angry when what he thought of her was exactly what she'd led him to think.

Denys believed she had jilted him for Henry Latham, and a more lucrative career in New York had been part of the bargain. In choosing to come back, she'd expected his enmity, so why was she angry at him for expressing it?

Because she hadn't realized how much it would hurt.

That was the real reason she was angry enough to spit nails. She was angry with herself. Hearing Denys say what he thought of her opened a wound inside, a wound she hadn't been honest enough with herself to admit was even there.

She'd ceased to care a long time ago what people thought of her, but Denys was different. He had always been able to get under her skin and slip past her defenses like no one else could.

And that feeling seemed to be mutual, or he would not have kissed her. He'd done it intending to prove the untenable nature of their partnership, but it was only untenable if he still wanted her.

He resented her, he might even despise her, he certainly did not want to forgive her, and he hadn't a shred of respect for her. But amid all that, the lust he'd once felt for her was still there.

That was a possibility she had refused to consider until now. During the weeks since Henry's death, whenever the possibility that Denys might still want her passed through her mind, she'd dismissed it and chided herself for her conceit. On the voyage over, it was the one scenario she hadn't rehearsed, the one contingency she had refused to plan for. Even last night, when Kitty had warned her, she'd managed to convince herself it was as likely as flying pigs. But now, her body still burning from his kiss, she no longer had the luxury of self-deceit. His desire for her was still there. And, as that kiss had so ruthlessly demonstrated, so was her desire for him.

Mortified, Lola groaned and buried her flushed face in her hands, heedless of the pedestrians streaming by. Her whole life, she'd lived by the knowledge that if anything was going to happen for her in this world, she'd have to make it happen. When Henry's will had dropped this chance in her lap, she'd known it would be up to her to make it work, and she'd dared to think that was possible. She'd hoped—foolishly, perhaps—that she could wipe away the past and start again. That she could erase the girl who'd taken off her clothes for men in a Brooklyn saloon and the cabaret dancer who'd allowed herself to be kept by her aristocratic lover. She'd believed that she, who had perfected the art of using sexual allure to entertain, could become an actress and producer worthy of respect. And yet, she had just behaved like the wanton everyone, including Denys, believed her to be.

The moment he'd hauled her into his arms, she ought to have shoved him away, slapped him across the face, and told him to keep his hands to himself. He'd kissed her, he'd even manhandled her, and not only had she allowed it, she'd relished every second of it, and she hadn't spared a thought for their partnership, her aspirations, and her future.

"Are you all right, miss?"

Lola lifted her head, turning to find a young man standing beside her, a young man in the pin-striped suit and ink-stained cuffs of a clerk, who was studying her with polite concern.

She pasted on a smile at once. "Yes, of course. Thank you."

He went on, and Lola took a deep, steadying breath, working to think with her head.

In choosing to come back here, she'd ignored some of the possible consequences, true, but even if she'd allowed herself to foresee today's events, would she have chosen to stay in New York and let this opportunity slip through her fingers?

Not a chance.

She'd spent years shimmying around a stage showing off her body, but she wanted to show the world she really could act. She wanted the critics who had heaped scorn on her for her performance in *A Doll's House* to eat the biting words they'd written about her afterward. She wanted respect, the professional respect garnered by the likes of Ellen Terry and Sarah Bernhardt, respect performers like her never got. And she wanted to learn the business side of things. She wanted to produce her own plays, see her ideas come to life in a way that was not only creatively satisfying but also profitable.

The Imperial was her chance to do all those things, and she wasn't about to let one stupid kiss get in the way. She might have blindly refused to see this coming, but she'd always known this partnership wouldn't be smooth sailing, so there was no point in crying at the first squall. What she and Denys had once had was over, and any lingering desires from their past could not be allowed to get in the way of the future—for either of them.

Denys must be made to see her not as his former lover, or as his former mistress, or as the woman who'd hurt him. She had to make him see her as his equal.

And just how, a rather deflating little voice inside her whispered, *are you going to do that?*

As if in answer, Denys's voice came back to her.

Can you contribute even one idea that would increase the Imperial's profits?

Of all the challenges he'd hurled at her a short time ago, that was the one she had the best chance of rising to, at least in the short term. She had no contacts in London yet, and she had no business experience at all, and she'd never seen a financial statement in her life. But she had intelligence, she had grit, and she had imagination. Those traits had carried her from the stockyards of Kansas City to the cabarets of Paris to a successful one-woman show in New York. Surely she could rely on them now.

With that, Lola's innate optimism and resolve began to return. She'd arrange that partnership meeting, just as she'd told Denys she would, and she could only hope he showed up because she intended to bring an absolutely brilliant business idea with her. She just had to figure out what it was.

She considered for a moment, then she pulled her handbag from under her arm, opened it, and extracted the cards Denys had given her earlier. The first thing to do was to keep her part of the bargain she'd proposed and find herself an agent. And perhaps, she thought, tapping the white card against the smooth kid of her gloved palm, she'd learn some valuable information and gain some ideas in the process.

Chapter 10

 Denys thought he'd made it plain to Lola that they could never be partners, and that kiss, though unintended, had provided ample proof of the reasons why. He soon discovered, however, that despite everything, she remained undeterred.

First thing Monday morning, he received her formal written request calling for a meeting, making him more determined than ever to find a way out of this. But his options were limited. The only means of escape he could see were to sell his family's share, buy her out, or find some way to break the partnership agreement. The first he still refused to consider, and the second he'd already tried, so the third was his only hope. He discussed the matter at length with his solicitors and spent two days poring over the partnership agreement, but to no avail, and he began to fear he might be stuck with Lola for good.

But then a note came from his friend Nick, inviting him to a private dinner at White's with Jack Featherstone and their other two closest friends, and Denys's spirits revived a bit. Being acquainted with Lola already, the other four men knew she was chaos in a corset. And they'd seen Denys's disastrous liaison with her play out in full, so they would appreciate why he had to keep that woman as far from him and his family as possible. And they were all men of business. They might have valuable advice to offer. He accepted Nick's invitation with alacrity.

The following night, he waited until after they had dined and the port had made its first journey around the table before he opened the topic weighing so heavily on his mind.

"Lola's back in town." Those words would impel any man to need a drink, and he immediately downed his port in one draught.

The initial response of his friends varied. Nick nodded, not seeming surprised, probably because his wife, Belinda, was one of the most influential ladies of society and heard every scrap of news almost the moment it happened. Stuart, the Duke of Margrave, raised one dark eyebrow with ducal impassivity and said nothing. James, the Earl of Hayward, gave a low whistle. Jack, ever irrepressible, actually laughed.

"You seem a bit rattled by this, old boy," he said. "Is there a problem?"

Denys stared at the man seated beside him, unable to believe Jack could ask such a question. "Lola's back. She's here," he added, as his friend merely grinned. "In London."

"I heard you. No need to keep reiterating the point." Jack faced him, settling back against the arm of his chair, drink in hand. "But I'm not sure how it signifies."

Denys proceeded to explain, but even after he'd offered an account of the past week's events—carefully edited, of course—Jack's amusement wasn't dimmed in the slightest. "By Jove, Denys, what a lucky chap you are."

"Lucky?"

"Yes. You're a bachelor, and you're in business with a beautiful, desirable woman. What single man wouldn't think himself fortunate in such circumstances?"

"This one," Denys assured him, and took up the port decanter to refill his glass. "I'd prefer the devil for a partner. Not," he added glumly, "that there's much of a difference in this case."

"It'll be a difficult transition at first, no doubt," Nick said from his other side, as Denys passed him the decanter. "You'll be dealing with someone who isn't halfway around the world, allowing you to make all the decisions on your own."

"That's not my objection."

"Then what is?"

"She has this notion we should make peace. Bury the past and work together. As colleagues." He paused for a swallow of port. "God, what a notion."

Nick shrugged. "Is it so absurd?"

James saved Denys from having to answer by pulling the bottle from Nick's hand. Clearly feeling that along with the port came the opportunity to offer an opinion, he offered his.

"Why can't you work together?" he asked as he poured himself more port. "Lola's approach seems quite sensible to me."

"Sensible?" Denys couldn't believe what he was hearing. "Sensible?"

"It is, rather," Stuart put in as he took the port from James. "You're partners in a very lucrative enterprise, and you can't conduct its business without her, at least not without strong-arm tactics and legal wrangling. What happened between you was a long time ago. You've both gone on with your lives and gotten over it." Stuart paused in refilling his glass, his gray eyes meeting Denys's across the table. "Haven't you?"

"Of course we have." As he spoke, he strove to keep his expression neutral. The last thing he needed was for his friends to perceive his desire for Lola wasn't quite as over as he'd wanted to believe. "There are no romantic considerations here."

"Well, there you are." Stuart set the port beside Jack and leaned back in his chair. "Anyone going to Ascot in June?"

Several assents were voiced and one or two horses mentioned before Denys could get a word in. "Damn it, gentlemen, I don't want to discuss Ascot. I'm in the devil of a mess, and I'd appreciate some suggestions on how to get out of it."

"I don't see what you can do," Stuart reiterated. "Unless you sell your shares, I'm not sure you have any way out of this, and why should you want one? Why does it matter?"

Denys didn't have the chance to reply.

"It seems we're back to my original question," Jack said. "What's the problem?"

"Lola is the problem." Denys glanced around the table, noting in bafflement their unenlightened stares. "Lola, the woman all of us—Stuart excepted—were once infatuated with. The very woman Nick was so enamored with that he tried to steal her away from me at one time, as I recall."

"You mean I tried to steal her back," Nick clarified, grinning at him. "Since I'm the one who introduced you to her in the first place."

"We both introduced them," Jack corrected.

"Either way," Nick resumed, "I failed. Even after all my invitations to dinner, my offers of expensive champagne, and my wittiest, most charming conversation, I cut no ice with her. For some inexplicable reason, she chose you instead. But Jack and I knew her first, so if anyone did the stealing, Denys, it was you."

"That's codswallop," Denys denied, feeling defensive all of a sudden. "You just admitted you cut no ice with her. And Jack didn't either. So don't tell me I stole her because she never belonged to either of you."

"I'm not sure Lola could ever belong to any man," Jack interjected with a laugh. "From what I recall, she always seemed very much in possession of her own heart and mind. I suspect that's what made her so fascinating."

"A characteristic which also makes her a poor prospect as a business partner," Denys pointed out, hoping they could steer clear of any discussion of Lola's more fascinating aspects.

"Why should it?" Nick asked. "Because the pair of you will see things differently? You'll disagree? Fight?"

"Yes, exactly. Partners need to be in accord."

"Not necessarily. Differing opinions and points of view can make a partnership stronger."

"You and I are partners in the brewery we own, Nick. If we fought all the time, we'd never get anything accomplished. And while we're on the subject of fights," he added, wanting to hammer home the fact that having Lola anywhere about was a disaster in the making, "what ultimately resulted from your association with Lola? You got shot, that's what. By Pongo here."

"My name is not Pongo," James said at once, his usual response to the uttering of his hated childhood nickname. "It's James. I am James Edward Fitzhugh, Earl Hayward, son of the Marquess of Wetherford. Honestly, after over twenty years of friendship, can't any of you call me by my actual *name*?"

"No," they all answered at once.

"Pongo only shot me," Nick said, reverting to the topic at hand, "because I got in the way. He was pointing the pistol at you, Denys, and, like an idiot, I stepped between you."

"And let's remember just why I was trying to shoot Denys, shall we?" James asked, joining Nick in this most inconvenient inclination to reminiscence. "Because he made a play for my girl! And right in front of me, too."

Recalling his idiotic behavior on the night in question, Denys began to wish he'd never started this discussion in the first place. "At the time, I didn't know the girl was with you, Pongo," he muttered. "I thought she was with Nick."

"Making the move one of pure retaliation on your part," Nick pointed out. "I know you were hurting and angry as hell because Lola had just left you, and three sheets to the wind besides, but still, you crossed the line there, old chap—"

"Did I?" he countered, his defensiveness increasing because he knew that accusation was true. "You let Lola live with you when she went back to Paris."

"I was there, too," Jack piped up, but he was ignored.

"She came to me as a friend," Nick defended himself. "She arrived on our doorstep and told me the play had closed, she couldn't find work in London anymore, and she didn't have money and needed a place to live until she could afford a flat of her own. What was I supposed to do? Toss her into the street?"

"You're my friend, damn it. You ought to have advised her to come back to me and allow me to take care of her. But is that what you did? No. And when Henry came after her, did you tell him to sod off? No, you told him where she was working."

"How could I have known he intended to spirit her off to New York? He was a friend of your family, for God's sake, and old enough to be her father."

"Thank you, Nick," Denys muttered. "That's such a comforting reminder."

"Gentlemen, please," Stuart cut in, "let's not have a row. I'm enjoying this evening, and I've no intention of allowing idiotic peccadilloes of our wilder days spoil it." He lifted his glass. "It's damned good to see all of you, something that doesn't happen often enough, to my mind."

All of them raised their glasses in hearty agreement with that sentiment, temptations to quarrel were laid aside, and the friendship that had lasted most of their lives was reaffirmed.

"Sorry, Nick," Denys said, rubbing a hand over his forehead. "That's all water under the bridge, honestly, and I don't blame you for what happened."

"Apology accepted," Nick said at once.

"What about me?" Pongo demanded good-naturedly. "Am I not entitled to an apology, too? It was my girl Denys attempted to abscond with the day after Lola left."

"Your girl?" Denys made a scoffing sound. "She was a barmaid you'd met the night before. And the fact that you seized the barkeep's pistol, pointed it at me after I'd barely asked the girl to dinner, and accidentally shot Nick in the process cancels out any right you might have had to an apology. We were both drunk and out of our senses. And on that note," he added, seeing the perfect opportunity to illustrate his concerns about his present situation, "what happened that night in Paris rather illustrates what I'm saying, doesn't it?"

"Why?" Jack asked, grinning. "Because it shows that you and Pongo are capable of behaving like a pair of horses' asses?"

Denys made a sound of impatience. "It proves that where Lola goes, anarchy follows."

"But why should any of that be true now?" Nick asked. "I still don't quite see what's so difficult."

"No?" Denys turned to Nick. "If our situation were reversed, how would you see it? More importantly, how would Belinda see it? You had quite a passion for Lola yourself once."

"That's different. Belinda is my wife. You're not married."

"I don't see the problem, either," James said. "Lola's an intelligent woman, and she certainly knows her way around a stage. Henry ensured she'd have the blunt to stand her share of any financial losses, should you have a play that fails. As a partner in a theater company, she seems well suited."

Denys winced, remembering his assessment to Lola of her attributes as a partner had been somewhat less complimentary. "I suppose," he muttered, "she does have a few things to offer."

"A fine concession," James said. "I think she'd be smashing. Stuart?" he added, turning to the man beside him.

"What I think, what any of us think, doesn't matter," the duke pointed out. "Denys is the one who has to work with her, and she did leave him for someone else."

Denys felt a hint of relief. "Finally," he said, "someone begins to see my side. Thank you, Stuart."

"You're welcome. But I have to say that your concerns do seem premature. Why not wait a bit and see how the arrangement works before you judge it?"

Denys considered, trying to find a way to explain without revealing his own vulnerabilities. "It's so damned awkward."

"Bound to be," Stuart conceded. "But that'll pass in time, I daresay."

"It'll cause tremendous gossip."

"Which, since you're a viscount and Lola's not a lady, hardly affects your reputation—or hers, either, for that matter. At worst, people will assume you've taken up with her again."

Glad that someone had grasped at least that much of his difficulty, he nodded. "Just so."

"You're thinking of your father," James put in.

"Of course I am. My father is a good man, and I'm fond of him. But I am also thinking of my mother, and Susan— all my family. When the scandal sheets find out about this, the whole business will be raked up and discussed *ad nauseum*. Speculation will run wild that Lola and I have rekindled our affair. We'll be the talk of society."

"Only until people see there's nothing to the gossip."

Denys thought of that damnable kiss in his office and resisted the impulse to shift guiltily in his chair. "Yes, well," he mumbled, "until they do, it'll be a painful and embarrassing situation for the entire family. It was difficult enough for them to endure it all the first time—"

"Oh, for God's sake," Nick interrupted with a groan. "You made a fool of yourself over a woman. It's happened to us all. When will you stop flogging yourself for not being the ever-perfect son?"

"I know you don't worry about things like that, Nick," he shot back. "You gave up being Landsdowne's perfect son before any of us were out of short pants."

Nick grinned, unperturbed. "You've met Landsdowne. Were he your father, would you give a damn what he thought?"

Denys sighed. "I suppose not," he conceded. "But I can't make light of what this sort of talk would do to my family. I care about them. I care how they would feel, and I care what they think. And in any case, they are not the only ones to consider. There's Georgiana as well."

The other four men stared at him, and their surprise led him to assume a nonchalant air. "We've been seeing a bit of each other this season. Well, I am thirty-two, you know," he added, their silence impelling him to explain. "Time's getting on. I have to start thinking of the future."

Jack gave a shout of laughter at that, and Denys turned to the man beside him with a frown. "Really, Jack, you seem to find my situation endlessly amusing."

"Well," Jack began, but Denys cut him off.

"We all hold aristocratic titles, and we know it's our

duty to marry, and marry well. Even you finally accepted that fact."

"I would not have done if Linnet hadn't been the perfect wife for me."

Denys considered Georgiana—her grace and restraint, her charity work, her impeccable reputation and background, her fastidious nature, their fond childhood. "And Georgiana would be the perfect wife for me."

"Not perfect enough to impel you to actually propose, however."

He scowled in the face of that irrefutable point. "Just because I haven't doesn't mean I won't. I am . . . considering it."

"It's probably too late now. You've known Georgiana since she was born. If she has half the brains I think she has, she gave up any hopes about you ages ago. I would have."

He opened his mouth to fire off a smart reply about Jack's brains, but Nick deprived him of the chance.

"Surely, Georgiana and your family will all understand this arrangement with Lola is a business partnership, one forced upon you. Your private relationship with Lola is history, you've assured your family on that point, and once you've explained it all to Georgiana, there should be no cause for worry."

"In theory that seems so reasonable." Denys took another swallow of port. "The reality, I daresay, will be much less so."

"Why?" Nick countered. "Don't they trust you?"

"Of course they trust me. It's just that—" He stopped, the brutal truth hitting him square in the chest.

I don't trust myself.

That admission, silently made, was galling beyond belief, and when he glanced around the table, the faces of his friends told him he might just as well have said it out loud.

"For God's sake," he muttered, "let's forget the whole bloody business. I don't know why I ever thought any of you could offer suggestions that might help."

"It's not our job to help," Jack told him with cheer, giving him a hearty slap on the back. "We're your friends. Our job is to tease you mercilessly about your foibles, rag you about your upright, honorable nature, and point out to you when you're being a complete dolt."

"Thank you, Jack." He took a swallow of port. "I feel so much better about it all now."

Stuart spoke before Jack could reply. "If it's suggestions you want, I have one." He paused, leaning forward in his chair. "Stop kicking against the pricks."

Denys stiffened. "Accept the inevitable, you mean. That's an easy thing to say. Not so easy to do."

"Only if you're not over her."

That was the heart of the matter. Over the years, he'd convinced himself he was over Lola, but that kiss had dispelled any such illusion. He wasn't over her, not completely, and he didn't know if he ever would be.

There was only one way to find out.

And suddenly Denys knew what he had to do. Time and distance hadn't rid him of his desire for Lola, so taking such pains to avoid her wasn't going to accomplish a thing. Working with her was the only way to demonstrate his resolve, reaffirm his choices, and prove to himself that her reappearance didn't make any difference to his life at all.

It wouldn't be easy. As things stood now, he had to draw on all the fortitude he possessed just to be in the same room with her without wanting to ravish her or wring her neck. But with time and sufficient strength of will, surely he could get past that. Perhaps this situation would accomplish what years of time and distance had not, and he would become immune to her charms once and for all.

"You're right, Stuart. I didn't choose this partnership, God knows, but I suppose I've no choice but to accept it." He straightened in his chair. "After all, when a man's caught in a hurricane, it's better to be a reed than an oak."

"A sound principle," Jack approved, raising his glass, "and an apt analogy, for Lola Valentine is one hell of a hurricane."

Denys couldn't argue the point. Reed or oak, he knew he'd be facing some torrential headwinds in the days to come. He just hoped he could weather the storm without been wrecked all over again.

LOLA THOUGHT DENYS would keep avoiding a meeting with her, all the way to January if he could. But four days following her call at his office, she received a note from his secretary, granting her request and inquiring if five o'clock one week hence at his lordship's offices would be acceptable.

Such unexpected capitulation on Denys's part was quite a surprise, but though it gave her little time to prepare, her resolve to prove herself remained unaltered.

She had called on Mr. Lloyd Jamison as she'd intended, and whether it was due to her success in New York working with Henry, her role in Lord Somerton's latest play, or her new position as the viscount's partner, the theatrical agent happily accepted her as a client, despite her refusal to consider any role that involved kicking up her legs or singing bawdy songs.

For her part, she had found Mr. Jamison to be an engaging and likable man, and though she had little desire to employ an agent, she agreed to allow him to represent her acting interests. She also took the opportunity to make use of his extensive knowledge of London theater.

Thanks to that interview and the reports sent by Denys's office, as well as what she learned about balance sheets and income statements from an accounting clerk she hired, Lola had a much stronger understanding of the financial workings of theater in general and the Imperial in particular than she'd had before. But two nights before her meeting with Denys, she still hadn't come up with a single idea to increase the Imperial's profits.

She had never lacked for ideas. She'd built an entire

show around them. She knew she could do some innovative things with Shakespeare if given a chance, but though she trusted her creative instincts, she couldn't expect Denys to do so. He would never agree to setting *Two Gentlemen of Verona* in the American West or allowing Kate to be in on the joke when Petruchio made his famous wager, unless she could convince him her business acumen was as sound as her creativity.

Lola set down the theater's latest financial report and leaned back, resting her weight on her arms and staring at the documents spread all around her on the floor of her suite, frustrated. She'd hoped to find some weakness in the Imperial's current operations that she could exploit, but there didn't seem to be one.

No, when it came to weaknesses, the only one she could see was her own. When Denys had hauled off and kissed her, she'd surrendered in mortifying fashion, and every time she recalled those passionate moments in his office, her body began to burn, but not with the indignation a woman ought to feel in such circumstances. No, when she recalled Denys's mouth on hers and his arms around her, she felt the unmistakable burn of desire.

She tilted her head back, closing her eyes, memories coming over her in a flood—memories of other hot kisses they'd shared, kisses long ago, in that brief, blissful window of time when she'd allowed herself to fall in love with him, when she'd opened her heart and surrendered her body and chosen to believe in fairy tales.

Lola sat up, shoving aside the past, reminding herself that this was real life. Denys had not only kissed her, he'd used that kiss as proof they couldn't work together, and he'd ripped her abilities to shreds. If she didn't challenge his contentions and disprove them, if she couldn't make him start to see her as an equal and a colleague instead of as his former mistress, then he'd be proved right, and the partnership would be doomed.

Lola frowned at the documents spread around her, thinking hard. The Imperial made a hefty profit. It was well regarded and efficiently run. As things stood, there just didn't seem much room for improvement in theater operations. Anything with the potential to increase profits would have to involve some sort of radical change.

Radical change.

Something flickered within her, something forged by the documents before her, her interview with Jamison, and a chance remark made by Kitty during their supper. Suddenly alert, she worked to form this vague glimmer into an idea, and when she succeeded, she felt a jolt of jubilation and hope.

She rummaged through the stacks, pulling out various reports, then she spread the selected sheets in front of her to study them. A few minutes' perusal confirmed that her idea could not only work, but it could also make the Imperial significantly more profitable. There was only one problem.

Denys would never agree. He'd never been one for radical change.

That irrefutable fact deflated her, but only for a moment. Her purpose was to prove she could hold her own as a partner, and this idea, properly presented, would accomplish that. He didn't have to agree to implement it, but it would force him to admit he'd been wrong about her ability to come up with business ideas. Lola allowed herself a moment to savor the sweetness of that possibility, then she picked up her pencil and reached for a blank sheet of paper. She still had a lot of work to do.

Chapter 11

Two days later, thanks to another session with the accounting clerk and the hiring of a typist at Houghton's Secretarial Service, Lola came to her meeting with Denys loaded for bear. She had a fully-fleshed-out business plan in her portfolio, and she felt confident, prepared, and ready to defend her idea and fight for her rights. She wasn't even nervous.

Until she saw him.

He wasn't behind his desk when she entered his office. Instead, he was seated on the horsehair settee at the opposite end of the room having tea, and as he set aside his cup and rose to greet her, she noted in surprise that he was in his shirtsleeves, his jacket off and his cuffs rolled back. This casual state of dress made him seem less like the ruthless man of business she'd come to expect and much more like the Denys she used to know. Caught off guard, she came to an abrupt halt just inside the door, her hand tightening around the handle of her leather portfolio.

"Good afternoon," he said, and glanced past her. "Thank you, Dawson. You may go."

The secretary departed, and Lola felt an absurd jolt of nervousness when she heard the door click shut behind her.

Denys gestured to the tray beside him. "Would you care for tea?"

She'd come for a battle. She hadn't expected tea. Lola took a deep breath and started forward, but with each step, her uneasiness increased, and she stopped again, still several feet away.

Denys tilted his head, giving her a quizzical look. "Is something wrong?"

"Tea, Denys?"

"Well, we are in England, Lola. Tea's not particularly extraordinary."

"No, but it's . . ." She paused, considering. "Unexpected."

"I daresay." He gestured to the settee behind him. "Shall we sit down?"

She glanced at the comfortable leather furnishings and the tea tray laden with sandwiches and cakes, and a poem she'd learned in childhood flashed through her mind. " 'Will you walk into my parlor?' " she quoted wryly, returning her gaze to his face as she started forward again. "Is that it?"

He smiled a little. "You did ask to walk into this par-

ticular parlor," he reminded. "But you needn't worry. I
don't bite."

"No? You could have fooled me." Lola made a rueful
face as she sat down on the settee and placed her portfolio by her feet. "You've been baring your teeth at me
ever since I got to town."

"Yes, about that . . ." He paused and sat down beside
her. "I have always prided myself on being a gentleman, but my behavior since your arrival has been anything but gentlemanly. And my remark the other day
and my conduct . . ." He paused, grimacing. "Both were
beyond the pale. I must apologize."

His words ought to have been reassuring, and yet,
they had the curious effect of making her even more
apprehensive. Lola tried to shake it off, telling herself
not to look a gift horse in the mouth. "Apology accepted. So, we have a truce, then?"

"I hope so. That is the reason I requested we meet at
five o'clock."

She frowned, uncomprehending. "What does the
time of day have to do with it?"

"Your American Indians smoke a pipe with their
former enemies, don't they, to symbolize a peace
accord? We British do that with tea. Speaking of
which . . ." He turned toward the tray beside his seat.
"You take plenty of sugar in yours, if I recall. And you
prefer lemon to milk."

Astonished, she stared at his back as he added the
requisite ingredients to her cup. "I can't believe you remember how I prefer my tea."

He turned, holding out her cup and saucer, along with a napkin. "Of course I remember."

Those words, the low intensity of his voice as he said them, froze her in place, and when she looked up, she could see in his dark eyes a hint of the tender, passionate man who had slipped past all her defenses all those years ago. Her throat went dry.

"Would you like a sandwich?" he asked, and his voice broke the spell, for it was once again properly polite. "Or would you prefer the walnut cake?"

She took the tea things, striving to recover her poise as she laid the napkin across her lap. "Cake, please. What?" she added as he chuckled.

"I don't know why I even asked," he said, cutting a hefty wedge from the iced cake on the tray. He placed the cake on a plate and faced her as he offered it. "You always did have a sweet tooth."

She took the plate, and the moment she did, another memory from early childhood flashed through her mind—sitting at the kitchen table in her Sunday dress, the tulle underskirt scratchy against her legs, and her mother across from her with the blue willow china spread out between them.

No, no, Charlotte. You've forgotten to remove your gloves again. Oh heavens, I fear you shall never learn to do it properly.

Heat flooded her cheeks at her mistake, and she glanced around, but there was no table near her on which to put her tea things.

Denys perceived her difficulty at once. "Let me help," he said, taking back the tea and cake.

"Thank you," she mumbled as she pulled off her gloves, her cheeks burning. Never had the class difference between them seemed greater than it was right now. "Your English tea is something I'm not used to," she added, even as she wondered why she felt the need for an excuse. "Even when I lived here, I never could quite get the hang of it."

That made him laugh, and she frowned, taken aback. "Why are you laughing?"

"I'm not laughing at you," he assured at once. "It's just the way you talk, your colorful American expressions. 'Get the hang of it,' for example. It's charming." He paused, and his smile faded. "I'd forgotten that."

She feared she was the one being charmed here. Damn it, she'd come prepared for a fight, not for this. "Why are you being this way?" she whispered painfully. "Why are you being so nice?"

"Isn't that a good thing?"

It ought to be, but it wasn't. And that was the problem, a problem she'd sensed the moment she walked in the door today. Denys, angry and resentful, was a man she'd been prepared to meet ever since she'd decided to return. She could hold her own with that man any day of the week. But Denys when he was like this made her feel much too vulnerable.

"Of course it's a good thing," she answered, forcing a hearty certainty into her voice that she didn't feel in the least. "I just wish I knew what inspired this about-face on your part."

"Nothing earth-shattering. I was railing about our situation to my friends—you remember Stuart, Jack, Nick, and James? Anyway," he went on, as she nodded, "I was expressing my views about this partnership—"

"And peeling paint off the walls in the process, I bet."

The wry answering look he gave her acknowledged the truth of that. "I'm sure you'll be pleased to know that my friends found my predicament quite amusing."

She couldn't help grinning at that. "Did they?"

"Oh, yes. They pointed out that I was being an utter idiot."

"And what was your response? Did you tell them to go hang themselves from the nearest tree?"

His mouth twitched. "No, actually. I . . ." He paused and lifted his hands in a gesture of surrender. "I was forced to agree with them. And with you. Neither of us wants to sell," he went on before she could express her astonishment at this most unexpected change of heart, "so working together is the only viable alternative."

"Do you think you can do that?"

"I shall have to."

"You don't . . ." She paused over her next question, not sure she wanted the answer. "You don't still hate me?"

"I never hated you." He looked away, drawing a deep breath. "Despite how much I wanted to. And," he went on, returning his gaze to her face, "in trying to decide what to do with you, I realized that resenting you, fighting with you—whether it be about our past as lovers or our future as partners—is a futile exercise. The only thing to be done is to accept the situation and learn to work within it."

It was just what she'd hoped for, and yet she didn't find it the least bit reassuring. "Are you sure that's how you want to play it?" she asked. "You wouldn't rather take a piece of my hide?"

"An intriguing notion." His lashes lowered, then lifted. "Which piece did you have in mind?"

Her heart slammed against her ribs, and her teacup rattled in its saucer.

Dismayed by such an obvious display of nervousness, Lola lifted her cup from its saucer and gulped down the rest of her tea, but though it was hot and sweet and strong, she didn't feel fortified by it. Instead, she still felt as skittish as a colt.

Seated beside her was the man she remembered from long ago, the one man who'd made her break all her own rules about keeping stage-door johnnies at arm's length. The man whose kisses had made her head spin and her knees go weak, whose tenderness had softened her hard, cynical shell, whose passion had stolen her heart. This was the man she'd fallen in love with. And it had been a huge mistake.

Her gaze lowered to his mouth, and the kiss they'd shared a week ago was suddenly vivid in her mind. Her lips tingled. Her body flushed with heat, and her heart began thudding in her chest so loudly that when he spoke, she had to strain to hear what he said.

"Would you care for more tea?"

Lola stiffened in her chair. "No, thank you. I'd prefer it if we could come straight to business."

She grimaced at the tartness in her voice, aware of how rude she must seem in light of his hospitality, but she didn't know how much more of Denys being nice she could handle in a single day. "Sorry if I'm rushing you," she added, shoving her teacup toward him as her mind grasped desperately for a viable reason to speed things along so she could get out of here. "It's just that I . . . I have plans this evening."

He took her cup and saucer from her outstretched hand. "Of course. You're going to the theater, I suppose?" he asked, turning away to set aside their tea things. "Or the opera, perhaps?"

She had only an instant to decide, for any hesitation smacked of lying. "Opera. By the way," she rushed on before he could ask what was playing at Covent Garden tonight, "I received those financial statements from your office. Thank you for having them sent over."

"No thanks are necessary," he said, and to her relief, his voice was brisk and businesslike, expressing no further curiosity about her fictional plans for the evening. "Is there anything you wish to ask me about the state of the Imperial's finances?"

"No, everything seems quite in order. I have lots of questions, of course, but I think we can save them for another day. Today, there is something else I would like to discuss. I feel it's important."

"Certainly." He settled back against the arm of the settee, and for the first time since she'd reentered his life, he seemed receptive to hearing what she had to say. She couldn't predict how long this new cooperation would last, of course, but she knew this might be her only chance to demonstrate her worth as a partner.

She took a deep breath. "You asked me the other day what of value I could possibly bring to a partnership between us. I'd like to use this meeting to answer that question."

A hint of regret crossed his face. "I would ask that you forget what I said. I was frustrated, and I spoke in anger."

"But you meant what you said. It's all right," she added before he could reply. "Your question was a fair one. I realize that in the normal course of events, you would never have considered going into business with me, and your father certainly wouldn't. But though I don't have Henry's experience, or connections, and I know I have a lot to learn about business, I do have one of the things you asked me about."

She reached into the portfolio beside her, pulled out the proposal she'd spent the past two days working on, and handed it to him.

"What's this?" he asked as he took it.

"A way to make the Imperial more profitable."

Using his thumb, he flipped through the thick sheaf

of carefully compiled documents. "You've gone to a great deal of work," he said slowly, and there was something in his voice she couldn't quite define. Chagrin, perhaps, or surprise. But when he looked up, his gaze was thoughtful, assessing, and she could only hope that meant he was beginning to see her in a different light. "I hadn't expected this. I'm . . ." He paused and laughed a little, as if confounded. "I'm impressed, Lola, I admit."

Pride and a sweet sense of gratification rose within her, but she didn't have long to enjoy it. "Unfortunately," he said as he turned and set the sheaf of papers on the table beside the tea tray, "we don't have time today for a discussion of anything complicated. I only allotted an hour for this meeting, you see, because, like you, I am going to the opera. Unlike you, however, I have to return to the other side of town in order to change to evening clothes."

She felt a jolt of dismay. "You are going to Covent Garden, too?"

"Yes. I'm sorry now that I didn't allow more time for our meeting, but all decisions for the current season have already been made, and I did not anticipate that you would wish to discuss new business, particularly something as complex as this seems to be."

"I see."

He must have sensed her disappointment, for he stirred in his seat and glanced at the clock.

"I still have a bit of time before I have to return to the West End, I suppose. Why don't you tell me the gist of what you are proposing? I'll read the details later, and we can discuss it at our next meeting."

"Of course." She sucked in a deep breath and took the plunge. "If we truly want to increase profits, we should expand the acting company, extend the season, and make the Imperial into a repertory theater."

He blinked, seeming startled, and she feared he was going to tell her she was out of her mind. But he didn't. Instead, he was silent so long, she couldn't imagine what he was thinking. "For heaven's sake, Denys, say something."

He shook his head, looking as if she'd just poleaxed him. "I don't know what to say. You've just presented me with a very creditable idea."

She was so relieved he hadn't scoffed at her and dismissed the idea as ridiculous that she couldn't help chaffing him. "You needn't sound so surprised," she said, making a face. "I do occasionally have good ideas."

He tilted his head, studying her. "You truly took my doubts about you to heart, didn't you?"

"I took them as a challenge."

"I keep forgetting challenges don't deter you. They just spur you on."

He sounded rueful, and she grinned. "I am ornery that way. So my idea could work?"

"It could. It's an idea I've considered myself, as a matter of fact. But there are difficulties . . ." He paused and leaned forward as if eager to discuss it further, but as he rested his forearms on his knees, his clasped hands brushed her thigh. She jerked at the contact, an involuntary move that sent her plate with its slice of cake tumbling off her lap. It hit the floor carpet by her feet with a thud—icing side down, of course.

She grimaced. "I'm so sorry. How clumsy of me."

She leaned down, but as she reached for the plate and its contents, he leaned down as well, his hand closing over hers to stop her. "It's all right," he said, a strange, fierce undercurrent in his voice. "Leave it."

Lola looked into his eyes, paralyzed as the touch of his hand spread warmth through her body, sending it along her spine and down to her toes, to every fingertip and the top of her head. She stared at him helplessly as that warmth pooled in her midsection and deepened into desire. He felt it, too. She could see that in his eyes.

Oh, no, she thought. *No, no, no. Pull away, Lola. Pull away now.*

She didn't move.

His thumb brushed back and forth over the back of her wrist, and she recalled their kiss the other day and all the ones before it, of what being his woman had been like. A month ago, she'd feared this partnership wouldn't work because Denys hated her, but now, she feared it wouldn't work because he didn't hate her at all. She couldn't decide, suddenly, which prospect was worse.

"Reed," he muttered under his breath, and let her go. "Not oak."

She frowned, not sure she'd heard him right, for her

dazed wits couldn't see what reading and oaks had to do with anything. "I beg your pardon?"

"Nothing." He rubbed a hand over his face and glanced at the clock. "We're out of time."

"Yes, of course." She jerked to her feet, relieved, and glad to end this meeting before she did something truly stupid.

He also stood up, but strangely, neither of them moved. He wasn't touching her, but he might as well have been, for she could still feel the imprint of his palm over the back of her hand.

"I hope you enjoy the opera this evening."

The opera? For a moment, she could only stare at him, then she remembered. "Oh, yes, the opera," she said with a forced laugh. "Of course."

He frowned a little, studying her far too closely for her peace of mind, but when he spoke, his voice was perfectly natural. "Have you ever been to the opera before?"

Not with you.

She almost said it aloud, but checked herself in time. It was true that Denys had never taken her to the opera, or the theater, or anywhere else where his family or his friends might see them together, but there was no point in bringing that up.

It doesn't matter now, she told herself, but that was a lie. It mattered. Even after all these years, it still mattered. It still hurt.

She felt cold, suddenly, afraid he'd see, and she forced herself to paste on a smile. "Of course I've been to the opera. I know America is terribly uncivilized, Denys," she added, making her voice as light as she could manage, "but we do have opera there, you know."

He smiled, responding to the teasing. "No need to spring to your country's defense, Lola. I wasn't being snobbish. And I know you have opera, for I attended one there two years ago. At the Metropolitan."

"Yes, I'd heard you were in town." The moment the words were out of her mouth, she wanted to take them back, for now he might think she had been keeping track of his doings, and she hadn't been, not really. "Jack was living there at the time, I remember. I never saw him," she added at once, "but I'd often see his name in the gossip columns. And yours, too, of course, when you came. You and James. And Nick. Some Knicker-bocker who'd swindled you—it was in all the papers. I couldn't help hearing about it."

She broke off, aware that these completely unneces-sary explanations were only reinforcing her fears of what he'd think. Hoping she could at last escape, she retrieved her gloves and bent to reach for her portfolio. "I hope you and your family enjoy yourselves tonight," she said as she straightened.

"Oh, I shan't be with the family. I'm—" He stopped, took a breath, and let it out. "I'm attending with a friend."

The friend was female; his hesitation made that clear, and Lola was suddenly assaulted by a new and differ-ent sort of hurt—the sharp, quick sting of jealousy.

She tried to quash it at once, for she'd no right to it, no right at all. She'd always appreciated she wasn't right for him, aware of the vast difference in class between them. In the end, she'd left him because of it. There was nothing to be jealous about now.

And she could not fault his choice of companions. Unlike her, Lady Georgiana Prescott was born and bred to the world he moved in, just the sort of girl she'd hoped he would find when she left, the sort who could sit beside him at the opera without being a slap in his family's face. She was glad for him. *Glad*, damn it.

Keeping her smile in place, she edged toward the door. "I hope you enjoy yourselves."

"Thank you," he said as he walked with her to the door. "I expect we shall see you and your companions strolling about the foyer during intermission?"

Lola felt a pang of alarm. "Oh, but surely you and your friend won't want to come down for refreshments. The concession stalls are always so crowded, and the lines are so long."

"True, but I like to stretch my legs during intermission. And my friend likes milling about the foyer at intermission."

"Does she, indeed?"

The acidic question was out of her mouth before she could stop it, and she wanted to bite her tongue off.

"Why, yes," he answered, looking at her far too closely for her peace of mind, and when he began to smile, Lola's cheeks grew hot, and she felt as transparent as glass. Cursing this damnable inclination to jealousy, she worked to again force it away as he went on, "She enjoys seeing who's with whom, what the ladies are wearing—that sort of thing. I thought all women enjoyed that. Don't you?"

"No," she said firmly. "I don't stroll about. I like to remain in my seat."

"I see." He moved to open the door for her, and she breathed a sigh of relief that she was finally escaping. Her relief, however, proved premature, for he stopped, the door half-open. "You're in a box, I hope? That way, you can have refreshments brought to you."

Lola had to bite back a sigh of exasperation. One harmless lie, and suddenly she was in a tangle of them. "Oh, no," she answered. "A box is far too grand. We're in stalls. You know," she added, forcing a laugh, "where all the plebeians sit."

He didn't laugh with her. Instead, his smile vanished, and he tilted his head to one side, studying her. "You always did have quite a chip on your shoulder about the difference in our position," he murmured.

"Did I?" Her own smile faltered a bit, despite her best efforts to prop it up. "Or did I just have a more realistic view of my place in the world than you did?"

She didn't wait for him to reply. "Thank you, Denys," she said, and held out her hand. "I know you didn't want this meeting or this arrangement."

"No," he agreed, shook hands, and quite properly, let go of her at once. "But I'll rub along. I appreciate the effort you've taken to demonstrate your abilities as a partner, and I shall be interested to read your proposal."

"You're not just saying that to pacify me and get me out of your hair?"

"On the contrary. As I said, you've brought up an idea I've sometimes considered myself. We can discuss it in depth at our next meeting. I hope to see you and your companions later this evening." He bowed. "But if not, have an enjoyable evening, Miss Valentine."

With that rather formal farewell, he stepped aside to let her depart, and when she'd crossed the threshold, he closed the door behind her, leaving her baffled by his change of heart, bemused by his new spirit of friendly cooperation, and exasperated with herself for losing her wits so thoroughly.

Why had she ever said she was going to the opera? Denys loved opera. She ought to have remembered that and chosen theater instead. Still, what was done was done.

She'd have to follow through now. The lights were always lit during the performances at Covent Garden so the posh people could see and be seen. If he looked for her and found she wasn't there, he might conclude jealousy had kept her away, and that notion was just too humiliating to contemplate. And besides, if both of them were seen publicly with other people, Kitty's prediction about gossip surrounding them might be headed off at the pass.

With that perhaps overly optimistic possibility in mind, Lola tucked her portfolio under her arm, slid on her gloves, and put her wits to work.

If she was going, it was clear she'd need an escort, and if attending the opera was going to dampen gossip about her and Denys, her escort would have to be a man. But as Lola reckoned up the number of single men she knew well enough for such an invitation, she knew finding an escort wasn't going to be easy. She knew so few people in London these days, although if she were still in New York, she'd probably have had the same problem. On both sides of the Atlantic, she'd been living like a nun.

Lola stared at the panels of the closed door, her mind working frantically. What about James? He might be in town, he was single, and she certainly knew him well enough to invite him to attend an opera. But as she thought of him, she knew she couldn't ask him. She could not gad about London with one of Denys's friends even if he'd once been a friend of hers as well. That wouldn't be right. But there was no one else, absolutely no one.

She might be able to get by with insisting she'd been there, even if he mentioned looking for her and not finding her. Still, he'd no doubt ask how she and her companions had liked the performance. He might even ask her about them, which meant she'd have to invent more lies, and she really did not want to lie to Denys, even about something innocuous—

"Miss Valentine?"

The voice startled her out of her contemplations, and she turned to find Mr. Dawson standing behind his desk, watching her in some puzzlement, and she realized she must have been dithering here for quite some time.

"Can I be of help?" he asked.

Lola took a quick glance over the handsome, sandy-haired young secretary, and he suddenly seemed like the answer to a prayer.

"Why, yes, Mr. Dawson, I believe you can. Tell me . . ." She paused, giving him her prettiest smile. "Do you like opera?"

Chapter 12

 If bending like a reed in the wind was to be his strategy in weathering the storm that was Lola Valentine, Denys knew he'd have to be quite a flexible chap in the coming days.

Their meeting had been a necessary first step, and thankfully, it hadn't been as tortuous as he would have predicted. They'd had tea, discussed business, and made small talk for a full hour, and the notion of ravishing her on the settee had only crossed his mind three times. That wasn't too bad, all things considered.

Still, as flexible as he was willing to be in regard to Lola, there was one rule he knew he would have to adhere to at all times. He could not touch her.

That particular maxim was one no gentleman ought

to find difficult, he thought with chagrin as he sat in his seat at the Royal Opera House. But when he'd unthinkingly put his hand over hers this afternoon, the effect on his body had been immediate, nearly destroying his control before he could even begin to prove he had any. Touching an unmarried woman's bare hand was one of those things a gentleman simply did not do, but with Lola, all the rules of propriety he'd been raised with never seemed to matter much.

As if to prove that contention, Denys suddenly realized the view through his opera glasses was no longer the stage but the seats below. He'd begun looking for her without even realizing it.

Does she, indeed?

Her question and the prickly tone of her voice as she'd asked it came echoing back to him, and he couldn't help a sense of satisfaction as he appreciated its cause.

She was jealous.

His smile widened into a grin as he savored this quite unexpected turnabout. In his infatuated youth, he'd paced outside her dressing room at the *Théâtre-Latin* countless times—along with all the other stage-door johnnies—and he'd nearly driven himself mad wondering if he would ever be allowed through her door. Every time he had returned to Paris, he'd observed the besotted faces of his friends as they'd watched her dance or listened to her talk. Hell, Henry had stolen her right from under his nose. So when it came to Lola, jealousy was an emotion he'd often had cause to feel.

The notion that the tables might be turned was a sweet one to contemplate.

There was no cause for Lola to be jealous, of course, not on this particular night. He lowered the pair of opera glasses, his gaze sliding to his companion for the evening. There was no doubt that Belinda, the Marchioness of Trubridge, was a beautiful woman, but she was also the wife of Denys's best friend.

Lola wouldn't know that, however, having never seen Belinda, and he felt a hint of regret that she had declared an intention to remain in her seat. Still, it was probably for the best.

He raised the opera glasses, but his view of the stage receded almost at once, replaced in his mind's eye by Lola's face, the proud lift of her chin and her burning cheeks. Lola, jealous? He still found it hard to believe. And yet . . .

Irresistibly drawn, he once again tilted the opera glasses down and began studying the seats below. Sure enough, he'd only scanned two rows before his theory was proved right, and he saw her down in the stalls below.

Not that there was much to see from this angle, for he was high above and almost directly behind her. But one glance over the auburn hair piled high atop her head and the pale, creamy skin of her neck and back above the deep vee of her evening gown was enough to confirm her identity. His body, traitor that it was, responded at once, and arousal came over him—another test of his new resolve.

He worked to hold fast against it. He didn't try to deny its existence, for that was pointless. Instead, he strove to find equilibrium within it, knowing that was the only way he would ever conquer it.

She was facing the stage, not looking at her surroundings, but even if she had been glancing around, she'd have to turn almost completely in her seat and crane her neck to catch sight of him up here, a less-than-subtle move that would surely draw attention to her. Denys, secure in that knowledge, was able to put his newfound resolutions to the test, but only a few moments made him appreciate what a pleasurable agony it was going to be.

Her dark red hair gleamed with incandescent fire beneath the chandeliers, beckoning to the heat inside him. Against the deep rose pink fabric of her gown, her skin was like rich cream, evoking in his memory its velvety texture.

"Looking for someone?"

Belinda's voice intruded, and Denys was forced to lower the glasses and give his attention to his companion. He did it slowly, giving himself plenty of time to paste an expression of bland indifference on his face, for Belinda had shrewd eyes and keen instincts. "No," he said, glad the phrasing of her question enabled him to answer truthfully. He'd already found the person he'd been looking for.

Belinda's blue gaze was steady, her expression impassive. "Very wise of you," she said. "So many people are inclined to stare at each other during the opera, aren't they? I daresay you are the subject of much scrutiny and gossip." She paused. "At the present time."

"True." Deciding to take the delicate hint, he returned his attention to the stage, but only moments later, the performance broke for intermission, and his attention was drawn irresistibly back to the seats below.

It was easy to find her again, for amid the gentlemen in black evening coats, matrons in dark-hued velvet, and debutantes in pastel chiffon, she was like an exotic tropical bird amid a flock of crows, pigeons, and sparrows. As for her escort—

Denys swerved his gaze to the right just as the fair-haired man beside Lola turned his head to say something to her, a move that revealed a profile Denys knew well. He tensed in his seat, appalled, not quite able to believe his eyes.

Dawson? Of all the men in London, Lola was gallivanting about with his own secretary?

A myriad of emotions struck him one after another. Anger, jealousy, frustration, pain—each shot through him like a jolt of electricity, burning away reason, propriety, and restraint. He wasn't a reed bending in the storm. Instead, he was an oak struck by lightning, cracking straight down the center.

Of all the men in London she could have crooked her finger at, she'd chosen a man Denys knew, a man he worked with and liked. It was like Henry all over again. Damn her, couldn't she at least have the decency to take up with someone he didn't know?

He watched as the couple rose to their feet and joined the throng streaming toward the exits, belying her declaration that she preferred to stay in her seat during intermissions.

His gaze followed them out the doors, and the moment they had vanished from view, he lowered the opera glasses and stood up. "I think I shall stretch my legs a bit," he said, setting the opera glasses with painstaking care on the little table between them.

"Is that—" Belinda paused, tilting her head back to meet his gaze with a somber one of her own. "Is that wise?"

He was in no frame of mind to be dissuaded. "No," he answered, and with that terse concession, he left the box. It wasn't wise at all, but he was going to do it anyway. Because it was too late to bend like a reed in the wind.

INVITING MR. DAWSON MIGHT have been a stroke of pure desperation on her part, but as she watched him weave his way toward her through the crowd after purchasing her a champagne cup, she was glad things had turned out this way. Denys's secretary was intelligent, considerate, and very pleasant company.

He'd been a bit reluctant to accept her invitation, expressing concern that his employer wouldn't like it, but Lola hoped Denys would be relieved she'd taken up with someone else. After all, if she was seen around town with a man much closer to her own class, society might dismiss any notion that she and Denys were re-kindling their affair. It was a faint possibility, true, but Lola had always been an optimist. She chose to hope for the best.

"Here we are," Mr. Dawson said, halting in front of her and holding out the small goblet of cognac and champagne with a little bow.

"Thank you," she said as she accepted the glass. "You are a gallant man to brave that line of people on my behalf."

"Not at all. It was my pleasure." He took a glance around. "It is quite crowded this evening, isn't it?"

Lola didn't miss the anxiousness in that look. "You mustn't worry. You won't be in trouble for this, I promise you."

"Even if I lost my job," he said, looking at her again, "this evening would make it worthwhile."

Oh, dear, she thought, noting the admiration in his gaze with dismay, and suddenly the secretary's acceptance of her invitation seemed less like a stroke of good luck and more like a serious problem, and when she glanced past Mr. Dawson's shoulder, the sight of Denys's tall form at the other end of the room confirmed her theory, for he did not look the least bit relieved. He looked furious. Although he had no right to dictate where she went and with whom, as she watched him start toward them with a purposeful stride and a grim expression, she decided it might be best to avoid reminding him of that particular fact.

"Would you like to go backstage?" she asked. Tucking her arm through the secretary's, she turned her back on Denys and began propelling Mr. Dawson toward a nearby corridor.

"I should adore it, Miss Valentine," he answered, keeping up with her hurried steps as she strode down the corridor. "But will they allow us?"

"Of course they will," she said, crossing her fingers that she could spy some old acquaintance amid the stagehands flitting about who would let them through. "But we'll have to be quick," she added, hastening her steps even more, pulling him with her around a corner and into another corridor, but a few moments later, when she heard Denys's voice behind her, she knew they hadn't been quite quick enough.

"Miss Valentine?" he called, and though Lola was inclined to want to ignore it, Denys's incisive voice brought her companion to a halt, impelling her to stop as well.

Still, she had no intention of allowing Denys to call Dawson on the carpet for her invitation, so she turned around and hastened into speech. "Why, it's Lord Somerton," she said brightly, trying to sound surprised. "Good evening, my lord. What are you doing wandering the corridors of Covent Garden?"

"I have need to speak with you, Miss Valentine. It's important. Dawson," he added before she could come up with objections, "will you excuse us, please?"

The young man hesitated and glanced at Lola, who

gave a nod of assent. Denys's implacable expression told her there was no escape, and at least this way, she'd keep Dawson out of trouble.

"Good evening, sir," the secretary said, bowing. "Miss Valentine."

Denys waited until the secretary had traversed the corridor and turned the corner before he returned his attention to her. "Just what the devil do you think you're doing?"

Though his voice was calm, there was anger in his dark eyes, making it clear that any progress they'd made this afternoon toward a permanent truce had now been obliterated. But why? He'd known she would be coming this evening. Surely he'd known she wouldn't come alone. And besides, he could have stayed in his seat. Instead, he had sought her out. Why?

Whatever his reasons, Denys in a fury was not something to take lightly. Like all good men, when he lost his temper, he lost it thoroughly.

"You should not be talking to me," she pointed out, hoping to dampen his anger with a reminder of propriety. "If someone of your set were to notice that you followed us back here, the story would be in all the scandal sheets quick as the wink of an eye."

His mouth tightened, showing that he appreciated the truth of that, but if she'd hoped it would impel him to depart, that hope was dashed. "You cannot go gadding about London with my secretary. It is highly inappropriate."

"He said you wouldn't like it, and I can see he

was right. But really, Denys, why should it matter to you?"

"It's understandable you would break the rules," he went on without answering her question. "But Dawson has no such excuse."

"What rule have we broken? The one that says an unmarried woman can't go about with a man unchaperoned? It's so sweet of you to be concerned for my reputation," she added, though she was pretty sure consideration for her was the last thing on his mind right now, "but it isn't necessary. As for Mr. Dawson, you mustn't censure him for any of this. I can't go to the opera alone. Even I wouldn't defy society to that extent. So I asked Mr. Dawson to come with me. As I said, he warned me that you wouldn't like it, but I persuaded him to come anyway. Any blame for this lies with me."

Denys studied her face for a moment, then he gave a deep sigh. "I suppose I'm the last man on earth who should condemn another for succumbing to your charms," he muttered. "God help any man who tries to hold out when you decide to be persuasive. Regardless of who invited whom," he added before she could reply, "when we are finished here, you will bid him good evening and part from his company."

"Now, wait just a minute," she said, infuriated by such high-handed arrogance. "You have no right to dictate with whom I spend my evenings."

"I do when it's a violation of company policy. You cannot fraternize with an employee. It's not done."

"Fraternize?" he echoed, rolling her eyes. "That's ridiculous. It's only one evening at the opera. And anyway, he isn't my employee. He's yours."

"In point of fact, he is our employee. You are my partner in the Imperial, and the Imperial pays a portion of Mr. Dawson's salary."

"Is that what's got you in such a lather?" She took a sip from her champagne cup, studying him over the rim. "Don't you think you're being a bit too punctilious?"

"Am I? If my secretary were female, would it be acceptable for me to squire her about town and take her to the opera?"

She made a sound of derision at that ridiculous notion. "As if you'd ever hire a female secretary! And you certainly wouldn't take her to the opera. If a cancan dancer wasn't good enough to be seen about town with you, a female secretary wouldn't be either. And as I said before, we really cannot afford to be seen together. So, if you will pardon me?"

She started to step around him to return to her seat, but Denys moved as well, blocking her departure.

"Wait," he ordered. "What do you mean, 'not good enough'? Is that—" He broke off, comprehension dawning in his face. "Oh, my God. Is that what you thought?"

"It doesn't matter," she hastened to say. "I always knew the lay of the land."

"It's clear you didn't understand a damn thing." His voice was tight. "Damn it all, I was—" He broke off as a pair of stagehands appeared in the corridor, pushing a cart of props. He waited until they had passed by and disappeared, then he reached for the handle of the door beside him and opened it.

Lola watched, frowning in puzzlement as he leaned through the doorway to peer into the room beyond. "What are you doing?"

He straightened, but he didn't answer her question. Instead, he grabbed her by the arm. "Come with me," he said.

Lola felt her stomach give a nervous lurch. "But what about Mr. Dawson?" she asked, glancing desperately over her shoulder as Denys began pulling her across the threshold into the darkened room beyond. "We can't just leave him—"

"Hang Dawson. The fellow is well aware of your position as my partner and should have known better than to accept a social invitation from you. Let him return to his seat and enjoy the performance. You and I are going to thrash this out."

That would be like thrashing with sharks, but Denys gave her no opportunity to escape the encounter. He pulled her into what seemed to be a storage room. In the light that spilled from the corridor, she could make out the shadowy outlines of props, scenery canvases, and racks of costumes. The space seemed far too intimate, especially when he closed the door behind them, and she decided it was best to go on the offensive before he could put her on the defensive.

"Why did you drag me in here?" she demanded, turning to face him in the darkness. "You have no right to manhandle me in this manner—"

"What really happened six years ago?" he interrupted, cutting off any attempt on her part to gain the upper hand. "Why did you really leave me?"

Chapter 13

 There it was, the question she'd been dreading, thrown down like a gauntlet. She'd have to address it, of course, but not here, in a room so dark she couldn't see his face, with him standing so close that she could feel the heat of his body.

"I am not going to explain myself to you when we're standing in a storage closet at Covent Garden," she said, and turned to reach for the door handle. She'd only managed to open the door a crack, however, before he flattened one palm against it and slammed it shut.

"Oh, yes, you are," his voice murmured beside her ear, "because we are not leaving here until you do."

"For heaven's sake, Denys," she mumbled, turning around carefully in the tight space. "It's pitch-black in here."

"I can remedy that."

Thankfully, he took a step back from her, and she was able to take a breath. But any relief was short-lived, for a moment later, she heard the rasp of a match, light penetrated the dark, and he once again stepped closer to her, reaching up to turn the knob of the gas jet on the wall sconce beside the door. "Now then," he said as he lit the jet and blew out the match. "Answer my question. Why did you really leave me?"

She wanted nothing more than to duck and run, but with that option unavailable, she lifted her chin and countered his question with one of her own. "Why did you never take me to the opera?"

He frowned, clearly not comprehending the parallel. "You know why. It would have caused a scandal. We had agreed to be discreet."

"Yes. Because I'm not the sort of woman a man like you could ever be seen with in public, not amid your family and friends."

"Is that what you meant a moment ago when you said you weren't good enough?" He looked at her askance, as if this was somehow a surprising notion. "Don't tell me you've got it into your head that I regarded you as inferior to me."

"Well, you did say just the other day that I bring nothing worthwhile to our partnership. That I only seem to have one particular talent."

He grimaced at the reminder of his own harsh words. "As I told you this afternoon, I was angry when I said that, and frustrated, and though my frame of mind is no excuse for what I said, I'd ask again that you forget it. In any case, I was speaking in reference to business matters. As to our private affairs, I have never thought of you as inferior to me, and I can't believe you would think so."

"It's not a matter of what I think. It's a fact of life."

"You are referring, I suppose, to my title? Lola, you are the last person from whom I would have expected to hear about class distinctions."

"Why should you be surprised? Class distinctions exist. That is a fact, and I never rail against facts, no matter how unfair they might be. In the eyes of the world, I am your inferior. No one, particularly in your precious British society, would argue the point."

"I would argue it! For God's sake, Lola, I intended to marry you. Do you think I would ever have contemplated such a course if I thought of you as my inferior?"

"Yes." She paused a second. "If you couldn't keep me any other way."

He sucked in a deep breath, confirming he knew there was at least some truth in her words. Nonetheless, he chose to debate the point. "I wasn't intending to 'keep you,' as you put it. I was intending to make you my wife."

"And I couldn't let you do it. I couldn't let you ruin your future, so I—"

"Wait," he interrupted, holding up a hand to stop her flow of words. "You left me for another man, you broke my heart, and wrecked my life, and now you are trying to tell me that you did it all for *my* sake?"

"Yes." She watched the skeptical lift of his brow. "Mostly," she amended.

He gave a short, harsh laugh and rubbed his hands over his face. "Forgive me if I'm not grateful for my part of the favor."

"I don't expect you to be. But tonight, you have a woman with you who is elegant, beautiful, obviously a lady. With her, you won't ever have to worry anyone will turn against you for marrying her. Lady Georgiana Prescott is perfect for you."

He blinked as if surprised. "Lady Georgiana?"

"I saw you two up there. Not that it was easy to find you, by the way," she added, hoping to lighten the moment a little by confessing she'd been looking. "I had to practically turn all the way around in my seat before I spied you with her."

"Actually—"

"She's a lady. She's part of your world. I'm not a lady of the *ton*, and I could never have become one. And why the hell are you smiling?" she demanded, as his lips curved upward. "I'm baring my soul here, and you're smiling?"

"Sorry." Despite the apology, he made no effort to wipe the smirk off his face. "It's just that I'm not with Lady Georgiana this evening."

That took her back a bit. "The woman sitting next to you isn't Lady Georgiana Prescott? Black hair," she added as he shook his head. "Strands of pearls round her neck, midnight blue evening gown. Well, who is she, then?" she demanded, as he continued to shake his head.

"Jealous?" His smile widened into a grin, and the only reason she didn't find it insufferable was because it meant his anger had faded. "There's no need to be."

"Damn it, Denys, who is that woman?"

"Not Lady Georgiana. But the next time I see Nick," he added before she could reply, "I'll be sure to tell him you think his wife is perfect for me."

"His wife?" She felt a surge of relief, followed at once by irritation because she knew she shouldn't be feeling anything of the sort. "Well, how was I supposed to know? I've never met her. Either way, the point's the same."

"Point?" he scoffed, his grin vanishing. "What point? That you had some harebrained idea to be self-sacrificing? Not," he added at once, "that I necessarily believe you. Self-sacrifice has never been your strong suit."

"I didn't just do it for you," she reminded. "I did it for my own sake as well."

"Because Henry made you a—what was it?—*a better offer.*"

She winced. Those words sounded every bit as brutal as she'd intended them to be when she'd spoken them.

"I'm sure I'm an idiot for asking," he murmured, "but why was Henry's offer to make you his mistress better than my honorable proposal of marriage?"

"Making me his mistress wasn't Henry's offer. He

wasn't the least bit interested in doing so, and neither was I. Henry already had a mistress, a very respectable woman. He wanted to protect her good name."

Denys stared at her, looking understandably skeptical. "You mean it was all a charade? You allowed yourself to be used as a front to protect some other woman's reputation?"

"Yes. Her name is Alice van Deusen. She's the headmistress of New York City's finest finishing school for girls. Henry met her when he was living here and she was on a tour of England with a group of her pupils. They fell in love, and that's why he returned to New York. But because he was already married, they had to keep their affair a secret. If anyone found out she and Henry were lovers, Alice and her school would be ruined. I know I can trust you not to tell anyone about her."

"Of course, but why would you agree to such an arrangement? Why would you allow Henry to use you in such a way?"

"It was convenient for me as well as for Henry. He protected Alice's good name, and he made a lot of money by backing my show. But I was protected, too, for no man would dare make advances to me, or try to take advantage of me, not with Henry to deal with. And I made money, too, of course. And I learned acting the proper way. But the important thing to me at the time was that I got a fresh start, away from—"

"Away from me," he finished when she fell silent.

She swallowed hard. "Yes. Going with him kept me

in the world where I belong. Oh, Denys," she added
with a sigh as she watched his lips press tight, "you and
I both know what your people thought of me. To them,
I was a gold-digging tramp."

"And you cared so much what my family thought."

"I did care! I cared for your sake. I'd already put a
wedge between you and your family, and I couldn't
bear to make it wider. And what if you started to blame
me for it?"

"I wouldn't have done."

"That's an easy thing to say, but with your family
disparaging me at every opportunity, after months or
years of being cold-shouldered by your friends—"

"My friends would never have done such a thing.
Do you really think Nick, Jack, James, or Stuart cared
tuppence about your background?"

"Their wives would have cared."

He inhaled sharply, and his head went back, demonstrating she'd touched on another hard truth. "None of
my friends had wives back then," he muttered, but he
didn't look at her, making it clear he knew just what a
feeble argument he was making.

"I knew they'd have wives at some point, and it's
women who rule society, Denys. You know that as well
as I do. Do you think they would have accepted me?
Me, a cabaret dancer, a woman most of their husbands
had been infatuated with at one time or another? And
even if they did swallow it down for your sake, they'd
never do more than be civil. And no other women of
your British *ton* would have even gone that far."

He shook his head, looking at her again, fighting what she was saying. "You don't know that."

"That's where you're wrong," she cried. "I do know. I know far more than you realize. Did you ever stop to think about what our life would have been like? No dinner invitations, no one coming to tea, no house parties at Arcady, everyone you know giving you the cut, one by one—"

"I didn't think things like that mattered to you."

"They matter to *you*, Denys. And to your family. And your friends. Anyone who chose not to turn their backs on you would suffer guilt by association. I couldn't do that to you."

He didn't seem impressed by the knowledge that she'd left him for his own sake. He plunked his hands on his hips and scowled at her. "I don't suppose you could have told me any of this at the time?"

Guilt nudged her, and she swallowed hard. "No."

"Why the hell not?"

Face the music, Lola.

"I was afraid if I started explaining why I was leaving, I'd lose my nerve."

"Nerve? Nerve's not something I'd say you lack. In fact, I'd say doing what you did took plenty of nerve."

She heard the bitter edge of his voice, and it hurt deep down, like pressing a bruise. "If I had tried to explain, you wouldn't have accepted it. You'd have found a way to persuade me to relent, so—" She broke off, took a deep breath, and forced herself to say the rest. "So I made you hate me. That way, I knew you wouldn't try to come after me."

"Well, you were right about that," he muttered. "Is there a single reason I should believe any of this?"

"I wouldn't blame you if you didn't, but it is the truth."

His gaze raked over her, a long, hard, searching gaze, and she found herself holding her breath because she had no idea if he'd accept her explanations, but just when she thought this conversation had been a waste of breath, he gave a nod.

"All right, then," he said abruptly. "I may be an utter fool to think you did any of this for my sake, but I'm choosing to believe you. But," he added before she could feel any relief, "I still resent you like hell for not being honest with me. I didn't deserve what you did to me or the way you did it."

"No," she agreed, "you didn't. And though I realize it's no excuse, I didn't plan any of it. My only plan was returning to my old life in Paris so that I could consider my future without you around to muddle my thinking. Henry came and told me you intended to propose marriage, and he'd just offered to take me to New York when you showed up, and I knew I had to go. I was ruining your life. Sure as I was that it would be a mistake to marry you, I know that if I'd stayed, eventually you'd have persuaded me to change my mind."

She bit her lip, looking at him. "You were never very good at taking no for an answer, and I was never very good at resisting you."

His mouth curved a bit, a wry, one-sided smile. "As I recall, you spent the better part of two years resisting me. Hell, it took a year before you let me into your dressing room."

She gave him a rueful smile in return. "I kept hoping you'd give up and go away, and yet, I was always hoping you wouldn't. And you were so good to me, and that was always my weakness."

His smile vanished. "And yet, as good as I was, you wouldn't have considered marrying me."

"No. The truth is . . ." She paused, and swallowed hard. "I didn't deserve you. And," she added, as he opened his mouth to make some sort of gentlemanly protest, "you certainly didn't deserve to be saddled with me, for I'd have made a horrible peeress. I have no idea what society ladies do all day. Have tea, I suppose, and go to parties, and shop. And pay calls, though what they all find to talk about—" She stopped, took a breath, and cut to the chase. "Marriage doesn't work for people like us, Denys. People who are as different as we. Like has to marry like."

"You don't think love could have overcome our differences?"

Longing twisted her heart, but she forced it ruthlessly away. There was no place here for self-deceit. "No, I don't."

"How cynical you are."

"Why?" she shot back, defensive all of a sudden. "Because I don't believe in fairy tales?"

"Sometimes fairy tales do come true."

"And love conquers all?"

"Sometimes."

She thought of her father hunched over the kitchen table, head in his hands and an empty bottle of whiskey by his elbow. "I don't think so. Love can be . . . a terrible thing."

"Or a wonderful thing."

"Either way, love didn't have much to do with it."

"It had everything to do with it. I loved you, damn it all!"

This was the heart of the matter, and the part of this inevitable conversation she'd been dreading the most. "But that's just it, Denys," she said softly. "You didn't love me. Not really."

"What? My God, is that what you think? Didn't I make my feelings plain enough at the time? I was head over ears—"

"You were infatuated with me, yes. You had a passion for me, yes. Had anyone asked, you'd have said of course you were in love with me. In the throes of passion, you often declared that love to me. But passion is all it was. It wasn't love, not the kind that lasts. How could it have been?" She shook her head. "You didn't even know me. You still don't."

He stared at her as if unable to believe what he was hearing. "Of course I know you. Lola, I've known you for nearly nine years."

"The amount of time doesn't matter. What do you

know of me? Of my life? Of my thoughts, my feelings, my experiences, my . . . my past before you met me? Practically nothing. We spent so little time together."

"It's odd how differently we see the situation." He paused, his gaze skimming over her, a long, slow perusal that seemed to burn right through her clothes and made her want to bolt for the door. "You might be right about when you were living in Paris, since I was in London and traveling back and forth to see you whenever I could, which wasn't nearly often enough. But here in London, it was different. Here, you and I spent a great deal of time together. That was why I brought you here."

"Yes, and there we were, meeting in secret in an illicit affair, with your having to sneak in and out of that little house in St. John's Wood." As she spoke of their arrangement, she tried to sound dismissive, but with his heated gaze roaming over her, her words came out in a breathless rush. Mortified, afraid he might guess what she was feeling, she forced a little laugh, hoping to make light of it all. "We were trying so hard to be discreet. I can't think why we bothered since everyone in society already knew all about us."

"And you say we've spent no time together? We spent nearly every afternoon in that house, Lola." He stirred, moving a bit closer. "Alone, together."

"Yes, but . . ." She paused, her face growing hot, but it wasn't the close, stuffy confines of the storage room that made her feel as if she were melting into a puddle. It was his heated, knowing gaze. "If you'll recall, we didn't spend much of our time there engaged in conversation."

He gave a caustic chuckle, acknowledging the truth of that. "No," he murmured, his gaze pausing at her mouth, his amusement fading. "I suppose not."

The gong sounded, indicating that intermission was nearly over, but neither of them moved.

Their gaze met, and locked, and suddenly, the past six years seemed to vanish as if they'd never existed, and the erotic summer afternoons they'd spent together were as vivid in her mind as they'd ever been.

He was standing a foot away, not touching her at all, and yet, in her imagination she could feel his hands on her, untying laces and unfastening buttons, gliding down her bare arms and over her hips, pulling her closer. She could feel his arms, wrapping around her and holding her fast. She could taste his mouth, opening over hers, arousing her.

Lola jerked back, flattening her back against the door, fighting desires that were supposed to be long gone, desires that had almost been the ruin of both of them.

But here, now, with him standing right in front of her and all the raw passion of the old days suddenly in his eyes, those desires seemed impossible to suppress. She did it, though, by using other, more ruthless memories, memories of what their affair had cost them both and the wreckage it had wrought. Her dreams and his finances in ruins, her heart and his pride in pieces, her self-respect shredded, and his, too. And all for what?

He eased closer. "Lola," he began, but she interrupted, for she knew whatever he'd been about to say wouldn't be good for either of them.

"We'd better go back, or our companions will think we've vanished off the face of the earth. And God knows what people will say if they notice we've both been missing during the entire intermission."

Her words seemed like the fall of a stage curtain. The desire in his face vanished, and yet, she knew it was still there, concealed by the polite demeanor of a gentleman.

"It's probably too late to worry about that," he said, sounding resigned to the fact. "I have no doubt our mutual absence has already been noted, and stories about us are probably being invented as we speak. It's my fault," he added. "I cornered you back here. I wasn't . . . thinking."

"Don't apologize, not on my account. My reputation's long gone, so gossip about us wouldn't affect me. It's different for you." She hesitated a moment, wavering, then she said, "You should tell Lady Georgiana about this conversation before she hears gossip about our mutual absence from others. If you care how she feels, and what she thinks of you, and if you . . . if you . . ." Her voice failed suddenly, but she took a breath and forced herself to say the rest. "If you intend to marry her, you don't want her hearing malicious rumors about us and thinking the worst. Ours is a business partnership and nothing more. Make sure she understands that."

As she spoke, Lola felt leaden. Doing the right thing

was supposed to make one feel good, wasn't it? So why did she feel so awful?

Desperate to leave and end this conversation, she turned her back. "As for Mr. Dawson," she added over her shoulder as she reached for the door handle, "you're quite right that it's inappropriate. I won't see him again."

An easy promise to keep, she knew. With her body on fire because of Denys, any notions of another man's easy, friendly companionship had already burned to dust and ashes.

She opened the door, but Denys's voice stopped her before she could get away.

"You're wrong, you know."

She stilled, her fingers on the handle. "About what?"

"I did love you."

Her heart twisted in her chest, joy and pain and overwhelming sorrow. She squeezed her eyes shut. A sob rose in her throat, but she caught it back before he could hear it, thinking of the girl who'd taken off her dresses and pranced around in a corset and netted stockings for the men in a Brooklyn saloon. In Paris, she'd actually worn a dress, and the men had been wealthier, and the drinks wine and absinthe instead of Irish whiskey and rye, and all the songs sung in French instead of English, but the woman had been the same: a bold-as-brass femme fatale with a kissable pout, a sultry voice, and great legs, who tucked money into her garter with a wink and a smile. Denys believed what he said, she knew, and yet, she also knew he believed in a lie. Slowly, she opened her eyes and turned her head to look at him over her shoulder

"What you loved was the illusion of me, an illusion I invented years before I ever met you. The real me, however, is someone you don't know at all. Hell, Denys," she added with a brittle laugh as she opened the door and walked out, "you don't even know my name."

Chapter 14

In the days that followed, Lola spent a great deal of time reflecting on her conversation with Denys at the opera, but no matter how many times she considered it, she still couldn't fathom her own sudden burst of frankness. In returning to London, she'd known she would have to explain to Denys why she'd left, but she certainly hadn't intended to tell him anything about the life she'd had before they met.

You don't even know my name.

What on earth had impelled her to point that out? Doing so had probably piqued his curiosity, and she feared she may have kicked over a hornet's nest. Now, he'd keep asking questions, delving into her background, perhaps discovering the girl underneath Lola Valentine's bold and brassy façade. Lola didn't want him to find that girl. In fact, there were times when she didn't even want to remember that that girl had existed.

During the next few days, she spent a lot of time wishing she'd just kept her mouth shut, and it was a good thing her first rehearsal came on Monday, for it provided an excellent distraction. Even if she did have to put up with Arabella Danvers.

"Really, Jacob, is it necessary for Miss Valentine to be quite so zealous in her reading?"

The actress's voice from the other side of the table yet again overrode Lola's reading of her part, and she stopped, managing to stifle an exasperated sigh as she lowered the script in her hands.

"I appreciate that in light of past events, Miss Valentine wants to offer us some reassurance regarding her abilities," the other actress went on, and Lola didn't know which she found more irritating—Arabella's tendency to talk about her as if she weren't in the room, or these continual reminders to her peers of her inexperience. "But we've already had a full day, and if she insists on speaking her lines with such painstaking histrionics, her small part may keep us here all night as well."

Lola had to bite down, hard, on her lower lip to stop herself from pointing out that Arabella's almost continual interruptions to discuss the nuances of the plot and her criticisms of her fellow actors were the real reason all of them were still here well into the evening. But she did not want to earn the reputation of being difficult to work with, and she couldn't afford to be seen as arrogant. Unlike Arabella, she didn't have a long line of successes under her belt to mitigate such behavior.

She could only hope Jacob Roth would take Arabella to task, but the director was either a tactful man who didn't want his star performer storming out in a snit on the first day of rehearsal, or he'd worked with Arabella often enough that he didn't find her behavior irritating. Either way, he'd been choosing to ignore the woman's remarks all day, and he did so again. Without comment, he gestured to Lola that she should resume.

Arabella, however, gave her no opportunity to do so.

"Miss Valentine's enthusiastic rendition is commendable, I am sure, but hardly necessary. Today is just a table read, after all."

"Since it's only a table read," Lola countered before she could stop herself, "then why are you making such a fuss?"

Beside her, Blackie Cowell gave a stifled snicker, and when she glanced sideways at him, he gave her a wink. Blackie was dark and witty, every bit an Irishman, and he was also a talented actor, and she was glad he'd been chosen to play Cassio, Bianca's love interest. Blackie was one of the few people here who didn't seem to mind she'd been cast. Grateful to have him as an ally, she gave him an answering wink, but before the table read could resume, they were interrupted.

"Good evening, everyone."

At the sound of Denys's voice, chairs instantly scraped the floorboards as those seated around the table stood up. "Lord Somerton," Jacob greeted him as he entered the rehearsal hall. "Good evening."

"Jacob." He paused beside the other man and glanced around, his gaze flitting past her without a pause. "Working late, I see."

"You as well, it seems."

"Unfortunately, yes. From my window, I noticed that the lights were still on over here, and I wondered why you were being such a slave driver toward these poor actors on their very first day."

Jacob did not enlighten him. Instead, he smiled. "They can discover how amiable I am at a later date. Still," he added, pulling out his pocket watch, "it is almost eight o'clock. Let's stop for today, everyone. We'll resume tomorrow morning."

Sighs of relief greeted this decision, though Lola suspected from Arabella's face that she wasn't among those happy to end for the day.

She started to join those leaving the room, but Denys's voice stopped her. "Miss Valentine? If you and Jacob would be so good as to remain behind, there's something I wish to discuss with the two of you."

She remained by her seat as Denys talked to Jacob, and her fellow actors began heading for the door. All but one.

"My, my," Arabella murmured, pausing beside Lola on her way out as other actors streamed past them, "the grass certainly doesn't grow under your feet, does it, dear?"

Lola looked into Arabella's hard, beautiful face, saw

the derision there, and realized the other woman was aware of her true position here. "I see you know of my good fortune."

"Everyone knows."

Lola sucked in a breath, feeling as if she'd just been punched in the stomach. "Already?"

Arabella smiled, seeming to sense her dismay. "There's a word for women who accumulate a fortune the way you have, you know."

Lola tamped down any hint of what she felt, for she refused to give Arabella that sort of satisfaction. "I'm sure there is," she murmured with a shrug, and was rewarded for this show of indifference by the frustration that flashed across the other woman's face. Thankfully, Arabella let the matter drop, stepped around her, and walked out of the room without another word.

"Ugh," Lola muttered, shuddering as she turned away. "What a poisonous woman."

Those words were barely out of her mouth before she noticed that Denys and Jacob had stopped their conversation and were standing by their chairs waiting for her, and they must have overheard at least part of the conversation. Reminding herself that it was probably best not to voice her opinions out loud, she resumed her seat. "What is it you wish to discuss, my lord?"

Denys took the chair opposite her and waited until Jacob had also resumed his seat at the head of the table before he spoke.

"I have a decision to make," he said at last, "and I am honestly not sure which way to proceed. Jacob knows about your participation in the Imperial already, Miss Valentine. I told him myself that day at the Savoy."

"I daresay many people know," she answered with a sigh.

He didn't seem at all surprised by that announcement, and she didn't know if that was because he and Jacob had overheard her entire conversation with Arabella a moment ago or because he was already fully aware of the gossip. "My question is, should a formal announcement be made?" He glanced from Jacob to her and back again. "I'd like opinions from both of you."

Before either of them could reply, however, a door banged in the distance, and footsteps sounded in the corridor. "That must be Dawson," Denys explained. "I asked him to fetch some sandwiches before I came over. Given the lateness of the hour, I deemed it unfair to detain the two of you without at least providing some sustenance. Good evening, Dawson," he added, looking toward the doorway as the secretary came in with a large basket in his hands. "That didn't take long."

Dawson nodded to Lola as he circled the table to Denys's side, but he didn't give her his usual smile of greeting. "Miss Valentine," he said, and looked away again at once.

His reticence didn't surprise her. When they had parted company after the opera the other night, they had agreed it would be best if they did not fraternize, as Denys had put it, in the future.

"Rosetti's only had ham and tongue sandwiches re-

maining, sir. No chicken or watercress. Understandable, since it is quite late. Will there be anything else?"

"You might be sure all the gaslights are turned off in
the theater, then you may go. Leave one burning by the
door on your way out. I'll extinguish it when we leave."

"Very good, my lord." The secretary departed, and
Denys opened the basket. "So," he resumed as he
pulled out two paper-wrapped sandwiches and handed
one to Lola, "should the company be told formally of
Miss Valentine's position? Jacob?" he added, holding
out the sandwich in his other hand to the director.

Jacob waved it aside, shaking his head. "Thank you,
my lord, but I am dining shortly with friends," he explained. "As to your question, it might be best to let
sleeping dogs lie. If Miss Valentine is to be merely a
silent partner—"

"Miss Valentine has no intention of maintaining such
a limited role, Jacob," Denys said, and there was an
unmistakably wry note in his voice. "On the contrary,
she intends to be involved in every aspect of running
the theater."

The director's heavy dark brows rose, then fell. "Ah,"
he murmured, and there was a wealth of implication in
the word and in the meaningful glance exchanged between the two men. Clearly, that afternoon at the Savoy,
both of them had thought she'd be long gone by now—
or at least shunted off to the side—and Lola couldn't
help feeling a bit of satisfaction that she'd upset that
particular applecart.

"What are your thoughts, Miss Valentine?" Denys

asked, turning to her. "Should we announce your position to the company or not?"

"Since they already seem to know," she countered, "why bother with a formal announcement?"

"It might diffuse further speculations."

"Or make them worse," Jacob put in. "I must confess, I have been concerned about the possibility of gossip ever since Lord Somerton informed me of the situation. A formal announcement could underscore and perhaps inflame an already awkward situation."

"The awkwardness will probably be temporary," Denys pointed out. "After all, ours is not a situation wholly without precedent. Henry Irving manages the Lyceum, for example, and acts in many of his own productions."

"Henry Irving does, yes," Jacob said, and as if fearing she might take offense, he turned to her. "I don't doubt your abilities as a performer, Miss Valentine," Jacob said at once. "If I had, I'd never have cast you in my play. But don't be surprised if there is a perception among your peers that you are being favored for roles because you are an owner. And because—"

He broke off, but his glance at Denys told her what he had not said, and suddenly, her prior relationship with Denys seemed like a giant elephant in the room.

Jacob sensed it, too, for he gave a cough. "My point," he hastened on, "is that Miss Valentine needs to be prepared for some hostility."

"I understand that, Mr. Roth," she said, "but I came into this knowing full well what I was getting into. The news of Henry's bequest to me was already beginning to circulate in New York when I left, and it was bound to arrive here sooner or later. Even if I were not intending to be actively involved, we could never have hoped to keep this partnership a secret for long. I realize that I will be the subject of much gossip and speculation, but other than performing to the very best of my ability, there's little I can do about it. I can only hope . . ." She paused and swallowed hard. "I can only hope my performances prove worthy enough that people will come to see there's more to me than my position or my past."

"Either way," Denys put in, "neither of you seem to feel a formal announcement is necessary?" When both of them shook their heads, he nodded in acquiescence. "Very well then, we will leave the situation as it stands."

"If that is all, my lord," Jacob said, shoving back his chair and standing up, "I shall be on my way."

"Yes, that is all. Thank you, Jacob."

The other man departed, and with his departure, the situation suddenly seemed far too intimate for her peace of mind. "I should be going as well," she said, but Denys's voice stopped her before she could stand up.

"At least stay and have your dinner. After all," he added, gesturing to the basket, "I can't possibly eat all this by myself."

Lola hesitated. Lingering here, having dinner with him would give Denys ample opportunity to probe further into her past. She'd left her real name behind her over ten years ago, along with that dingy saloon in Brooklyn, and the last thing she wanted to do was talk about it, especially with him. "Given the possibility of gossip," she began, but he interrupted her excuse.

"It's a bit late to stop that, as we've just been discussing. And as partners, we will have to talk about the Imperial from time to time, whether in front of others, or alone. We can't do business together and simultaneously avoid each other."

That made her smile a little. "This is quite a turnabout from two weeks ago. Now you're the one wanting to cope with our situation."

"And you want to avoid it. Why?" he asked before she could reply. "Because you don't want to tell me your real name?"

"That just slipped out," she mumbled. "I never intended to tell you anything about it."

"An admission that hardly helps you in your quest to regain my trust," he countered dryly.

She was hardly in a position to argue it. "What if we discuss my proposal instead?" she countered lightly. It was clear she hoped to evade any inconvenient questions by changing the subject, but he had no intention of letting her do so.

He studied her for a moment, considering his options. A gentleman should not probe into a woman's private affairs, especially when she so clearly did not want to discuss them. On the other hand, after her rather shattering announcement at Covent Garden, she could hardly expect him to leave it there. He'd been trying to do that for three days, without success, and when he'd looked out the window earlier this evening and seen the lights still on over here, he'd seized the opportunity to find out more without a moment of hesitation. "Before we discuss your proposal," he said at last, "something else needs to be done first."

"What is that?"

"We have to introduce ourselves. After all, we can't dine together if we don't know each other, can we? The more you evade this," he added, smiling as she made a sound of exasperation, "the more curious you make me."

"Oh, for heaven's sake," she muttered, "I don't see why it matters. There aren't any legal considerations, if that's what's worrying you. I had my name changed by deed poll over ten years ago."

He didn't reply. He merely reached into the basket and pulled out her business proposal, which he'd instructed Dawson bring over with the sandwiches. He held it up, giving her an inquiring look across the table.

She scowled back at him, and for a moment, he thought she was going to refuse to answer, but after a moment, she surprised him. "Charlotte," she said with a sigh. "My name is—was—Charlotte Valinsky."

Lola, of course, was a shortening of Charlotte, and the first syllable of her surname echoed that of her stage name, but any similarities ended there. The impressions conveyed by the two names were as different as chalk and cheese.

"It is a pleasure to make your acquaintance, Miss Valinsky," he said, and bowed to her across the table. "Viscount Somerton, at your service."

That made her smile a little. "I'm not sure it's done this way," she murmured as she began unwrapping her sandwich. "Isn't someone else always required to make a social introduction?"

"In this case, I think we can bend the rules a little."

"To what end?"

"To give ourselves a fresh start."

"A fresh start," she murmured, and her smile faltered. "I seem to need a great many of those."

"Two's not that many, Lola."

"I've had more than two, I'm afraid." She didn't elaborate. Instead, she gestured to the basket. "Is there something to drink with these sandwiches? I'm thirsty."

Another diversion, he noted. "So, Miss Valinsky," he said as he opened the basket and pulled out a bottle of beer, "now that we've introduced ourselves, why don't you tell me more about yourself?"

She licked her lips, looking a bit desperate. "Why do you want to know things about me? I don't see why it matters now."

"It always mattered, at least to me." Holding the bottle in one hand, he rummaged in the basket for a corkscrew. "But after our conversation the other night, I've come to appreciate that you were right. In many ways, I don't really know you. And when I think back to our time together, I realize that though you were always very good about listening to me talk about my life, my family, my friends, you somehow always managed to avoid telling me anything about yourself. You shared almost nothing with me about what your life was like before we met."

"Perhaps because I didn't want to do so," she suggested, and though her voice was light, he wasn't fooled.

"I daresay." He paused, one hand in the basket, watching her, waiting.

The silent scrutiny seemed to goad her. "For a man with such good manners, you're being terribly nosy," she grumbled. "Don't the British consider it bad form to pry into someone's private life this way?"

"Very bad form," he agreed, and pulled the corkscrew from the basket. "But in this case," he went on as he began to open the beer, "I think it's necessary. Trust is important to any partnership."

She laughed, but he didn't think she was amused. "If you think knowing my past is going to help you trust me, you couldn't be more wrong. The opposite is probably closer to the truth."

"I disagree. It's not what you tell me that signifies. It's the act of doing so."

"I don't understand what you mean."

"I think you do," he said, "but I'm happy to explain. I want you to—what is the American expression?—go out on a limb. Take a risk. Show some vulnerability. If you want this to be a true partnership, you'll have to earn back my trust." He paused, watching her as he pulled the cork from the bottle. "Which means you'll have to offer yours."

"You want me to tell you something about myself?

All right, I will." She lifted her chin, bristling, rebellious, her gaze meeting his across the table. "I used to take off my clothes in front of men when I danced, for money. Is that far enough out on the limb for you?

"Sailors, mostly," she went on when he didn't speak. "In the taverns by the docks in Brooklyn before I moved to Paris. I sang and danced and took off my clothes, and the sailors would toss money at me." She paused, looking steadily at him across the table. "The more clothes I took off, the more money I made."

Denys managed to hold her gaze, for he saw the defiance in her eyes, daring him to be repulsed, but repulsion for her was not at all what he felt. Instead, he felt anger, anger at those sailors, at the tavern keeper, at her relations. God, she couldn't have been more than sixteen years old. Where had her family been, and how could they have allowed her to come to such a pass? Why hadn't they taken better care of her?

He thought of what it must have been like for her, to be young and alone and desperate, and it hurt, imagining her that way, with lusty men all around her. Still, he wasn't about to veer off just because what she told him was hard to hear.

"Well?" she demanded when he didn't say anything.

"Well, what?" He pushed anger aside, knowing the worst thing he could do right now was show it, for she'd surely misunderstand its cause. Instead, he looked steadily back at her. "Am I supposed to be shocked?"

"I don't know! You're the one who comes from a world of rectitude and propriety."

"I'm not shocked, so put that in your pipe and smoke it, Lola." He held out the bottle to her. "Beer?"

She didn't move to accept it. Instead, she scowled, seeming almost put out by the fact that he was taking her bald announcement with such equanimity. "All right, perhaps you're not shocked. But you can't possibly approve."

"No, but why should that matter?"

She took the bottle from him. "It doesn't."

"But it does," he said, noting the proud tilt of her head, realizing the truth, startled by his discovery. "Is that why prying answers out of you has been like opening oysters?" he asked. "Because you thought I wouldn't approve of your past?"

"No," she said at once, and watched him raise an eyebrow. "All right, yes, a little. Damn it, Denys," she added, as he began to smile. "I don't see what's amusing about this."

"You care what I think," he said, and laughed a little in sheer disbelief. "Another turnabout. Life is full of surprises."

"I don't know why it's such a revelation." She lowered her head, staring at the bottle in her hand. "I always cared what you thought of me. Why do you think I never told you anything?"

He studied her bent head, his momentary amusement fading at her soft confession, and he didn't know what to say. There had always been a part of her that had seemed out of reach, untouchable. Perhaps that had been the very thing that had always made him so determined to have her and keep her. And yet, in the end, she'd still slipped away from him.

"Anyway," she said before he could think of a reply, "what I told you ought to have shocked you right out of your proper British sensibilities. Why it didn't, I can't think."

"I suppose . . ." He paused, considering as he unwrapped his sandwich and began to eat. "I suppose in the back of my mind, I suspected you might have had some experience of that sort," he said at last, licking a bit of tongue paste from his thumb. "But I didn't dwell on it."

"You didn't want to dwell on it, you mean."

"No," he admitted. "Either way, I'm sure you had good reasons for the choice you made."

"Maybe. Or maybe I just liked doing it."

He heard the defiance in her voice, but he refused to be drawn. "That's possible," he said. "But I doubt it."

"What makes you say that?"

"Simple logic. If you liked it, I assume you'd still be doing it." He nodded to the bottle in her hand. "Don't you want that beer after all?"

"Beer?" She turned the bottle in her hand to read the label, and when she did, her expression of distaste made him laugh again.

"Really, Lola, you at least have to taste it before you turn up your nose. It's from my own brewery."

"Your family owns a brewery?"

It was another deflection, he knew, but he didn't press her to return to the subject of her past, not yet. Instead, he decided it was best to give her a bit of room to breathe. "Not the family. Nick and I own it. We started it three years ago. My father put up the initial capital, but we paid him back."

She looked at the label again and smiled. "Lily-field's," she read, and looked up. "Why that name? Another partner?"

"Not a partner, no. More like a story. A wink and a nod to true love."

"True love?" She looked at him dubiously. "And beer?"

"It sounds incongruous, doesn't it? Nick was courting Belinda at the time, and she told him she wouldn't have him because he was a lily of the field, and that if he wanted to prove his worth to her, he had to find himself an occupation."

"A lady of the *ton* demanding a peer work for a living?"

"Belinda's American. But it wasn't just that. Nick was rather an irresponsible scapegrace—we all were back then, as you know. Nick was stone broke and thinking his only way out of the mess was to marry an heiress. So he hired Belinda to find him a wife and ended up by marrying her himself. I'm not sure if you know, but Belinda is quite a famous matchmaker."

"I did know that. As I said, I read the society papers." She began to laugh. "So now, Nick and Jack are not only friends, but also brothers-in-law. That must make for some rather wild family parties."

"On the contrary, they've both settled down quite

happily to matrimony. But when he was courting her, Nick had to prove to Belinda he wasn't a lily of the field, so he decided to form a brewing company and make beer. His estate, Honeywood, grows hops, you see. My estate, Arcady, does the same, which is why he pulled me in to be his partner. We manage it together."

"I see." She lifted the bottle to her lips, took a swallow, made a face, and set the bottle aside.

He laughed. "Is it so terrible?"

Her answering look was apologetic. "I don't much care for beer, so I'm not a fair judge. But it must be good."

"If you don't like beer, then how do you know?"

"She married Nick, didn't she? So I'm assuming you two must have made a success of this brewery."

"We have, actually. Nick wasn't the only one whose life changed. So did mine. The brewery enabled me to pay off my debts. In addition, I started taking responsibility for my life. My father saw that I was serious about turning over a new leaf, and he began handing over management of the family's investments to me, one by one. Along the way, I discovered—much to my surprise—that I had a genuine talent for business. Most peers don't, my father included. He was happy and relieved to be able to hand all the family investments over to me. He's quite proud of how I turned my life around, I think."

"I don't doubt it. You're the apple of his eye."

"No, I'm afraid my sister, Susan, holds that honor." He leaned back with his beer and his sandwich, studied her for a moment, and decided to try again to satisfy his curiosity. "But don't think I haven't noticed this latest attempt to divert me, Miss Valinsky," he said gently. "We were discussing you."

"I suppose you want to know how I came to such a pass," she murmured. "Taking my clothes off, I mean."

"Only if you want to tell me."

"I did it for the same reason most girls do. I needed money."

"What about your family?" he asked and resumed eating.

"My family." She smiled a little. "My father was a Lithuanian immigrant, a butcher by trade. He went west, and he ended up in Kansas City, where he set up his shop."

This was the first time she'd ever mentioned a thing about her family—another topic she'd always been adept at avoiding. "And he met your mother there?"

"Not exactly. My mother was from Baltimore. Miss Elizabeth Breckenridge, of the Baltimore Breckenridges. Very wealthy and very high-society."

He couldn't help being a bit surprised, perhaps because Lola had been so positive in her assurance that marriages across class lines didn't work. "A girl of good society married a butcher? She must have been very much in love."

"Love?" Lola laughed, but she didn't seem amused.

"She married him before ever meeting him. He wanted a wife, you see, and in the frontier towns, there wasn't much of a selection. So he did what many other men did. He advertised for a wife in the Eastern papers. My mother answered his advertisement. They corresponded for a few months, then she married him by proxy and came west to join him."

"You read about such things in penny dreadfuls," he murmured. "I didn't think they happened in real life. Why did she do it?"

"She was very young, not even sixteen. When I try to imagine her motives, I think she must have been very romantic, very idealistic, and probably a reader of those penny dreadfuls you mention. Her own life must have seemed terribly boring by comparison to the wild western frontier."

"In other words, she ran away from home?"

"I think she must have done, but I don't know for sure. The truth is, I don't remember her very well. She left when I was five."

"Left?"

"She went back to her people."

"What? She abandoned you?"

"I suppose reality wasn't as romantic as the penny dreadfuls." She shrugged as if it didn't matter. "Anyway, her father was a very powerful man, and somehow, he got the marriage annulled, very discreetly, of course. Which means that I . . ." She paused and looked at him. "I'm a bastard child. Legally, anyway."

"If you ever feared I'd judge you for that, your fear was misplaced," he said gently. "I couldn't care two pins."

"Yes, well, my mother remarried, a very wealthy man of her own class, a Mr. Angus Hutchison, and she had five sons with him."

"I'm sorry." Such easy words to say, and so inadequate.

"I went to see her once. When I was living in New York, before I went to Paris, I took the train down to Baltimore. She wouldn't see me. She told her butler to tell me she didn't have a daughter, she didn't know who I was or what I was talking about. She wiped me out of her life, you see. Like wiping a slate clean."

Denys's anger, banked for a short while, came roaring back, and he vowed that if he ever returned to America, he would pay a call upon Mrs. Angus Hutchison of Baltimore.

"In America, one can do that, you see," Lola said, breaking into his thoughts. "Start over, change your name, become someone else. It's different here—at least, it is for people like you. If I had married you, there wouldn't have been any way out of it, for either of us."

"You think I would have wanted a way out," he said slowly. "You think I would have abandoned you?"

"I . . ." She frowned, staring down at the bottle of beer on the table. "I don't know. But either way, I couldn't have made you happy."

He tilted his head, studying. "I'm beginning to see why you think so."

She roused herself, shaking her head. "Anyway, my father was shattered when my mother left. He took to drink. He stopped working, lost his butcher shop, he even sold his knives. He wanted to die. He finally succeeded. He drank himself to death when I fifteen."

"Is that why you had no money?"

She nodded. "I'd been taking in laundry, singing in the local saloon, trying to make enough to keep body and soul together, and my father hadn't been much help. After he died, and the rent came due, I didn't have quite enough to pay it. I knew the girls who served the whiskey in the saloon got tips if they . . . smiled pretty, if they flirted. So that night, when I sang, I lifted up my skirt a bit—not much, just enough to show an ankle, and one of the cowboys tossed me two bits."

He frowned. "Two bits?"

"A twenty-five-cent piece. That's when I really began to understand how it's done."

"How what is done?"

She met his eyes across the table. "Making men want you."

His chest hurt, like a fist squeezing his heart. One heard about girls going down the road to ruin, but even in his salad days, he'd never thought much about how, precisely, that happened. Now he knew.

"The next morning," she went on, "I learned making men want you had consequences."

"What happened?" he asked, his voice a harsh whisper to his own ears, his fingers gripping the beer in his hand so tightly, they ached.

"One of the cowboys who'd seen me waving my ankles around came to my place. He told me he knew I was all alone in the world, and he offered to help me out. 'Take care of me,' was how he put it."

I'll take care of you.

His own words came echoing back to him, and his dismay deepened, bringing a sense of shame he'd never felt before. "And what was your answer?"

"I told him no. He didn't take it kindly."

"No," Denys muttered, feeling sick. He remembered her declaration that she'd only been with two men, and he wondered if this was the other man, if her only other sexual experience had been an assault. "I don't imagine he would."

"He shoved me down on the floor," she said, and Denys squeezed his eyes shut. "But I managed to grab the Erie on my way down, and I bashed it over his head."

He felt a relief so great, it shook him down to his bones, and it was several moments before he could speak. "What's an Erie?" he asked, opening his eyes, easing his death grip on the beer bottle in his hand.

"A cast-iron skillet. Knocked him out cold. He had ten dollars in his pocket, and I took it. I went straight to the train station, got a ticket on the first train out, thinking to go as far away from Kansas City as I could get.

I got all the way to New York on that ten dollars. I was thinking I'd sing there, work in a music hall, or something. But my voice wasn't good enough. So . . ." She paused and gave a shrug. "That's how I ended up at the dockside taverns in Brooklyn. It started with waving an ankle, then a flirty little flip of the back of my skirt . . . it kept getting easier, to go a bit further. And it seemed harmless, I made money, I got an apartment in Flatbush and learned to keep a knife in my garter. Eventually, I got enough money to get to Paris."

He expelled his breath in a deep sigh. Then he sat back and raked a hand through his hair. "Hell," he muttered.

Unexpectedly, she smiled. "I know you asked, but that's probably a lot more than you wanted to know."

"No, I'm glad you told me. And I'm just glad you were all right. That no man . . ." He stopped, then tried again. "That no man ever forced you . . ."

In it was a question, and she answered it. "No, Denys," she said quietly. "No man ever forced me."

She looked down, and absently began turning the bottle on the table round and round. "Denys? May I ask you a question now?"

"Of course."

"You mortgaged Arcady to finance that play for me, didn't you?"

She phrased it like a question, but the certainty in her voice told him she already knew the answer. "Yes," he admitted. "How did you find out? Henry told you, I suppose."

"Yes, that night in Paris. Why did you do it?" She gave him no chance to answer. "Did you do it because you truly believed I had talent?" She stopped turning the bottle, and looked at him. "Or was it just because you wanted to sleep with me?"

Chapter 15

 Denys did not want to be the one answering questions, especially not the question she'd just asked him. But he also knew trust and truth had to run both ways. "My initial motive was lust, yes," he admitted. "But," he hastened to add, hoping to soften the rather callous motives he'd possessed at the time, "it's not that I didn't think you had talent."

She gave him a rueful look. "What you mean is that you didn't think about my talent, or lack of it, at all."

He gave a sigh. "No, I didn't. Truth be told, I didn't care. I wanted you, and I would have done anything to have you. That's a . . ." He paused, swallowing hard. "That's a rather frightening thing, when I think about it."

"I'm sorry the play was such a disaster. I wish I'd been better."

"That's not your fault. You weren't ready for the part. How could you be, with no preparation and no training? I suppose I knew, deep down, that you weren't ready to take it on, but as I said, I didn't dwell on it. I wanted you with me here in London, but every time I voiced the idea, you laughed and shrugged it off and said something about how a girl has to eat or how you weren't about to risk losing a good place. In the end, it seemed the only way to get you to come to London was to toss what you wanted most right into your lap."

"That wasn't what I wanted most," she objected, then bit her lip, as if regretting her words.

"No?" He shouldn't ask, he told himself. He shouldn't open old wounds this way. "What did you want?"

"You," she said simply. "But I didn't want to be your mistress."

He would have liked to say that wasn't what he'd been offering, that his intentions had been honorable from the start.

He slid his gaze away.

"You said the other night that I'm cynical," she went on in the wake of his silence. "And maybe I am. My life before I met you wasn't the sort that would make any girl believe in fairy tales. But when you came along, and I kept saying no, and you kept coming back, I started to think for the first time that maybe fairy tales could happen in real life. You told me you'd gotten me an audition for a play in London, and later, when I actually got the part, it seemed as if everything I'd ever wanted was being handed to me on a silver platter." She paused and cleared her throat. "Denys, when I came to that audition, it was already a foregone conclusion I'd get the part, wasn't it?"

"Yes." The admission felt torn out of him, those old wounds opening up.

"Looking back, I wonder that I didn't see that at the time," she said musingly. "It seems so obvious now. And it wasn't as if I was some naïve innocent girl back then." She shook her head as if in disbelief at her own lack of perspicacity. "It's amazing how blind you can be when you're happy. I'd begun to believe that you were my knight in shining armor, you see. That you'd love me and marry me, and I'd be a great and successful actress, and we'd live happily ever after. But life . . . isn't like that."

Denys shut his eyes. A couple of weeks ago, everything about their past had seemed so straightforward. In his version of events, she'd always been the one who'd wronged him. Many times, particularly right after her departure, he'd asked himself why she'd left him for Henry, but never had he been able to set aside his sense of betrayal, his broken heart, and his wounded pride long enough to see things from her side, or to admit that he had a great deal of culpability, too. Until now.

He opened his eyes, forcing a laugh. "I begin to appreciate why you don't like talking about yourself. In doing so, the truth about oneself is laid bare, isn't it? And it isn't always a pretty picture. I was no knight in shining armor, Lola."

He met her eyes across the table. "The truth is, the

notion of marrying you never entered my head until after you'd returned to Paris. Only then, when I realized I was losing you, did I decide to propose marriage. You said the other night that I didn't love you, and I can see now why you felt that way because even though I'd told you many times how much I was in love with you, that I was mad for you, that I couldn't eat or sleep for wanting you, even I didn't realize until you'd gone back to Paris that I loved you enough to marry you."

He took a deep breath. "So, all those months and months I was pursing you, while you were thinking me some kind of heroic figure, my true intentions were actually quite unsavory."

"Hmm." She ate the rest of her sandwich, studying him as she did so, and he had no idea what she was thinking. But after a minute or two, she shook her head. "No, Denys," she said. "It won't work."

He frowned, puzzled by this enigmatic reply. "What won't work?"

"This attempt to paint yourself as some sort of cad. Sorry, but I don't believe it. I never have, and I never will. So, to quote your own words back at you, put that in your pipe and smoke it."

He smiled. "A fitting analogy, isn't it? I think we are only now, tonight, truly smoking that peace pipe."

She smiled back, a tentative smile. "I think you might be right," she said, and lifted her bottle of beer. "To partnership?"

He lifted his own bottle and clinked it against hers. "To partnership."

Their eyes met as they drank, and his mind went back to the first night they'd ever dined together. He didn't know why. Other than sharing a meal, that night had little in common with this one. It had been one of the finest restaurants in Paris, not a picnic dinner of sandwiches. They'd drunk wine, not beer. And he'd spent most of the evening trying to figure out how he was going to seduce a girl who danced like she was made for sin but who wouldn't let him even step past her dressing-room door.

"Speaking of partnership . . ."

Her voice drew him out of the past, reminding him this wasn't Paris, he wasn't that wild man about town anymore, and seducing her wasn't his priority nowadays. Hell, it wasn't even on the table.

He took a deep breath. "Yes?"

"I know we've decided that it's not necessary to make an announcement of our partnership to the acting company, but I wonder if you could make a different one."

"What's that?"

"Maybe suggest that certain members of the company keep their interruptions of their fellow actors during rehearsal to a minimum?"

He grinned. "So I should take your side against Mrs. Danvers? Is that what you really want me to do, partner?"

"Oh, I suppose not, when you put it like that. But the woman is so damned irritating."

"What do I care?" He deliberately widened his grin. "I'm not the one who has to work with her."

She sniffed. "That's rather a selfish attitude, partner."

"I don't know why you need me anyway. Turn your charm on her, and she'll come around."

She gave him a wry look as she leaned across the table and tossed her empty bottle and the paper from her sandwich into the picnic basket. "As much as I appreciate your faith in my ability to be charming, in this case, it's wasted. I couldn't charm Arabella if I waved the part of Lady Macbeth and a thousand pounds under her nose."

"You underestimate yourself." He laughed. "I don't know how I ever managed to gain the upper hand with you at all, honestly."

"Because you're so nice. I told you, that's always been my weakness."

"Nice, am I?" He studied her, remembering some of her other weaknesses—the way her knees would buckle whenever he kissed her ear, and the long, slow caresses that melted away her resistance, and he didn't feel nice at all.

She must have sensed what was passing through his mind. "I should be going," she said abruptly, and jerked to her feet. "It's late."

"Of course." He forced naughty thoughts away, stood up, and reached for the picnic basket, then gestured to the doorway. "I'll walk with you."

"We never did talk about my proposal," she remarked as she waited for him in the corridor, and he turned off the gas jets in the rehearsal hall.

"No, we didn't." He joined her in the corridor, and by

the light Dawson had left burning, they walked to the end, where they paused by the door that led to the alley. "Why don't we meet about it Saturday afternoon after you finish rehearsals?" he suggested. "I don't believe I have any fixed engagements that day."

"Saturday?" She shook her head. "I can't. I have plans that afternoon."

He wondered suddenly what her plans might be, but he knew he couldn't ask. He also knew he shouldn't want to know.

"Perhaps we can meet the following Saturday instead?" she suggested.

"Of course. Shall I order tea?"

"If you want it."

"Do you want it?" The moment the words were out of his mouth, he wanted to kick himself in the head. "What I mean," he added at once, hurling himself onto safer ground, "is that tea's not really an American habit, so if you would prefer not to have it, just say so."

"Tea would be lovely, Denys, thank you." She gave him a rueful smile. "Just remind me to remove my gloves beforehand. I'm prone to forgetting that sort of thing."

He chuckled, remembering how she'd looked, tea things in her gloved hands and a look of chagrin on her face as she'd realized her predicament. "I shall endeavor to keep you up to snuff," he assured her.

He opened the door for her, pulling his latchkey out of his pocket as she walked through, but when he'd extinguished the last light and started to lock the door behind them, her voice stopped him.

"You should take the other exit, at the front of the theater. You'll reach the mews more quickly that way."

"And leave you to navigate a London alley alone and secure a hansom on your own? At night? I'll do no such thing."

"It's only a few dozen feet from here to the Strand, and only a few blocks from there to the Savoy. I shall be quite all right."

"I am not allowing you to walk alone, and I don't care if your hotel is only a few blocks away. This is not a debatable point, Lola," he added, as she began to argue.

"Denys, you can't do this. The Strand is a busy street, filled with carriages carrying your sort of people back and forth to the theater. And the Savoy is just the sort of hotel where someone you know is likely to be out front getting in or out of a taxi. We'd be seen."

"It's a bit too late to worry about that. I'm sure we were seen together that day at the Savoy when I dragged you into that lift. And at Covent Garden, too. We are living in the same city, working together, seeing some of the same people. I agree that we shouldn't draw attention to our partnership if possible, but it's pointless to duck and hide. If we're working together, we're going to be seen together—sometime, somewhere, by someone. You said it yourself the other night: When we were having an affair, we tried to be discreet, and everyone knew. If we make no effort to hide this partnership from the start, it won't stop people from thinking things, but perhaps they'll grow tired of speculating about us more quickly and move on to some other scandal."

"I doubt your family will see it that way."

"Leave my family to me. I've informed my father that I intend to carry through with this new arrangement, and if he doesn't like it, he's well within his rights to take back control of the company. He has chosen not to do that. He trusts me."

Even as he said it, Denys felt a flicker of uneasiness, for he suspected it was going to be a long time before he was worthy of that trust where Lola was concerned.

She sniffed. "I'm sure Conyers doesn't consider you the problem. I'm the one he doesn't trust. Either way, I still think it's best if we aren't seen sashaying along the Strand side by side."

"Very well. You will at least allow me to escort you to a taxi stand and see you safely into a hansom. It would be unconscionable for me to allow any lady, even if she were not a friend of mine, to walk home alone at night."

"Friend?" She tilted her head, giving him a dubious look as if she might not have heard him right. "Are we becoming friends now?"

Friendship would make the partnership easier and more pleasant. His gaze lowered. But only if he could manage to remember it was platonic.

He jerked his gaze back up to her face and forced himself to say something. "I don't know. We could make the attempt, I suppose. We've been everything else, after all," he added, striving for a nonchalance he didn't feel in the least. "Why not try being friends?"

She smiled that wide, radiant smile, and as always, he felt as if he were standing in the warmth of the sun. "Friends it is, then," she said. "But—" She broke off, drawing her brows together in a seeming attempt to look stern. Given the faint dusting of freckles across her nose, the attempt failed utterly. "But if we're to be friends, you can't call me Miss Valinsky ever again."

He laughed. "I have been duly warned. May I call you Charlotte?"

Her stern expression dissolved, and her nose wrinkled up. "Not if you expect me to answer."

"Don't you like the name Charlotte?"

"It's not that. I meant just what I said. I've been Lola Valentine for a long time now. If someone called me Charlotte, I'm not sure I'd realize that person was talking to me. In fact," she added softly, ducking her head, "I'm not sure I even remember who Charlotte is anymore."

"I think you do."

She looked up, seeming startled by the certainty in his voice. "What makes you say that?"

"If you didn't think that girl was still somewhere inside you, you wouldn't have told me I didn't really know you."

"Maybe." She shook her head. "I don't know. But, either way, I'm accustomed to being called Lola, so perhaps you should just continue to address me by that name."

"If that's what you prefer. And it does make things easier for me. Fresh starts are all very well, and I'm trying my best to adapt to this new situation, but calling you by a different name would take some getting used to." He gestured to the alley behind her. "Shall we?"

"Why don't I wait here, while you hail me a cab?"

He agreed to that compromise, and a short time later, he was standing at the entrance to the alley, watching her walk to the hansom at the curb. Fresh starts and being friends were all very well, but as he studied the brilliant fiery glints in her hair beneath the streetlight and the graceful dancer's sway of her hips as she moved, Denys could feel his desire for her still lurking deep within him, and he didn't know if he'd ever be able to think of Lola Valentine as just a friend, even if her name was really Charlotte Valinsky.

Chapter 16

 Denys knew Lola was right about the gossip, and that it would be best if they avoided each other as much as possible when they were not conducting actual theater business.

Given his determination that her return would not be allowed to change his life in any way, avoiding her ought to have been an easy thing for him to manage, especially since the last thing he'd wanted a few weeks ago was to be anywhere near her. But in the days that followed their picnic in the rehearsal hall, steering clear of Lola proved to be one of the hardest things he'd ever done.

He often found himself staring out his office window at the Imperial, wondering how she was getting on. Twice, he almost changed his dinner plans with friends so that he could dine at the Savoy, just on the chance that he might see her there. It was a fortunate thing that St. John's Wood was not within the proximity of his daily round, for if it were, he'd have been unable to resist having his driver take him to the office via that route.

Every day, he invented excuses for why he ought to go across the street—he could ask Jacob how the play was coming along, or examine the premises, or discuss possible maintenance issues with the janitors—oh, his imagination fashioned many reasons why the Imperial needed his personal attention right now, but fertile as his imagination became, he forced himself to stay away. For both their sakes, that was the best course.

He could not, however, stop himself from thinking of her. She entered his thoughts countless times—in the middle of business meetings, on the street if he chanced to pass a woman with red hair, or when his carriage took him past Covent Garden.

He'd actually thought being near her would help him get over all this, but as the days passed, he began to fear he'd been far too optimistic about the ability of familiarity to breed contempt.

What you loved was the illusion of me, an illusion I invented years before I ever met you. The real me, however, is someone you don't know at all.

Was that true? Denys stared down into his breakfast plate, pushing around eggs and bacon with his fork as he considered her declaration in light of what he now knew about her. But as he contemplated the things she'd told him about herself, he feared the knowledge didn't help him much, for the more he knew her, the more he wanted to know. The more deeply he explored, the deeper he wanted to delve. And if he went too deep, he feared it would sink him for good and all.

The voices of his family flowed past him, but lost in thought, he didn't hear a word, for he was thinking of a play six years ago and a callow chap who'd mortgaged his estate in order to seduce a girl.

He closed his eyes, sinking into memories of their afternoons together—the scent of her, the taste of her, the feel of her skin. All as vivid, and as erotic, as they'd ever been.

"Denys?"

The prompting voice of his mother broke into his reverie, and Denys looked up, appalled that he was now having passionate thoughts about Lola at the breakfast table. "I beg your pardon, Mama," he said after a moment, "but I was woolgathering. What did you say?"

"I asked if you would be joining us in the brougham tomorrow, or taking your own carriage."

He stared back at her blankly, for he didn't know what she was talking about. "Tomorrow?"

His mother's gaze slid sideways, toward her husband, and the uneasy glance the two exchanged wasn't lost on him. He'd forgotten something important, he realized, some social obligation, but for the moment, he couldn't remember what it was.

"Oh, Denys won't ride with us, Mama," Susan put in before their mother could answer his question. "He's always working in that office of his, even on Saturdays.

Surely he'll take his own carriage from Bedford Street to Regent's Park."

"I suppose." Lady Conyers gave a sigh and turned to him. "You work much too hard, dear. And during the season, why, it's absolutely uncivilized for a gentleman to slave away in an office."

Denys looked from his mother to his sister, utterly at sea. "Regent's Park?"

Susan laughed. "Oh, my, you have been working too hard, dear brother, if Mama's flower show has slipped your mind. And with Georgiana helping her make all the arrangements, too."

Good God. Georgiana. He'd forgotten all about her.

Aware that the other members of his family were staring at him, he felt impelled to fashion a reply. "I didn't forget," he lied, careful to keep any hint of his dismay off his face. "I just couldn't remember for the moment where they'd decided to hold it. After all," he added hastily, "Georgiana was suggesting so many possible locations for you to consider before she left for Kent, that it was impossible to keep track. Now, the various venues are all a jumble in my mind."

It was a poor excuse, and he knew it, for he saw his parents exchange another meaningful glance, but thankfully, they seemed inclined to accept it at face value.

"It was all very confusing, I know," his mother remarked. "We had quite despaired of finding somewhere suitable." She picked up her tea and took a sip, looking at him over the rim of her cup. "I believe they returned from Kent on Wednesday, did they not?"

He had no idea. But his mother's limpid, inquiring gaze suggested it would be wise to dissemble about this as well. "I believe so, yes. I haven't yet had the opportunity to call, however."

"Of course." There was a hint of reproof in her voice he chose to ignore. "As I said," she added, setting down her teacup, "you've been working far too hard this season."

With that, she turned her attention to Susan, but as she inquired about the girl's dress for an upcoming ball, Denys found little relief in the change of subject, for he was forced to face the fact that during the past three weeks, the woman he was considering to be his future wife had occupied none of his attention. He hadn't answered her letters; he hadn't even read them. In fact, other than a brief consideration of her during his conversation with Lola at Covent Garden, he hadn't spared so much as a thought for Georgiana during the entire time she'd been away.

Of course, many things had been going on in his life of late. Any man might find himself a bit at sixes and sevens in consequence—

He stopped that attempt to justify his lapse of gentlemanly conduct straightaway, for he knew there was no justification. He was thinking to marry Georgiana, for heaven's sake. How could he have forgotten about her so completely?

Even as he asked himself that question, he knew the answer.

Denys set down his knife and fork, shoved back his

chair, and stood up, intending to remedy his lapse in gentlemanly conduct at once.

"Forgive me, ladies," he said, bowing to his mother and sister. "But I must be on my way. I have a great deal to do today if I'm to take tomorrow away from the offices."

He turned to go, but then paused and looked at his mother. "You are quite right, Mama. I have been spending too much time working. Will you be so good as to inform my secretary which events you would most like me to attend in the coming weeks? I shall make every effort to fulfill your wishes on that score and spend more time enjoying the season with our family and friends."

That accommodation pleased her, he could tell, but it didn't make him feel much better. As he left the dining room, he was still dismayed by his own forgetfulness, aggravated by the reasons for it, and feeling guilty as hell. He'd vowed that he would not allow this partnership with Lola to have any effect on his private life, and so far, he was not doing very well at keeping that particular vow.

"Be a reed, Denys," he muttered, raking his hands through his hair as he traversed the corridor to the front of the house. "Not an oak."

As he turned toward the stairs, he noticed the butler in the foyer, and he paused, one hand on the newel post, one foot on the bottom step. "Monckton?"

The butler turned from the mirror on the wall he was attempting to straighten. "My lord?"

"Have my carriage brought around in half an hour, would you?" he said and started up. "And have Henry fetch a posy of forget-me-nots from the flower girl on the corner, if you please."

Thirty minutes later, attired in a gray morning suit and top hat suitable for paying calls, Denys came down to find his carriage waiting at the curb, with a pretty bouquet of forget-me-nots on the seat and his driver standing by.

"To 18 Berkeley Square," he said, and stepped into his carriage.

He knew it was time to put his priorities back in the proper order and start arranging his future, but as his carriage carried him the few short blocks to the Marquess of Belsham's London residence, Denys couldn't shake the uneasy feeling that his future was going to be about as exciting as watching paint dry.

DURING THE WEEK that had followed her picnic supper with Denys, Lola immersed herself in the play. Due to Arabella's arrogant tendency to offer unsolicited suggestions and advice to her fellow actors, Lola in particular, there were several more late nights at the rehearsal hall during that week.

At first, Lola had been worried that Arabella's near-constant criticism of her abilities would cement the notion that she was only here because of the men she had slept with, but as the days passed, the opposite outcome had proved closer to the truth. The more criticism Arabella heaped on her, the more other members of the company had been inclined to give her the benefit of the doubt, especially since Arabella didn't only pick on her but on them as well.

It was plain the conduct of Jacob's diva was causing his patience with her to erode, a fact in which Lola couldn't help taking some satisfaction. By Friday, he'd begun cutting Arabella's comments off midsentence with terse comments of his own, and actors had started speculating how long it would be before a full-on quarrel erupted. Lola had offered no opinion knowing it was best to keep her mouth closed and her mind on her work. She was not only an actor in the company, she was also an owner, and as Denys had pointed out, owners did not play favorites or take sides.

Regardless of the emotional upheaval, work had proved a blessing. During rehearsals, when she was reciting lines and immersing herself in the play, when she was grinding her teeth in exasperation at Arabella's latest interruption, or trying to accept Jacob's vision of her role rather than impose her own, she was able to put Denys out of her mind and concentrate solely on what she'd come here to accomplish.

Unfortunately, she couldn't work all the time, and in between, there were the gaps, the times when she was alone, and there was nothing to do but think.

She wasn't used to gaps like that. In New York, she'd had her own show, one that needed the constant replenishment of new songs and new dance routines to keep it fresh and entertaining. Any spare time she had, she'd spent it honing her skill at dramatic acting, and there'd been little time or energy left for things like reflection and contemplation.

But here in London, in spite of Arabella's desire to keep all of them slaving away, she had far more time on her hands than she'd ever had in New York, and she had few friends here to distract her.

Nights were the worst, for she would lie in bed, wide-awake, thinking of her conversations with Denys at Covent Garden and in the rehearsal hall, the sandwiches and confidences they'd shared, and she'd wonder what had impelled her to be so forthcoming. In the whole of her life, she'd never talked about herself as much as she had during the past few weeks.

How? she wondered, staring up at the plasterwork ceiling that gleamed stark and white in the darkness of the room. How had he managed to wheedle one of the most sordid details of her past out of her? As he had noted, she'd always been very adept at deflecting conversation away from herself, especially with him.

You shared almost nothing with me about what your life was like before we met.

She'd left Charlotte Valinsky behind on her eighteenth birthday, the day she'd bought a steamship ticket from New York to Paris, and when she'd stepped aboard that steamship with a ticket that had Lola Valentine's name on it, she'd never looked back. During her time with Denys, she had exercised painstaking care and a great deal of ingenuity to deflect any questions and keep her past life hidden from him. Dancing the cancan and singing suggestive French songs was just risqué enough to titillate and intrigue a gentleman of Denys's class, but that was a far cry from stripping off most of her clothes for the randy sailors who worked the boats of the Bay Ridge Channel. She'd always been afraid if Denys knew the depths to which Charlotte had sunk, it would drive him away. Five nights ago, she'd finally told him the truth—a piece of it, anyway—for that exact purpose.

She'd hoped telling him about it all now might impel him to stop looking at her with the old desires in his eyes, that her confession would ensure he'd make no further attempts to kiss her, or seduce her, or steal her heart again. She'd given him up once for his own sake, and if she had to do it a second time, she feared it would annihilate her.

But her attempt to push him away by throwing some of her past in his face had backfired. He hadn't been repelled, or shocked. He hadn't even seemed particularly surprised. If driving him away was her goal, telling him about her burlesque dancing hadn't been particularly effective. Lola bit her lip and stared at the ceiling. Perhaps she ought to tell him what had finally made her stop doing it. What would he think of her then?

Her heart twisted in her chest. She squeezed her eyes shut, but if she thought that would blot Denys from her mind, she was mistaken, for her imagination could still conjure his face and remember the desire in his eyes. She could still hear his voice, vibrating with masculine need.

Nice, am I?

Aching warmth spread through her limbs at the memory of that question and an answering desire began to overtake her. The way he'd looked at that moment had been anything but nice. That searing kiss in his office—that, too, had not been nice. Denys, she well knew, could also be very, very naughty.

Her breathing deepened as memories flooded her mind, memories of their afternoons in St. John's Wood. The unbearable anticipation of waiting by her window, watching for the carriage that would bring him to her door. Of being in his arms, of his mouth on hers, his hands undressing her, caressing her, bringing her to blissful completion.

Lola groaned and turned on her side. She could not go on thinking about him this way. She'd go crazy, or worse, she'd do something stupid, or allow him to do so, and they'd ruin everything. And then what would happen? Another name, another place, yet another fresh start?

Her eyes tight shut, Lola worked, just as she had so many times before, to forget those afternoons in St. John's Wood, to forget his kisses and his caresses and the one brief blissful time in her life when she'd allowed herself to fall in love.

IT WAS A long time before Lola could finally fall asleep, and after a grueling rehearsal the following morning, during which Arabella chose to be particularly trying, the flower show in Regent's Park was a very welcome distraction.

"I needed this outing, Kitty," she said, as they walked the path of the park's Inner Circle, making their way to the grounds of St. John's Lodge. "You have no idea how much I needed this."

"Arabella?" her friend guessed at once, offering a glance of sympathetic understanding.

Lola's gaze slid away. "Partly," she mumbled, and made a great show of shifting her white parasol to a better angle. "The woman is just so impossible. She has to stop and discuss everything. It's quite trying."

"Oh, I know," Kitty agreed. "I was there the other day, hanging up the backdrop for Desdemona's bedroom scene to see how it looked, and she happened to be there at the time, worse luck. She told me at once how completely wrong it was for her scene, and she demanded to know how on earth Jacob Roth had chosen someone to do the scenery who can't paint for toffee."

"Did you just want to strangle her?"

"Rather! She's lucky I wasn't wearing a necktie that day."

Lola laughed, smoothing her own dark blue necktie against the base of her throat, taking a moment to wickedly imagine possibilities. "I'm just glad we were able to end work today when we did. As it was, I had to run all five blocks back to the Savoy in order to have time for a bathe and a change of clothes."

"Well, it was worth it, for you do look a treat," Kitty said, sliding an appreciative glance over her flounced white skirt, blue-and-white-striped bolero jacket and blue-dotted white waistcoat. "Are these puffy sleeves the newest fashion?" she asked, fingering one of Lola's dark blue gauntlet cuffs.

"Yes. Leg-o'-mutton sleeves, they're called."

"They make your waist look so tiny, don't they? I do hope the fashion lasts."

"It won't," Lola assured, and they both laughed.

It felt good to laugh after a sleepless night and a trying morning. And to be outdoors on such a fine day. She breathed in deeply, noting with heartfelt appreciation that the air up here in Regent's Park was fresher and sweeter than the dank air down by the river. Being here, her heart already felt lighter, and all the tumultuous feelings of the night before slid into their proper perspective. Her worries about the future and what disasters might happen down the line seemed to just float away, carried on the warm May breeze.

By the time they arrived at St. John's Lodge, the flower show was already fully in progress. The wrought-iron gates of Lord Bute's private residence had been thrown back, inviting anyone who had purchased a ticket to enter the grounds.

Once their tickets had been properly punched by one of Lord Bute's footmen, Lola and Kitty were able to join the throng strolling amid the white tents that had been erected on the marquess's lawn.

Though the show was open to anyone who had been able to afford a ticket, there was nothing crude about the arrangements. A string quartet played the music of

Mozart and Vivaldi, liveried footmen carried trays of champagne, lemonade, and canapés. Lola felt as if she'd stepped into a duchess's garden party. It was lovely.

In honor of the fine day, the walls of the tents had been rolled up, and beneath their shade, long tables covered with pristine white cloths displayed the finest flower specimens from London's finest gardens in glittering crystal vases. A card written in an elegant hand identified each bloom, the garden in which it had been grown, and the name of the person responsible.

"The Countess of Redwyn," Kitty read, as they paused before a stunning pink peony. "Heavens, you'd think she grew the bloom herself. Why doesn't her poor gardener receive any credit, that's what I'd like to know."

"He should," Lola acknowledged. "It's a lovely thing." Glancing over her shoulder, she spied a tent displaying vases of her own favorite flower. "C'mon," she said, pulling Kitty's arm. "Let's go look at the roses."

They walked across to the rose display, admiring the blooms for some time before the heat impelled them to a search for a footman with refreshments.

They spied one handing out flutes of champagne to an elegantly dressed group of ladies and gentlemen near the first tent, and they started in that direction, but they were still a couple of dozen feet away when Lola spied one man in particular amid their circle, a man whose back was to her but whose tall, wide-shouldered frame made him easy to recognize.

She froze, suddenly paralyzed. Her heart leapt in

her chest, a sensation borne of dread, excitement, and something else—something a lot like longing. She knew she should turn around before he saw her, but her feet could not seem to obey her mind's command.

He turned his head toward a slim brunette in pale blue silk who stood beside him, and when the girl leaned closer, putting her hand on his arm as she murmured something close to his ear, the gesture of familiarity told Lola the woman must be Lady Georgiana Prescott.

Seeing them hurt like fire, for they looked so splendid together, so right. They were surrounded by others whose elegance and wealth completed the picture. On Denys's other side stood a black-haired man whose profile was distinctly familiar to her.

Jack, she realized, but the ghastly situation enabled her to take no pleasure in seeing someone who she'd once, long ago, considered a friend. On his arm was a slim, elegant blonde—his wife, no doubt.

Talking to the couple was a vivacious, dark-haired girl who bore such a striking resemblance to Denys, Lola knew she must be his sister, Lady Susan. The lady who stood beside her, a stout woman whose dark hair was streaked with gray, had to be his mother, Lady Conyers. And behind the group, facing her, stood a silver-haired, handsome man whose smiling, friendly countenance made him seem so different from the haughty earl who'd contemptuously shoved a bank draft in her face so long ago.

The sight of Earl Conyers was the last straw. It snapped her out of her momentary paralysis, and she hastily whirled around before any of them could see her. "Oh, God, Kitty, we have to leave."

"But we've only just arrived." Kitty reached out, plucking a flute of champagne from the footman as he walked by. "Why should we leave?"

"Because," she hissed, "Denys is here."

"Somerton? Where?"

"That way." Lola jerked a thumb over one shoulder. "Don't look," she added in desperation as Kitty leaned sideways, trying to look past her. "He's scarcely twenty feet away from us."

"Is he?" Kitty didn't seem the least bit surprised. In fact, there was a little smile playing around her lips, and an awful idea flashed through Lola's brain.

"You knew he'd be here," she said, her eyes narrowing as she watched her friend shift her weight in decidedly guilty fashion. "It's an unbelievable coincidence that he would be at the same event we are when there are hundreds of things going on in London now, and yet, you are not the least bit surprised. You knew he'd be here, didn't you?"

Her friend wilted a bit beneath her gaze, confirming her guess. "I thought it was a possibility," she mumbled.

"What would ever lead you to believe he'd be at a flower show?"

Kitty tugged self-consciously at her ear. "Lucky guess?" she ventured, but when Lola's gaze narrowed still further, she gave a cough and proceeded to explain. "I heard tell that Somerton's mother is the . . . ahem . . . patroness of this . . . umm . . . show."

"What? Oh, my God." All the implications of the situation struck her, and she felt suddenly sick, and furious, and humiliated. If Denys saw her, he'd think . . . oh, God, it didn't bear imagining what he would think.

"How could you do this to me?" she demanded. "How?"

"Well, it isn't as if you don't have the right to attend. It's a public event, open to all. Even those of us in the lower classes are allowed to come," she added, unmistakable bitterness in her voice. "They just don't think we can afford to buy their outrageously expensive tickets."

"It doesn't matter that we're allowed to be here. You've put both me and Denys in an impossible position, don't you see that?"

"No, I don't." Kitty gave a toss of her head. "Somerton's your business partner, isn't he? Why shouldn't you attend his precious mother's flower show? Why shouldn't you speak to him? Why shouldn't he come over here and speak to you? Maybe he'll escort us around."

Lola groaned, realizing just how clueless Kitty was about the social nuances of high society.

"Besides," Kitty added as she didn't reply, "I told you before that I want one of our lot to beat the odds. Serve his snooty family right if you married Somerton," she added, her voice bitter from her own heartbreak. "Knock 'em all into a cocked hat, it would."

"For the love of heaven, I told you there's nothing romantic between—" She stopped, that kiss in Denys's office and her own erotic imaginings from last night flashing through her mind. She took a deep breath and changed tactics. "You had no right to play matchmaker when we both know you only did it out of a desire for revenge and some cockeyed sense of social justice. How do you think this makes me appear, showing up at his mother's charity event?"

She could hear her voice rising with panic as she asked that question, and she paused to take a deep breath before she could speak again. "We have to leave."

"So you intend to go scurrying off as if you have something to be ashamed of? Are you supposed to avoid all the other events of the season just because he might happen to be at those, too?"

"That is not the point, and you have no idea what you've done, and we are leaving right now." She grabbed Kitty's arm, but when she glanced around she realized escape was impossible. She was hemmed in by the elegant Georgian house and three walls of wrought-iron fencing, and the only way out was through the gate, which meant she'd have to walk right past his family.

And if that wasn't bad enough, her quick survey of her surroundings revealed the awful fact that she'd been noticed. One by one, people were turning to look at her. She watched in dismay as, one by one, the people strolling casually about the grounds stopped walking and stared, their attention fixed not on the fine day or the flowers displayed, but on her.

Oh, God, they all know who I am, she thought in

horror. *Probably none of these people have ever met me, and yet, they know.*

She felt as if she were watching a terrible street accident unfold before her eyes as she saw heads lean together, mouths begin to move. Every single pair of eyes in the crowd now seemed fixed on her, or on Denys and his family and friends, and as their gazes darted back and forth with avid interest, it was easy to read their thoughts and hear their whispered speculations. They were all wondering how Lord Somerton's former—or was it current?—mistress had the gall to appear at his mother's charity event, and what was the earl going to do about it?

Wondering if she could just bolt for the exit, she cast a desperate glance over her shoulder and froze, horrified to find the earl staring straight at her. His face, so pleasant and good-natured a moment ago, was now flushed purple with anger. His lips were pressed tight, and beneath his hat, his dark gaze seemed to blaze with repressed outrage. Their gazes locked, and he stiffened, raising his chin to the haughty angle so fitting to his rank. Then, with nearly every eye in the place watching the scene, he circled the group he was with, and with slow, deliberate intent, so that anyone watching her would see his action, he took several steps toward her, then stopped, and turned his back.

Lola sucked in her breath, the blatant snub like a punch in the stomach. She knew she should look away, walk, go . . . somewhere, and yet, she could not seem to move. She felt pinned in place by a hundred gazes, like a butterfly tacked up in a display case.

Denys and the girl suddenly seemed to realize something was amiss. They lifted their heads from their intimate tête-à-tête, and that was when Denys saw her. His eyes widened in astonishment, he glanced around, then he returned his gaze to hers. In his face, she could see shock, and when he pressed his lips together, he looked every bit as angry as his father.

Was he going to cut her, too? She couldn't bear to see it happen, and yet, she could not seem to make herself turn away. And besides, where was there to go?

She stared at him helplessly, tears of mortification blurring him before her eyes. She wanted to die. *An earthquake would be ideal,* one that would split the perfectly manicured grass and allow the earth swallow her up. Unfortunately, despite what Denys's family thought of her, she was no witch and could not conjure up earthquakes with a magic spell.

God help me, she thought. *What am I going to do?*

Chapter 17

 She looked like a stricken doe surrounded by hunters. And the hunters, he noted as he glanced around, were out for blood. A glance at his father's face told him some of those hunters were in his own family. Denys moved, taking a protective step toward her, but a hand curled around his arm, stopping him.

He turned his head and found Georgiana staring at him, her gray eyes wide and appalled. "Denys, what are you doing?" she whispered. "You can't be thinking to actually walk over and speak to that woman?"

He returned his gaze to Lola. He'd never seen her look this way—mortified and frightened. It was so unlike her, and he knew she was waiting to see what he would do. "Of course I shall speak to her," he said, keeping his voice low and as matter-of-fact as possible.

"She is my business partner. We discussed that fact only yesterday, Georgiana."

"Being her business partner does not mean you can acknowledge her publicly!"

That sort of hair-splitting was so absurd he nearly laughed. "I see no way to be one without doing the other." He glanced over to where Lola was still standing on the lawn surrounded by a sea of faces, avid and eager for scandal, and he knew all of them were wondering what he intended to do. "We can discuss this later. Everyone is waiting on my action, and I cannot allow her to be humiliated this way a moment longer."

"Humiliated?" Georgiana tightened her grip on his arm before he could turn away. "If you speak to her, if you even acknowledge her, it is I who am humiliated," she choked. "Do you not see that?"

He shook his head, knowing what she was expecting, knowing he could not do it. "I will not give her the cut, Georgiana. Even for you, I will not do that."

She made a sound—surprise, outrage, pain—he didn't know which because he hadn't seen her display any of these emotions before, not since they were children. Without warning, tears welled up in her eyes. "I knew it," she whispered. "I've always known."

And then, Georgiana, admired by all for her self-control and restraint, began to cry. Her hand slid away from his arm, she ducked around him, and ran for the house.

Christ Almighty.

He couldn't go after her, for he had an even more pressing problem than Georgiana's tears. He took another step toward Lola, but he was stopped again, this time by an unmistakably masculine grip. He turned, ready to tell his father not to interfere in his affairs, only to find it was Jack behind him.

"Georgiana's right, old boy."

"I won't give Lola the cut, Jack," he muttered. "I won't."

"Acknowledge her, if you must. But you can't go over there and speak to her. If you do, everyone will see it as a slap in Georgiana's face. She doesn't deserve that."

"I know, but hell, Jack, I can't leave Lola standing there in limbo."

"I'll take care of Lola. You go after Georgiana. You must," he added, as Denys opened his mouth to argue. "Georgiana's the girl you're thinking to marry." He paused, his dark eyes looking into Denys's. "Isn't she?"

Denys knew the answer to that question, knew it with abrupt and absolute certainty, but he also knew his sudden realization didn't change the fact that Jack was right. He nodded. "Get Lola out of here."

"I'll run the gauntlet with her, never fear." He winked. "Right past Conyers and all the rest."

"Linnet won't like it," Denys felt compelled to point out.

"No," his friend agreed, and grinned. "But my wife has been angry with me many times before. I'm sure she'll be angry with me quite a few times more before I'm finally laid in the ground."

With that, Jack turned and started toward Lola, who was standing with her friend, pretending a vast interest in the roses and trying her best to ignore the fact that everyone within fifty feet was observing her.

He waited as Jack walked to her side, bowed to her, and offered his arm, and it hurt to know that he'd had to allow a friend the honor of rescuing her.

Jack and Lola started in his direction, her friend trailing a couple of feet behind them, and as they approached, Denys's gaze slid to his family. They stood huddled together about a dozen feet from him—Susan, with her hand over her mouth and her eyes wide, his mother, displaying all the stoic calm a lady could manage in these circumstances, and lastly, his father, stone-faced and grim. He met the reproach in the earl's eyes with an unwavering gaze of his own before returning his attention to the couple coming across the grass. As she passed, he bowed to her, a polite but brief acknowledgment that, though it might offend Georgiana, wouldn't be a public insult to her.

Lola gave him a nod in return and strolled on by, but though his duty to her was done, he waited until Jack had seen her through the gates and into the park before he turned his attention to the house and another duty, one that he suspected was going to be every bit as painful.

HE KNEW GEORGIANA well enough to know where he'd find her, and it didn't take long to confirm his guess had been right. For he'd barely started down the corridor to Bute's music room before the melancholy notes of a Chopin concerto floated to his ears. In the doorway, he paused, and seeing her over the piano reminded him of when they were children and they'd played duets together.

He felt now all the same warm affection he'd felt for her then, but that was all he felt, and he knew now it was all he would ever feel. He also knew it was not enough, not for him. It could never be enough.

The music stopped, and she looked up, and though it was a hard, hard thing to look into her eyes, he did it. They were dry now, no sign of tears, but he could still see pain in their gray depths. He took a deep breath, removed his hat, and said the only thing that a gentleman could say in such circumstances.

"I'm sorry, Georgiana."

She lifted her chin a little higher, a proud gesture that reminded him of Lola though he doubted Georgiana would have seen that particular comparison as a compliment. She swallowed hard. "Just what," she said in a choked voice, "are you sorry for, Denys?"

He suspected they both knew the answer to that question, but of course, it had to be said aloud.

"I've hurt you, and I'm sorry for it," he said simply. "That has never been my intent. I have a great deal of fondness and affection for you, and have always regarded you as a dear friend. But—"

He stopped as she closed her eyes, and he waited for her to open them again before saying the rest. "But I have come to realize it is not enough for marriage."

She did not reply. Instead, she lifted her hands from the piano, and they trembled a little as she clasped them together. She steepled her index fingers, pressing the tips to her lips, considering her next words with care. "But surely," she said at last, "fondness and affection—along with suitability, of course—are the perfect foundation for marriage."

He had been trying to accept that particular premise all his life. When she had returned last year from an extended trip to the Continent, he'd already decided he was done with crazy, ungovernable passions, and he'd worked to accept everyone else's notion that mutual affection and fondness were a better basis for a happy marriage than romantic love could ever be. He thought he had succeeded, but he knew he had not. "Some people say that's how it is."

Her hands opened in a gesture of bewilderment. "I don't know anyone who would say otherwise."

That premise might be true for most people, but he knew now, as surely as he knew his name, that for him, marriage without romantic love would be as cold and colorless as the North Sea in January.

Georgiana deserved better from matrimony than that. So did he.

"I would," he said. "I would say otherwise."

She shook her head, a sudden, violent movement of denial, and jerked to her feet, but when she spoke, her voice was low, controlled. "All my life, I've waited for you, Denys, because I've always known we would be perfect together. Our families know it, too. We are so well suited. We have many interests in common, we think alike about most things. Why, in the whole of our lives, we've never had so much as one disagreement."

"That's not love, Georgiana," he said gently.

She ignored that. "I waited for you, wishing, hoping that one day, when you were ready to settle down, I would be the one you chose. And then, she came along, and ruined everything. All my hopes . . ." Her voice broke, and she stopped.

He pressed his fist to his mouth, and it was a moment before he could reply. "I'm sorry. I never meant to hurt you. Having had my heart broken, I always vowed I'd never cause anyone else that kind of pain. That I have done it to you—"

"She broke it."

Her words cut through his like the lash of a whip.

"I beg your pardon?"

"Your heart was broken because she broke it, Denys. I am the one who picked up the pieces."

The former might be true, but though he could have quibbled about the latter, he chose not to. Let her believe that if it made her feel better.

"And now," she went on, her voice rising a notch, vibrating with repressed anger, "now, just as I begin to believe that everything I have planned for us could still happen, that the future I have wished for could be mine after all, she comes back, and all my good work is undone."

Good work, he noted, and plans, and wishes, but no mention of love. He began to wonder if his concern for her broken heart was unfounded.

"And now? Now I have stood by," she went on, "as a lady must, able to do nothing while that woman waltzes back into your life and chases after you shamelessly. And then, she has the unmitigated gall to show up here? Here, at your own mother's event, as if she feels she is entitled to arrive anywhere you happen to be."

"Well, she is entitled to be here," Denys pointed out reasonably. "She bought a ticket."

"You took her side," she said, and the anger formerly in her voice was gone. In its place was disbelief, the same wondering disbelief a child might display upon discovering that wishes are not reality, and life is not always fair. "You took her side instead of mine."

"It was not a matter of taking sides. Would you have had me ignore her? Give her the cut?"

She stared. "Of course you should have cut her. There was no other proper alternative."

"Be deliberately cruel, you mean?"

"Oh, please. I know why you didn't do it. Everyone knows why."

"Indeed?"

"Oh, Denys, must we pretend again today?" She looked at him, and the pain in her eyes seemed deeper, darker, mixed with anger. "She's your mistress. Everyone knows that."

He stiffened though he'd known all along this was

bound to be the way people's minds would run. "Then everyone is misinformed. She is not my mistress. She is my business partner. We discussed this only yesterday, Georgiana."

"Business partner," she scoffed, making short shrift of their conversation the day before. "Do you think I didn't see through that arrangement the moment I heard about it? And no, I'm not talking about our conversation yesterday. I heard about that woman and why she's here the day before I departed for Kent."

"Perhaps you did," he acknowledged, "but you did not hear about any of it from *me* until yesterday, and what you heard elsewhere is gossip."

"It is? Do you think I didn't see how you looked at her today?"

Of the many tumultuous emotions Lola always managed to evoke in him, he had no idea which ones he had displayed moments ago. But there was one thing Georgiana had concluded that he could dispute. "Whatever you saw, or think you saw, in my countenance earlier, you are nonetheless mistaken about the nature of my relationship with Lola Valentine. I can see," he added, noting the disbelief in her expression, "that I must be blunt about a very indelicate subject. A mistress is a woman that a man pays to sleep with him. Lola has not indicated any desire for such an arrangement with me, and I can assure you that if she were to do so, I would not dream of accommodating her. I have not made her my mistress, and I will not. Not now, nor at any point in the future, and I am astonished that you would think I could come to you, and look into your eyes, and give you false explanations of the situation."

Her shoulders went back. "I chose to accept those explanations. And live with them."

"But not believe them." He paused. "So my supposed mistress is to be tolerated, but not acknowledged?"

"If necessary." Had he still possessed any doubts about his decision before walking into this room, that answer would have banished them. He took a deep breath. "You may be willing to accept such an arrangement, but I am not. I will always think of you with fondness and affection, Georgiana, and I hope one day, you can once again regard me in that light." He bowed. "Good-bye, my dear."

"You'll regret this, Denys." There was pain in her voice, and there were tears in her eyes, but he couldn't help feeling that they weren't the pain and tears of heartbreak, but rather, the disappointment of thwarted wishes. "You will regret this one day."

He wouldn't, but a gentleman could never say such a thing. "That is quite possible," he said instead, and donned his hat. "Good-bye, Georgiana. I wish you every happiness."

HE LEFT GEORGIANA in the music room, but he did not rejoin his family in the gardens of St. John's Lodge. Instead, he left Bute's house by the front entrance and began walking. It was nearing sunset, and ominous clouds were gathering overhead, but he paid little heed to that. He needed to walk—to move and to think—so he simply started around the park's Inner Circle and kept going, over both bridges of the boating lake, across Hanover Terrace, and onto the Park Road.

As he walked, he thought of his youth, of how he'd ignored his responsibilities and the expectations of his loved ones. He thought of his cavalier seduction of a dancing girl and his even more cavalier disregard of the consequences. He thought of his heartbreak and his resolve to straighten out the mess he'd made of his life, and though he was proud of what he'd achieved, he knew the changes he'd wrought within himself had somehow sent him ricocheting to the opposite extreme. The callow, careless youth had become a man so fixed on duty and obligation and doing the responsible thing that he'd actually considered marrying a girl he did not love.

Lola's return was making him realize that neither man was the man he wanted to be. He felt chained by forces that were pulling him in opposite directions. On one side were obligation, duty, and expectation, his deep love for his family, and all the conventions and beliefs with which he'd been raised. On the other was only one thing: his deep, unwavering desire for one woman.

A drop of rain fell, tapping the brim of his hat, then another, and another, but he did not stop. When the road forked at St. John's Church, he veered left and kept walking.

Was there no middle ground? he wondered. Was

there no way for him to bend with the forces around him and not break? Was there no compromise? No stable, solid center, no eye in the midst of the hurricane where he could be content? That was what he really wanted.

In other words, he thought wryly, he wanted to have it all. And perhaps, like Georgiana, he could not quite accept that life wasn't willing to hand it over.

Ah, but what if he took it?

There was, he knew from schooldays, a Persian proverb, something about taking what you want, but being prepared to pay the price to the gods, whatever the price might be.

What price was he willing to pay?

He stopped on the sidewalk, and it was only then that he took stock of his surroundings. He was in St. John's Wood, walking along beside the pretty little villas of Circus Road, villas where many mistresses had been kept over the years by many young and callow gentleman of the aristocracy.

He walked farther along the road, then stopped again in front of a small stone house that stood behind a discreet wall of ivy-laced wrought iron, a house that had once belonged to him. The delphiniums planted in the urn by the gate were vivid purple in the twilight, and the granite façade of the house shimmered silvery gray in the rain. *It looks the same,* he thought, and tightness squeezed his chest. *It looks exactly the same.*

Memories swamped him, memories of walking up those whitewashed steps, of Lola at the top of the stair-

case and her radiant smile beaming down on him like
sunshine, of her running down the stairs and straight
into his arms, of him carrying her right back up.

He closed his eyes and tilted his head back, feeling
the raindrops spatter his face. He inhaled deeply, but
what he smelled on the breeze was not the dampness
of a spring day, but the delicate sweetness of jasmine.

The clatter of carriage wheels on the road opened
his eyes, and he looked over his shoulder as a growler
came up the street. It stopped beside him, but when he
saw the astonished face of the woman on the other side
of the window glass, her eyes widening in shock beneath the narrow brim of her white straw hat, he could
not share her surprise.

To him, her arrival seemed inevitable. Fate offering
him a choice: take what he wanted and pay the price,
or walk away for good and all. There was no middle
ground, no solid center. There was Lola, and there was
everything else.

She'd said he didn't know who she really was, and
that was true, because he now understood that she was
not at all what he'd thought her to be. She was not a
force beyond his control, she was not something to be
fought, or seduced, or conquered, or denied. She was
simply his woman, for now and for always, and even
if she broke his heart all over again, even if everything he'd tried to be was in ruins afterward, he did
not care.

He took a step toward her, then stopped. He'd already
made his choice, but he wasn't the only one who had

to choose, and he certainly wasn't the only one who'd have to pay the price.

He doffed his hat, watching as the driver climbed down from the box, pulled out the step, and opened the door for her. Hat in his hand, heart in this throat, he waited.

She didn't move, not to come out, nor to invite him in. "What are you doing here?" she asked, sounding bewildered, almost plaintive.

"The same thing as you. At least, I hope so."

She shook her head, as if denying it, but then she sighed, seeming to realize denials were pointless. "I didn't know you would be at that flower show. Kitty—my friend—she bought the tickets and asked me to go, but she didn't say it was your mother's event. Oh, God, Denys." She paused, lifting one white-gloved hand in a hopeless gesture. "If I'd known, I'd never have—"

"It doesn't matter." He rubbed a hand over his rain-soaked face, and he waited.

"And your sweetheart?" She gave a laugh that to his ears sounded forced. "I'll wager you had a great deal of explaining to do there."

"She's not my sweetheart, and that doesn't matter either."

A tiny frown knit her auburn brows together. "But you're going to marry her, aren't you? That's what the scandal sheets are saying."

"The scandal sheets will say anything if it will sell newspapers. The truth is, I had been considering the possibility of courting Georgiana, with perhaps a view to marriage, and had been spending much more time in her company this season than previously, but I had not yet indicated any serious attachment or intention."

She drew a deep breath. "Perhaps you haven't, but she feels a serious attachment to you. It was in her face. I saw it."

"Georgiana has harbored hopes about me since our childhood, and I fear my recent attention toward her fueled those hopes, much to my regret. But today, I made it clear to her that those hopes will never be fulfilled. I daresay Georgiana will make some man a fine wife, but she now knows that man will never be me."

The rain was falling harder now. His hair was soaked, and so were his clothes, but he didn't point that out. Though he had no idea what she was going to do, he didn't try to help her make a decision. He willed himself not to move. He hardly dared to breathe. And he waited.

And then, after what seemed an eternity, she slid back on the seat to allow him inside with her, and Denys's heart leapt in his chest with such force, it hurt.

He was across the remaining distance in less than a second. "The Savoy," he told the driver as he stepped into the cab. "If I don't tap the roof when you arrive there, keep circling Covent Garden and the Strand until I do."

And then, he was in the cab, Lola was in his arms, his mouth was on hers, and he knew he had just walked straight into the teeth of the storm. He knew the choice he'd just made might cost him everything he'd spent the past six years trying to earn. He knew he might have to give up all the trappings of his position and the pleasures of good society. He might even have to sacrifice the affection of his family and the respect of his father. But if that was the price to have the only woman he had ever loved, he'd pay it. He'd pay it gladly.

Chapter 18

 Lola knew this was a mistake, one that would probably wreck him, and her, and everything both of them were trying to achieve, but with his mouth on hers and his arms around her, she just couldn't summon the will to stop it. When he dragged her onto his lap, she wrapped her arms around his neck, and when his tongue touched her lips, she parted them in willing accord.

The kiss was full and lush. His tongue caressed hers with carnal strokes, sliding deeper, then pulling back. Her body was flushed with heat, aching with need.

He broke the kiss, but she had time for one gasp for air before he was tilting his head the other way to kiss her again. This time, it was a slow, drugging kiss that seemed to go on and on as he explored her mouth, tasting her, rediscovering her. *It's been so long,* she thought, and moaned against his mouth. *God, Denys, it's been so long.*

He broke the kiss again, and pulled back. Afraid he was calling a halt, she grasped the soaking-wet lapels of his jacket. "Don't stop," she gasped. "Don't stop."

"Who's stopping?" he muttered, and his hands came up between them. He pressed kisses to her face as he began unfastening the buttons of her jacket, waistcoat, and shirtwaist.

He yanked apart her necktie, then pulled apart the edges of her garments, and bent his head to trail kisses along the side of her neck.

By the time he slipped his hand inside the placket of her shirtwaist, her breathing was quick and shallow, and her body was flushed with heat, and when his fingertips caressed the swell of her breast above her corset cover, she moaned, sinking back against the carriage seat, her weight on her elbows.

He followed the move, undoing more buttons as he came over her, and she closed her eyes, tilting her head back, arching her breasts upward as he pressed kisses along her collarbone. He worked his hand beneath her chemise, to touch her bare skin, and the heat in her grew stronger, hotter, pooling in long-forgotten places—her breasts, her abdomen, and between her thighs.

His free hand grabbed handfuls of white silk and lawn, pulling up her skirt and petticoats, getting beneath. Then his hand glided up her thigh, and the heat of his palm burned through the thin nainsook of her drawers.

Suddenly, he withdrew his hand from her bodice and sank to his knees beside her, then he was shoving her skirts up against her stomach. He pinned them to her waist with his forearm, as his other hand spread across her belly.

And then he went still.

"Denys?" Panting, she opened her eyes to find him hovering above her, breathing hard, but other than the rise and fall of his chest, he did not move. In the last vestiges of daylight that peeked between the carriage curtains, she could see the desire burning in his eyes. "Why did you stop?"

"I want to be sure you really want to do this," he said, his voice ragged, his countenance harsh with the effort of holding back. "If you don't, then for God's sake, stop me now."

"You're the one who wanted me to go out on a limb, didn't you?" she panted, sucking in air, unable to get enough into her lungs, given the tight confines of her corset. "This is about as far out on a limb a girl can go, don't you think?"

"Is it?" His hand slid down over her belly an inch or two, then stopped again.

"Don't tease," she groaned. "Don't tease me."

"Go out a bit further on that limb," he coaxed, moving his hand closer to the apex of her thighs. "Tell me what you want."

"Touch me," she gasped, parting her thighs, but it wasn't much access, for her bent knee hit his arm. She jerked her hips, urging him on. "Touch me like you used to do."

He complied, his finger sliding between her thighs and into the gusset of her drawers. Sharp sensation speared her, and she cried out.

He began to caress her with the tip of one finger, light, delicate circles that spread pleasure throughout her body, the delicious pleasure of so many summer afternoons. "Denys," she moaned. "I remember this."

"So do I, Lola," he murmured, and leaned down to kiss her mouth. "You are still every bit as soft as I remember. And so, so wet for me."

He deepened the caress, sliding his finger between the folds of her feminine opening, overwhelming her with sensations she'd never thought to feel again, and she bent her arm to stifle her own panting sobs, for she didn't want the driver to hear. "Denys. Oh, God, Denys."

"Yes," he coaxed softly, "That's it. You're coming, aren't you?"

"Yes," she sobbed. "Yes, yes," and then she did, climaxing in exquisite waves, again and again. "Don't stop, don't stop."

"I won't," he promised, his fingers continuing to caress her, wringing the last shards of orgasm from her until she finally collapsed, panting, against the seat.

"I'd forgotten, Denys," she whispered in amazement. "I'd forgotten how it feels."

She opened her eyes, but it was dark now, and no light peeked between the curtains. But though she could barely see the outline of him in the darkness, she could hear the harsh rasp of his breathing.

"I want to be inside you," he muttered.

"Yes." As her eyes adjusted to the dark, she watched him slide his trousers and linen down his hips, and when he did, she sat up, reaching out to take him in her hand.

He groaned, tilting his head back, and she stroked him just as he'd shown her how to do so long ago. He was thick and hard and scorching hot, and she relished the velvety feel of him in her palm. But when she caressed the cleft at the tip with her thumb, he groaned again, and her enjoyment of this particular activity was abruptly stopped as he grasped her wrist and pulled her hand away. "Now, who's teasing?"

His grip tightened around her wrist, and he leaned back, pulling her with him.

He didn't say anything, but she knew what he wanted. Bunching up her skirts around her waist, she eased herself onto his seat, straddling his hips, her knees sinking into the cushion as he settled back against the roll and tuck leather behind him.

"Take me," he ground out, grasping her hips. "Take me inside you."

She smiled, savoring the order, for she knew it was also a plea. Holding her skirts up out of the way with one hand, she took his erect penis in the other and guided the tip through the slit of her drawers and between the folds of her opening. As the tip of his penis entered her, she slid her hand out from between their bodies, and the moment she did, he thrust his hips upward, his hands tightening as he entered her.

She cried out, her fingers grasping for the seat back on either side of his shoulders to steady herself as he pushed into her.

"Do you remember this, Lola?" he asked, going deeper, pushing harder.

Yes, she remembered this, the hot sweet fullness of him inside her. How could she ever have forgotten it? With him inside her this way, it was as if no time had passed, as if their last afternoon in the house on Circus Road had been only yesterday. She gave a frantic nod, rolling her hips, rocking to accommodate his shaft, working to take him fully.

But he seemed to want her to say it aloud, for his hips flexed, pulling back. "Do you?" he asked, and thrust again, harder, the head of his penis touching that exquisite place deep inside her, a place that she knew could bring even more intense pleasure than the one he'd caressed with his fingers moments ago.

"Yes," she panted, her hips working as she felt the pleasure rising, thickening, and she knew she was close to climax. She widened her knees, pressing down, trying to work her hips and bring that completion.

But he didn't let her have it. His hands tightened on her hips, pushing her back a little, making her groan in protest.

"Denys!"

"What about this?" he asked, his voice ragged. He flexed his hips, touching her deep, then he pulled back and flexed again in a teasing, tormenting caress. "Do you remember this?"

She began to sob, for she was hovering just on the edge, and this sweet, drawn-out pleasure was agonizing. "Yes, yes, I remember, Denys," she sobbed. "Finish it. Oh, please, finish it."

He kissed her mouth, hard, then he obeyed her frantic plea. His grip tightened, his fingers pressing hard against her buttocks as he brought her down to him, and he thrust upward.

She came in a rush so intense it made her dizzy, and her fingers clenched convulsively over the seat back as her body pulsed with wave after wave of pleasure.

Even awash in the sensations of her own climax, she knew he was close to his. "Come, Denys, come," she begged, tightening her inner muscles around his shaft, working her hips to bring him to the peak. "Take your pleasure."

With a hoarse cry, he let go of her hips, and his arms wrapped tight around her, as if even now, she wasn't close enough. He buried his face against her neck, and his breathing was hot and quick against her exposed skin. A violent shudder rocked his body, he thrust into her twice more, and his body went rigid as the warmth of his climax pushed into her.

He relaxed against the seat, and she collapsed against

his chest, her body still impaled, as she slid her arms around his neck.

His hand slid up her back, his fingertips caressed her neck. "I remember, too, Lola," he murmured, and pressed a kiss to her hair. "I remember every moment."

She closed her eyes, her cheek against the wet wool of his jacket, and she wished they could stay like this forever. The rain had stopped, and the only sound was the grating clatter of the growler's wheels and the other carriages on the street. A moment later, the carriage turned, and Denys pulled back the curtain a bit to look out. "We're on Charing Cross Road," he told her. "Just past Soho Square. We'll be at Trafalgar in a few minutes."

Disappointment pierced her, for she knew they were almost out of time. She willed herself to pull back, easing away from him into the seat opposite, pulling down her skirts as he fastened his trousers, and she grimaced a little at the wetness between her legs, even as she longed to have him inside her again.

That, she told herself as she began refastening her garments, was a foolish thing to wish for. Everything that was true six years ago was still true and would always be true. This story, no matter how many times they relived it, would always have the same ending. And the same heartbreak.

Her hands began to shake, and when she tried to form the knot of her tie, she couldn't seem to manage it. Her fingers fumbled, and she stopped, fighting back the sudden, stupid urge to cry.

"Allow me," he said, and turned to kneel in front of her. Grasping the ends of her blue silk necktie, he began to form a four-in-hand knot.

He was so close that as he worked, she could feel his breath warm on her face. She lifted her gaze to his eyes, and though the light was dim, she could see their steady, dark brown depths. She wanted, so badly, to kiss him, but she couldn't. That blissful moment had passed, and she knew it couldn't come again.

"There," he said. His fingers shifted the knot, settling it against her throat, but though his hands stilled, he did not pull away. He leaned forward, his forehead pressed to hers. "I want to stay with you tonight. Let me come to your room."

"At the Savoy? Are you mad? It's impossible to get you up to my room without being seen."

He lifted his head, exhaling a sharp sigh, acknowledging the hazards of such a plan. "I suppose you're right. Still . . ." He paused, toying with the lapels of her jacket, smiling a little. "There are other hotels. More discreet hotels."

"And then what?" she choked, forcing out the words. "A discreet house? In a discreet neighborhood."

His smile vanished. "No, actually. I'm thinking of a different sort of house." His gaze was unwavering as it met hers. "A pretty little place in Kent called Arcady."

She felt as if there were a fist around her heart, squeezing tight. "We've been through this before."

"You mean, you have. I was never given the chance to air my views on the matter."

"Talking about this won't change it. I'm not the woman for you, and we both know it. Didn't what happened this afternoon prove that?"

His palm tenderly cupped her cheek. "I think what happened this evening proved the opposite."

Inside, she began to shake. She could feel hope rising, cracking her resolve, but she thought of what had happened earlier that day, of how it had felt to be in the glare of society's hostile scrutiny, and she reminded herself that hopes about a future with Denys were futile. In the eyes of his people and the society he moved in, she was, and would always be, a slut. If she married him, the only revision of their opinion would be that she was a jumped-up slut. But she wasn't the only one who would pay the price. "We lost our heads tonight and had a tumble. It's hardly reason enough to join for life."

"Is that all this was to you? A tumble?"

Another crack fissured her resolve, and she knew she had to get away from him before she broke completely apart, and her heart and her resolve were in pieces. Desperate, she reached up, tapping her knuckles hard against the roof of the carriage. "I won't do this," she said as the vehicle began to slow. "I won't ruin your life again."

"Lola," he began, but she cut him off.

"You've repaired your relations with your family,

earned their trust, and made good. I won't destroy all that a second time." She took a deep breath. "I'm no good for you, Denys. You need to stay away from me, and I need to stay away from you."

"That's going to be difficult, I'm afraid."

It would be impossible, and she knew it. Looking at him, she knew that he knew it, too.

"You managed everything on your own before, and you can do so again. Make whatever decisions about the Imperial you like. I won't fight you."

"So that's your answer? Running away again?"

That hurt, like the flick of a whip, but she couldn't deny the pattern of her life. "I don't want to run out on the play. If you and I can stay away from each other, I'll be able to see it through to the end of its run."

"And then?"

"And then . . ." Her voice wobbled, and she paused, swallowing hard, willing herself to remember the goal she'd set for herself long before she'd ever met him. "If I do well, I'll be able to gain another dramatic role. Perhaps I'll join a repertory company in the North— Manchester or Leeds. Or I may go to Dublin, or back to New York."

"Still sounds like running away to me," he murmured. "I see why you've had so many fresh starts. And what about what happened here tonight?" he added before she could respond. "You're thinking we'll just forget about it, I suppose?"

"Yes." She managed to hold his gaze across the carriage. "We will."

"I won't forget, Lola," he said. "I'll never forget."

The tenderness in his voice was almost her undoing, but she knew she could not destroy his life again. For the second time, she was in love with him, and for the second time, it was going to break her heart. She could already feel it happening. Not in a Paris dressing room this time but in a dingy growler on a London street.

The driver opened the door, but when he pulled down the step, Denys didn't move to exit the vehicle.

"Go, Denys," she said, striving to keep any hint of the pain out of her voice. "Please, just go."

"I'll go if that's what you wish, but this conversation isn't over." He reached for his hat. "Not by a long chalk."

He stepped out of the carriage, donned his hat, and pulled his notecase out of the breast pocket of his jacket. "Take her to the Savoy," he ordered the driver as he pulled a note from the case in payment of the fare and put it in the man's hand. Then he bowed to her, turned away, and began walking across Trafalgar Square.

The driver folded up the step and closed the door. But Lola leaned forward, her nose pressed to the rain-streaked window glass, her eyes on Denys as he started across the square. Then the carriage jerked into motion and pulled forward, and he was gone from her view.

Desperate, she shoved down the window and stuck her head out, craning her neck, wanting to watch him as long as possible. "I love you," she whispered, but he had already vanished behind Nelson's Column, and her soft confession was lost in the mist.

Chapter 19

Denys had no intention of being deterred by one refusal. Not now, not when he had her in his sights again, not when they had another chance. The moment he'd seen her face through the window of that taxi, it had reaffirmed what he'd felt from the first moment he'd ever seen her. She was his woman. He belonged to her, and she to him. The question was how to make her see it that way.

Denys walked to the taxi stand on the west side of Nelson's statue, and as he waited for a hansom, he considered what to do next.

He'd told her their conversation on the topic wasn't over, but he knew more conversation about this wasn't going to change anything. He could understand her reluctance to face down society—the *ton* could be a vicious, unrelenting gauntlet. But the fact that her reluctance was on his behalf, not her own, was frustrating as hell, for he'd face them all down until the end of his days and die with no regrets. He could tell her that until he was blue in the face, however, and he doubted it would make a particle of difference. No, in circumstances such as these, words were useless. Action was what was needed here.

And since he'd rather cut off his right arm than see her looking as she had earlier today in Regent's Park, whatever action he took would involve much more than persuading her to the altar. It would have to be monumental, something along the line of melting a glacier or moving a mountain, which meant he couldn't do it alone. He'd need help.

And he'd need time. Time to plan, to make arrangements, to give Lola room to breathe, and hopefully, the opportunity to miss him. Fortunately, time was something he had a bit of, for she had said she wouldn't leave until the play was finished, and since she was an equal partner, the earl couldn't close down the theater or shut the play down without her consent.

In the interim, however, his family would need to be dealt with. If they hadn't already guessed, the flower show and his break with Georgiana would surely show them which way the wind was blowing, and he did not want to reveal his intentions and ignite a family quarrel prematurely. He remembered quite vividly the rows he'd had with his father on Lola's account the first time around, his mother's tearful pleas, the endless rounds of calls on him by aunts, uncles, and cousins, the reminders to think of his position and his duty and his family name. He had no illusions that it would play out any other way the second time around.

When it all proved futile, the reckoning would come, and when it did, he wanted it to be on his terms, in a time and place of his choosing. In the meantime, his best course was to go to Arcady. Going to Kent enabled him to avoid, for now, the parade of concerned relatives, and it might also pacify his family and quiet the gossip. It would also ensure that he wasn't tempted to see Lola, and it would eliminate the possibility he would encounter her accidentally. Leaving town was clearly his best course.

A hansom pulled up to the curb in front of him and stopped. "Where to, guv'nor?" the driver asked, hopping down from the back to pull open the hansom's wooden doors.

Denys considered a moment, then pulled out his watch and turned toward the streetlight to read its face. It was just past six, which meant he had plenty of time to put the wheels of his plan in motion and still catch the last train for Kent.

"White's," he said, and tucked the watch back in his waistcoat pocket. "And there's half a crown above the fare if we arrive there within fifteen minutes."

The driver earned that half a crown, depositing him in front of his club with three minutes to spare. By the time those three minutes were up, he had ordered dinner for five in a private dining room and dispatched a footman to South Audley Street with instructions for his valet. Althorp was to pack his things, inform his family he was off to Arcady, and meet him at Victoria Station in time to catch the nine o'clock train for Kent.

He then made liberal use of the club's telephone. His account was charged an exorbitant amount for the privilege, but he didn't mind that in the least. After all, when a man called out his heaviest guns, he ought to do it with flair.

LOLA TRIED TO be strong. She tried to focus all her attention on her work because that was the only thing she could control. She couldn't change the world, not Denys's world, anyway. She tried to tell herself that once she was gone, he'd be able to forget her, and she'd forget him, though she feared that sort of self-deceit wasn't going to work a second time. Most of all, she tried not to miss him.

In all aspects, she failed miserably. Every morning on her way to rehearsal, she studied his office as she passed, hoping to catch a glimpse of him—alighting from his carriage, walking along the street, or perhaps standing by his office window up above. She could have spared herself that particular torture by turning onto Southampton Street and entering the rehearsal hall by the side entrance, but though it was painful, she couldn't spare herself that pain.

Nor could she resist reading the society pages. That was an equally painful exercise, but she craved any information about him she could find. She wanted to know everything—the activities he was engaged in, the places he went, the people he might be with. By the time three days had passed, the papers had made it clear no announcement of engagement between Lord Somerton and Lady Georgiana Prescott would be forthcoming and that it was Lola Valentine's appearance at the flower show and her wanton disregard for propriety that had caused the breach. Somerton, it was said, was so pained by Miss Valentine's breathtaking lack of discretion that he'd gone to his estates in Kent to recuperate.

Lola stopped reading the papers after that, but during the three weeks that followed, avoiding the scandal sheets did little to help her to forget him. This was London, and reminders of him seemed to be everywhere—in the lifts of the Savoy, in the growlers that rolled past her on the street, in the flowers of the parks and those sold by the flower sellers around Covent Garden.

She tried to lose herself in work, but that, too, did little to relieve her heartache. She was grateful that her part in *Othello* was the minor one of Bianca and not the leading role of Desdemona, for she could summon little interest in the play, and this sudden bout of apathy both surprised and frustrated her. After years of training, dreaming, working toward a goal, to have it seem so colorless and unimportant was something she had never anticipated, and she didn't know quite how to cope. And though she'd been through all this emotional turmoil with Denys once before, it seemed so much harder this time. Unlike last time, she could not run away until the play had run, which meant she was stuck, like a fly in amber, until *Othello* came to an end. And then, she would have to go as far away as she could get. He'd said their discussion of marriage wasn't over, and she couldn't bear to keep having that conversation, for she knew at some point her resistance would disintegrate and she would give in. Where Denys was concerned, she'd always been weak as water.

By opening night, she wondered how she would endure two more months of this. She stared at her reflection in the mirror of her dressing room, at her colorless face and the circles under her eyes, and she tried to rouse herself from her apathy. She could not reenter London's theatrical world as this haunted creature. Her career as a dramatic actress might only span two months, but it wasn't going to begin with her looking like this.

She opened the fitted case that held her stage cosmetics, but she'd barely finished applying powder to her face and rouge to her cheeks when the door of her dressing room opened. Lola looked up from the rouge pot she was closing and froze as her eyes met those of Earl Conyers in the mirror.

"Leave us, please," he said to the other girls preparing for the performance, and they scurried out of the room at once. Her own understudy, Betsy Brown, was the last to go, and she gave Lola a curious glance as she ducked past the earl and closed the door behind her.

Lola closed the pot of rouge, took a deep breath, and stood up, reminding herself that she was about to go on stage in front of an audience that fully expected her to fail, and somehow, that made facing Denys's father a bit less daunting. By the time she turned around, she was composed and calm, and had even managed to paste a little smile on her lips.

"My lord," she said, bowing her head a fraction. "This is most unexpected. To what do I owe the pleasure?"

"I doubt it is a pleasure for you, Miss Valentine, and it is certainly not one for me. I shall come straight to the point."

"Must you?" She widened her smile deliberately and gestured to the bottles of champagne open on the table in the center of the room—gifts to the girls from admiring stage-door johnnies. "Surely you'll have a drink first?"

He shook his head, but Lola strolled over to the table to pour one for herself, for she could certainly use it. A filled flute of fortifying champagne in her hand, she turned toward him, lifting the glass with a sardonic flourish. "You may now come to that point."

The inference that she was giving him permission made the earl's face flush with color, but he didn't take issue with it. "I came to inform you that I have sold my share of the Imperial."

Whatever she'd expected, it wasn't this, and Lola couldn't quite hide her surprise.

"Yes," he said, and it was his turn to offer a little smile. "So you see? Your attachment to my son is over."

"Does Denys know about this?"

"Lord Somerton," he said with emphasis, "will be informed when he returns from Kent."

"I see. You didn't even bother to consult him?"

"What would be the point? I know his opinion on the matter already."

"Then you know the Imperial is something of which he is extremely proud, as he should be. And yet, you have sold it out from under him without a thought."

"You are to blame for that, young woman."

That flicked her on the raw, and though she didn't want to make more trouble between Denys and his father than she already had, she couldn't resist a smart reply. "My, my, who'd have thought a guttersnipe like me had so much power."

He ignored that. "Your new partner is a certain Lord Barringer, and he intends to bring you a very generous offer to buy you out. I would suggest you consider accepting it."

"Why should I? Your money didn't make me go scurrying off last time. Why should someone else's money do so?"

"Because there will be no reason for you to stay."

She might have already decided to go, but for the life of her, she just couldn't bear to admit it here and watch Conyers gloat. "Denys is not a reason?"

"He is the future Earl Conyers. He must marry, and she must be a girl of good family, but as long as you are here, and he is under your spell, he will never consider it. And he certainly cannot marry you."

"No? Why is that?"

"My dear Miss Valinsky, I know all about you."

Lola tensed, a sick dread knotting her stomach.

"When you returned to London," he continued, "I hired Pinkerton men to investigate you. I'd have done it years ago, when you were here before, but at that time, I had deemed my son's infatuation with you a temporary madness. He'd been involved with women like you before, you see."

She tried to don a blasé air. "Must have been the shock of your life when Denys decided to marry me."

The earl set his jaw, looking grim. "It was. And though you refused my money, you did have the good sense to accept Henry's offer and go back where you came from. When you returned two months ago, however, I immediately set the detectives to work. I know your father was a drunk, and you are a bastard. I know about the dockside taverns where you . . . danced, shall we say? And," he added, his dark eyes so like Denys's, and yet, filled with a contempt she'd never seen in his son's gaze, "I know about your association with Robert Delacourt. I know you are nothing more than a whore."

She sucked in her breath, feeling as if she'd just been backhanded. That, she supposed, was the intent.

Almost as if he read her mind, he nodded slowly. "Mr. Delacourt is well-known to Pinkerton's in New York. They know all about him, and they know all about his girls." His gaze raked over her. "Girls like you."

She shook her head. "But, you don't understand—"

"Leave London," he told her. "If you don't, or if you

ever return, I will give Denys the report from Pinkerton's. We'll see if he still wants you after that."

Denials and explanations died on her lips, for what was the point of them? "What makes you think I haven't already told Denys all about my past?"

He studied her for a moment before he answered. "Because I believe you genuinely care for my son, and you care what he thinks of you. If you didn't, you'd have taken the money I offered you when you left for Paris, or you'd have jumped at his proposal of marriage when he offered it, and let him find out after the wedding what you truly are. I think you see as clearly as I do that you could never make him happy and that matters to you."

She swallowed hard and said nothing. The earl and his Pinkerton men might have gotten some things wrong, but not that. That part would always be true.

"So," he went on in the wake of her silence, "what is left for you here but to be his mistress? Until he eventually tires of you?"

For pride's sake, Lola worked to marshal what she had on her side of the ledger. "I am a woman of business. I still own half the theater. I am still an actress, and London is still the world capital of theater. I am building a new career here—"

"A career? Oh, my dear." Conyers gave her a pitying smile. "I witnessed your last performance here first-hand. I've no doubt this evening will be similar. The theater has been a passionate interest of mine since I was a very young man, and I have never seen an actress with less skill than you. My son can't see it, of course, but others are not so blind. When you fail, Barringer won't consent to allow you an audition in any Imperial production, and I doubt other producers will allow you that privilege either."

Lola lifted her chin, a gesture that Denys would have recognized quite well had he been present. But her voice when she spoke was cool and dismissive. "Thank you for coming to inform me of the situation, Lord Conyers. Now, if you don't mind, I must dress."

"Of course." He bowed and departed, and Lola watched the door close behind him through narrowed eyes.

"I may have to leave London, my lord," she muttered, and raised her glass, "but I'm damned well not leaving as a failure. Not this time."

With that, she downed the remaining champagne, slammed down her glass, reached for her costume, and prepared herself to give the performance of her life.

THE APPLAUSE STARTED before the curtain even began to close, and the audience was on its feet before the hem hit the floorboards. The roar of the crowd impelled the actors to go out and take their bows, but when it was her turn, Lola was too stunned to move. During the past three hours, she'd been so driven, so focused on her performance, that now, when the play was over, she felt dazed.

"Lola, c'mon." Blackie grabbed her hand. "They're calling for us, love."

"Did I do all right?" she asked, yanking her hand out of his and gripping him by the arms. "Blackie, tell me the truth. Did I do all right?"

"All right?" Blackie laughed, shaking his head in disbelief, a grin splitting his dark, Irish face. "By God, you were brilliant." He grabbed her hand again, adding over his shoulder as he started toward the stage with her in tow, "Even Arabella might be pleased."

"I doubt that," she said, but her reply was drowned out by the roar of the crowd as Blackie dragged her onto the stage. Hand in hand, they stopped in the center and looked at each other, and then, Blackie gave her a wink, and they bowed together.

The audience was not satisfied, however, and it wasn't until they had offered two more bows that they could return to the wings. But even then, as fellow actors darted back and forth all around her, talking, laughing, congratulating each other, she still couldn't quite believe any of it was real.

A hand thumped her back in approval, and she turned as John Breckenridge, the star of the play, paused beside her. "In the beginning, I had grave doubts about you, Miss Valentine," he told her. "I was sure you'd fall on your face, but you proved me wrong. I've lost a fiver over it, but I don't mind. You were good. Truly good."

Her lips parted, but her throat closed up, and she couldn't seem to offer a reply. John Breckinridge was one of London's finest actors, worthy of the comparisons that had been made of him to Sir Henry Irving. Hearing praise of her performance from him was one of the sweetest things that had ever happened to her. "Thank you," she managed at last. "Thank you."

Jamie Saunders stopped beside him. "Good work, Lola," he said, and held out his hand to her. She shook it, and he turned to John. "I believe you owe me a fiver. I'll take it in ale at the Lucky Pig, thank you." He glanced at Lola. "Some of us are going to the pub at the end of the street to celebrate. You're welcome to join."

Lola considered, then shook her head. Leaving London would be hard enough as it was. "Thank you, but I'm exhausted. Good night."

She returned to her dressing room, and she was grateful it was empty. The moment she was inside and had closed the door behind her, her knees went wobbly, and she had to sit down.

She plunked down in front of her dressing table and stared, wide-eyed, at her reflection, trying to assimilate what had just happened. "I did it," she whispered. "Oh my God, I just did Shakespeare." Joy rose up inside her like a rocket, and she laughed out loud. "And I was *good*. How about that, Lord Conyers?"

But then, she looked down and saw her empty champagne glass on the powder-dusted surface of her dressing table, and all her joy died away.

She might have proved Conyers wrong about her talents, but she knew it didn't make any difference. She still had no future here. Not now.

Had Denys seen her tonight? she wondered. Or was he still in Kent? What if he came backstage to congratulate her? To take her to dinner as he used to do so long ago? What if he asked her to marry him? How many times could she say no before she weakened and said yes?

The door opened and she jumped, then let out a sigh of relief that it was only Betsy. The girl sat down at her own dressing table farther along the wall and reached for a jar of lanolin to remove her paint and powder. The cosmetics hadn't been necessary tonight, for Betsy had no part in the play, but as Lola's understudy, the girl had to be prepared to go on stage at any moment regardless.

At any moment.

"Betsy?"

The girl turned her head. "Hmm?"

"You know the part, don't you? You've been rehearsing Bianca, right? You haven't been slouching or missing your rehearsals?"

"Oh, no, Miss Valentine." The girl's eyes widened. "I know we're almost never rehearsing in the same rehearsal hall, so you don't see me much, but—"

"Good." Lola cut her off, and stood up. She grabbed her cosmetics case. "Be ready to go on tomorrow night. The part is yours from now on."

She walked out before Betsy could recover her surprise enough to reply.

DOING A SHOW was always an exhausting business, and Lola never failed to fall asleep afterward the moment her head touched the pillow. Tonight, however, sleep chose to desert her. She had promised Denys she would stay until the play's run ended, and she'd already broken that promise, but that wasn't what kept sleep at bay. No, what kept her tossing and turning was fear—fear that even though she was leaving, Conyers would still tell Denys about the most sordid aspects of her past. If that happened, Denys would come to the same conclusion Conyers had. He would think she'd prostituted herself.

She turned over with a groan and cursed herself for ever returning to London. And yet, how could she regret it?

Tonight, she'd achieved the one goal she'd set for herself in coming back. But far more important, she'd been given the chance to see Denys again, to be in his company, to have his arms around her and taste his kiss and revel in his lovemaking. How could she regret that? How could she regret those blissful moments together after the flower show?

He is the future Earl Conyers. He must marry, and she must be a girl of good family, but as long as you are here, he will never consider anyone else.

Conyers's voice echoed through her brain, and Lola turned onto her side with a moan, grabbing a pillow and holding it over her ear. That, of course, didn't help a bit.

What is there for you here, but to be his mistress?

Why? she wondered in despair as she tossed the pillow aside and rolled onto her back. Why couldn't society and his family just leave them alone? Why couldn't they just be allowed to be together as lovers? Why couldn't they just enjoy each other for as long as

it lasted? Why the hell couldn't anything with her and
Denys ever be simple?

You will always be his ruin.

As those words echoed through her mind, she felt the
truth of them more than ever before. Something seemed
to crack inside of her, crack wide open, and suddenly,
she was crying. Lola turned on her other side, curling
into a ball, but she couldn't hold it back, and for the first
time in years, she cried herself to sleep.

"GOOD MORNING, MISS VALENTINE."

The cheerful greeting of her maid woke her, and Lola
opened her eyes, blinking a little in the morning light.
Her eyes hurt, the dry, burning hurt that came after a
crying jag. "What time is it?" she asked, sitting up on
her elbows to find her maid at the foot of her bed with
a tray.

"Half past twelve," Marianne answered. "Your usual
time after a show. Would you like to dress? Or have
breakfast first?"

"Neither." She sat upright in the bed, shoved a lock of
her hair out of her face as she worked to clear her sleep-
clogged senses. "Marianne, I need you to do something
for me first thing. I need you to go to Cook's and arrange for us to return to New York."

The maid's lips parted in surprise, but she was too
well trained to question her mistress. "Of course. When
would you like to depart?"

"As soon as possible, so you'd best go now and make
the arrangements."

"Yes, ma'am. But won't you wish me to dress you before I go? And have breakfast sent up?"

"No." Lola sank back into the pillows. "I just want to go back to sleep. Feel free to have luncheon while you're out. And wake me when you return."

"Yes, ma'am."

The maid departed, and Lola closed her eyes, but just as she fell asleep, she was awakened again, this time by a knocking sound.

She sat up, looked through the open doorway of her bedroom and realized the knock she'd heard was coming from the outer door to the suite.

"Miss Valentine?" a muffled male voice called from the corridor.

Still dazed, her eyes heavy with sleep, Lola shoved back the counterpane with a sigh, got out of bed, and walked to the doorway of her room.

"Miss Valentine?" the voice called again. "Are you there?"

"Yes," she answered. "What is it?"

"Room service, ma'am."

Damn it, she'd told Marianne she didn't want breakfast sent up. She frowned, trying to think. Hadn't she told her that?

"Miss Valentine?" the voice called. "Breakfast and coffee."

Coffee? Lola lifted her head, her spirits lifting a bit. After the night she'd had, coffee sounded awfully good. "Just a moment, please."

She returned to her bedroom, opened the armoire,

and pulled out a soft green tea gown that buttoned in front. She slipped it on over her nightdress and did up the buttons, then shoved her feet into a pair of silk slippers. Dressed, more or less, she returned to the sitting room, retrieved a sixpence from her handbag, and walked to the door. She opened it, but though the man standing outside her door with a cart wore the livery of a Savoy footman, he was definitely not a member of the hotel staff.

"Denys?" She rubbed her fingertips over her sleep-dazed eyes, wondering if she was dreaming. "What are you doing here?"

Chapter 20

 He'd gotten her out of bed, he knew, and the realization made Denys catch his breath. To him, this was the time of day when she had always looked loveliest, when her dark red hair was loose and tumbled around her shoulders, when her face was bereft of powder and rouge, and he could see the golden freckles that dusted her nose and cheeks. He swallowed hard, fighting the impulse to shove the cart aside, lift her into his arms, and carry her into the bedroom.

But he won that battle by reminding himself that he was playing for stakes far higher than just a tumble in the sheets. Forcing desire aside, he bowed. "Good morning, Miss Valentine."

Using her fists, she rubbed her eyes again, making him smile, for the gesture was reminiscent of a little girl waking from a dream. "Why are you dressed like a Savoy footman?"

"Oh, this." He smoothed the waistcoat of his uniform. "Like it?"

Clearly confounded, she closed her eyes and shook her head, and when she looked at him again, her sleepy haze had dissipated, and she was frowning. "Denys, you can't be up here outside my rooms."

"Lola, isn't it a bit silly to tell me I can't do what I have already done?"

She leaned forward, sticking her head out into the corridor. "Someone might see you."

"So what?"

She pulled back. "Someone might recognize you."

"In this costume? I doubt it. Why do you think I'm wearing it? And if you want your coffee, which I know you do since you've just risen from bed, and you adore coffee first thing, you'd best let me in before it grows cold."

She bit her lip, considering. "If I don't, I've no doubt you're prepared to just keep standing out here, hovering in the corridor and knocking on my door until I let you in," she muttered after a moment.

He thrust his hands into his pockets and looked around with an innocent air, whistling.

Heaving a sigh, she pulled the door wide and stepped back. "Oh, very well," she said crossly. "You'd better come in. I never can seem to say no to you."

He met her eyes. "That's what I'm hoping."

He heard her soft gasp, but when she spoke, he was reminded that he'd only accomplished the first step of his plan, and there were still many more steps to take.

"You went to a great deal of trouble," she said, shutting the door and following him as he wheeled the cart into the sitting room of her suite and steered it toward a card table and chairs at the far end of the room. "Where did you obtain a Savoy livery?"

"From a Savoy footman, of course. I found one just coming off duty and bribed him to loan me his livery, take me through the kitchens, and bring me up in the service lift."

"You're crazy," she declared, shaking her head. "Just plain crazy."

"The footman didn't think so." Denys chuckled. "He wasn't the least bit surprised by my suggestion. Without blinking, he told me the rate for this service is a guinea. Evidently, gentlemen in hotel livery are sneaking in and out of ladies' rooms all over London nowadays. So many, in fact, that hotel footmen have established a price. It even includes a letter of character, in case the fellow is caught and given the sack. The maids have a similar system at work. Quite enterprising, really, when one thinks about it."

He poured coffee for her, stirred in milk and sugar, and held it out to her across the table. "Coffee?"

She took it, but she didn't move to drink it. Instead, she lifted her gaze above the cup to meet his. "I heard you were in Kent. When did you return to London?"

"Yesterday afternoon."

"Have you . . ." She paused and took a deep breath. "Have you seen your father?"

He frowned, looking puzzled. "No, why?"

She didn't answer that. "Why did you come back from Kent?" she asked instead.

"Lola." He smiled at her tenderly. "Do you really need to ask?"

"Last night," she whispered. "You were there."

"Of course I was there. Lola," he added, his voice softly chiding, "you didn't really think I'd miss your opening night, did you?"

Her hand shook, and he heard the cup rattle in its saucer. "What . . ." She paused, passed her tongue over her lips. "What did you think? Tell me the truth."

"I thought you were remarkable."

There it was, that radiant smile he loved. "Really?"

"Really. And if you don't believe me . . ." He paused and bent down beside the cart, reaching beneath the hem of the tablecloth to retrieve the morning papers he'd placed on the bottom shelf. Straightening, he held up the stack. "Perhaps you might care to hear a few other opinions?"

He dropped the sheaf of newspapers on the table and picked up the one on top, already folded back to the proper page. "According to *Talk of the Town*, you are 'the most stunning and welcome surprise to appear on the London stage in years.' "

He set it aside, and picked up the next one. "*The Times* says, 'Miss Valentine shines the moment she walks out on stage, rather like the sun peeking out unexpectedly between clouds on an overcast day.' "

"*The Times* said that?" She stared at him, understandably disbelieving. "*The Times*?"

"Yes, *The Times*. Congratulations," he added, grinning at her over the top of the sheet. "I think you are the only person in theater who has ever inspired the staid and stuffy *London Times* to wax poetic. And you've done it twice."

"Maybe, but the first time wasn't very pleasant poetry," she reminded. "Let me see."

She set down her coffee, pulled the paper from his hand, and scanned the page. "I don't believe it," she said, laughing as she read the review. "Praise from *The Times*. Who'd have thought it?"

"In honor of the occasion," he said, once again bending down beside the cart, "I've brought champagne."

He pulled out two champagne flutes and the pail containing an opened bottle of Laurent-Perrier reposing in ice chips.

"This is . . ." She stopped and pressed a hand to her mouth, letting the paper fall from her fingers. It landed, splayed out like a lopsided army tent, on the floor. She looked down, staring at it for a moment, then she looked at him, and to his utter astonishment, he saw tears in her eyes.

"Lola?" He came around to her side of the table, rather alarmed. "For love of God, why are you crying?"

"This is so different," she choked. "The last time

you and I had breakfast and read reviews, it was so awful."

"Which makes this all the sweeter." He took her by the arms and pressed a kiss to her freckled nose. "Doesn't it?"

She turned her face away and shrugged as if trying to dislodge his hands, but it was, he noted with relief, a rather halfhearted attempt, and he began to think he might have just taken another step forward. Slowly, he slid his arms around her waist. "So much sweeter," he murmured, and kissed her cheek. Then the corner of her mouth.

She stiffened, and for a moment, he thought she might pull away, but then, her arms came up around his neck, her mouth opened beneath his, and she gave a soft moan of surrender. This was his opening, and he took it.

Tilting his head, he deepened the kiss. His hands came up to cup her cheeks, and his fingers tangled in her hair, and when she pressed her body closer, tasting him with her tongue, the desire he'd been holding back flared up, and he worked to contain it at once. Pulling back, he gentled the kiss, suckling her lower lip, tasting her in small nibbles.

Given that their most recent lovemaking had occurred in a growler, he was determined that this time things would be much more romantic, and that meant taking his time.

Lola, however, seemed to have other ideas.

She grasped his wrists and guided his hands to her breasts. She wore no corset beneath her gown, and her breasts were full and lush in his hands, the nipples already turgid.

Lust surged in him, and he groaned, opening his palms, torturing himself for a moment before he once again pulled back.

She protested with a moan, her fingers tightening around his wrists to keep his hands on her, but he resisted, pulling his hands out of her grip. "Our lovemaking in the growler was far too rushed," he said firmly. "Today, I'm taking my time."

He fingered the top button of her gown, kissing her nose as he slipped it free. With the next button, he kissed her forehead, and with the third, her chin. By the time the gown was open to her waist, her breathing was quick and shallow, and so was his.

But he held on to his control, determined to wait until he'd made her lose hers. Once again, he pulled back, relishing her moan of protest.

She was wearing an odd sort of chemise under her gown, one that buttoned to her chin, and it took him a moment to realize what it was. "You've taken to wearing a nightgown under your dresses?" he teased. "Is this a new fashion I'm unaware of?"

"My maid's out," she murmured in a breathy whisper, and kissed him. "And there was this very insistent footman knocking at my door. I'm not sure . . ." She paused and kissed him again. "I'm not sure the

Savoy would approve of such brass on the part of their waiters."

"Desperate times," he said against her mouth, his control slipping, "require desperate measures."

"Are you?" she asked, nipping at his lips. "Are you desperate?"

Denys knew her attempt to take control of this seduction could not be allowed, or things would be over long before he'd accomplished what he intended to do.

To regain the upper hand, he wrapped an arm around her shoulders, bent down, and hooked his other arm beneath her knees, then he lifted her into his arms.

"Denys," she protested, laughing as he carried her toward the bedroom. "What about breakfast? What about the champagne?"

"There is authentic room service in this hotel." Once inside her room, he kicked the door shut behind him. "We'll have ice and food sent up later. Now," he added as he set her on her feet at the foot of the bed, "where was I?"

"I believe you were undressing me." Her words were blasé, but her tone was breathless, and he knew he was again in charge, but once he had unfastened the buttons down to her waist, his control was again tested.

"My God," he breathed as he slid her tea gown and nightdress off her shoulders and down her arms, exposing her breasts. "You are even more beautiful than I remember."

He let go of the garments, allowing them to catch at her hips, but when he cupped her breasts, she stopped him. "I can't," she said, pulling back, and he felt a jolt of panic.

He took a deep, steadying breath. "Can't what?"

"I just can't make love to you while you're dressed in a Savoy footman's livery." She fingered a button of the distinctive gold-and-black-striped waistcoat. "I live here right now, and I see footmen wearing this all the time. It's just too . . . strange."

He laughed, relieved as hell she wasn't calling a halt. "Are you telling me to get undressed?"

"Don't worry." She looked up, laughing, too. "I'll help you."

He let her remove the black jacket, striped waistcoat, and gold necktie of his footman's livery. His collar studs, collar, and cuff links followed. He even allowed her to slip his braces off his shoulders and remove his shirt. But when she began to unbutton his trousers, he stopped her.

"That's far enough," he chided. "I am undressing you, remember?" He ignored her protests, plucked her hands away, then cupped her breasts in his hands.

He caressed and shaped them, savoring their lush fullness. When he caressed her hardened nipples with his thumbs, she tilted her head back with a moan, arching into his hands, and when he pinched them lightly in his fingers, she gave a soft cry, and her knees buckled beneath her.

He caught her with one arm, wrapping it around her

waist, laughing softly as he resumed caressing her. "You always did like that."

"Yes," she gasped.

"I remember what else you like." He let her go, and sank to his knees in front of her, pulling her tea gown and nightdress down as he went, baring her entire body to his gaze—her small waist and generous hips, the gentle swell of her stomach, the triangle of auburn curls at the apex of her thighs, and down her slim, gorgeous legs. Taking a profound, shaky breath, he tilted his head back up. Looking into her eyes, he grasped her hips in his hands, pulled her closer, and pressed a hot, wet, kiss to her stomach.

She moaned low, arching into the kiss, her hands reaching back on either side of her hips to grasp the brass footboard. He moved lower, kissing her navel, and then lower still, pressing his lips to soft red curls.

She let out a soft wail, as his tongue raked over her, tasting her. Then he paused, lifting his head to look into her face. "Remember the first time we did this?" he asked.

She nodded, and her legs parted a little, but he ignored the hint. "You'd never done it." He laughed a little, his palm gliding over her hip. "It shocked you, I think."

"Well, of course it did." Her fingers raked through his hair, pulling him closer, and he relented. He kissed the crease of her sex, stroked it with his tongue. He savored her softness, her taste, the sounds she made. He relished her pleasure as it built and built, and when she was trembling all over, when her body was moving in frantic little jerks and he knew the moment was right, he flicked his tongue over her clitoris, and when she made that soft, sweet wail of feminine ecstasy he remembered so well, he took more pleasure in her climax than he had ever taken in his own.

He kissed her there one more time, and rose to his feet. She let go of the bed at once and wrapped her arms around his neck, burying her face against his chest, panting, her breathing ragged and hot against his skin.

He smoothed her hair, and when she pressed a kiss to his chest, his heart twisted, reminding him of all that was in the balance right now, and yet, his body was so tightly leashed, he didn't know how much longer he could hold out. His hands tangled in her hair, pulling her head back, and he kissed her. "I want you," he said, and let her go, bending to yank off his shoes and socks. "Do you want me?"

He looked at her again, watched her eyes widen, and he knew she remembered their first time together as vividly as he. How, after months of being held at arm's length, he'd finally gotten her to admit her desire was as great as his.

"You have to say it," he reminded her, smiling faintly as he unbuttoned his trousers. "Remember?"

He watched her as he shoved down his trousers and linen and pulled them off. Her lips parted, but as he looked on, she didn't speak.

"Well?" he prompted, tossing garments aside, standing naked in front of her.

She shoved a lock of hair back from her face and shrugged, trying not to smile. "Well, what?"

He grasped her at the waist, and she gave a shriek of laughter as he lifted her and plunked her bum down on the brass footboard. He pushed, sending her falling backward, and she was laughing before she even hit the mattress, but he was on the bed beside her before she could scramble away. "Want me?" he asked again, capturing her, rolling over her, pinning her with his body.

She was still laughing, but she pressed her lips together, trying to stifle it.

He wasn't deterred. "Very well. I can wait," he murmured, and nuzzled her neck. "You know I am a very patient . . ." He paused to kiss her throat. "Very persistent fellow."

He slid his arms beneath hers, resting his weight on his elbows, settling himself, and though his cock was hard as stone between her thighs and he was shaking inside from the effort of holding back, he strove to pretend he was shipshape and Bristol fashion. "Do you want me?"

He flexed his hips, sliding his cock against her, a long, slow, teasing slide.

"Denys," she gasped, and her hips rolled against his, but he held out, not entering her.

"You have to say it." When she didn't speak, he slid

his body down a bit, eased his hand between them, and touched her. "Admit it. You want me."

"Oh," she moaned, and he relished the sound.

"Not laughing now, are you?" he murmured, stroking her.

"Stop teasing."

"I think you're the one teasing," he said, the tip of his finger sliding up and down, in and out of her.

"I don't know what you mean," she gasped, shivering with the wicked excitement of this game.

"Yes, you do. Say it, Lola, say it."

"All right, yes, I want you," she gasped, jerking her hips, trying to urge him on. "I want you."

He pulled his hand back a bit, until only the tip of his finger touched her. Gently, he caressed her, circling her clitoris with the tip of his finger, then drawing back. "Are you sure?"

"Yes," she panted. "Yes, yes. Come inside me. Now, Denys, now. I want you so much, I can't bear it."

He shook his head, holding back, for even her desire was not enough. To get what he really wanted, he had to bring her to the very edge. Drawing a deep breath, he pulled back so that he could look into her face. "I love you," he said, sliding the tip of his finger inside her. "Do you love me?"

She didn't answer, and he pulled back, causing her to moan in protest. Her hips lifted as she tried to follow his hand, but he didn't let her have that scrap of satisfaction. "Do you love me?"

She was panting, desperate, her eyes closed. She nodded.

"Not good enough. You have to say it." He teased again, caressing, pulling back. "Do you love me?"

She was whimpering now, desperate, mewling sounds of need, but he did not relent. "Do you, Lola? Love me?"

"Yes," she cried on a sob. "I love you, Denys. I've always loved you."

That was everything he needed to hear. He kissed her hard, withdrew his hand, and entered her fully. "Love you," he told her, thrusting deep. "Now, and always."

She cried out, clenching tight around him, pushing with her hips, urging him on, but he wasn't about to let her set the pace. He fought to hold back, making each thrust just a bit deeper than the one before, building the pleasure, until at last, she came.

He was right behind her, climaxing in a white-hot rush of pleasure so intense, it seemed as if his entire body were on fire. The shudders rocked him, again and again, until at last, they subsided, and he stilled, his body easing down on hers, his breathing hard, mingling with hers in the hush of afternoon.

At last, he lifted his head. "There now," he murmured, pressing a kiss to her mouth, "was that so hard?"

He eased back, curling his arms beneath her, his weight on his elbows, but when he looked at her, his throat went dry, and his heart hurt, because she had never looked more beautiful than she did right now.

In the crack of sunlight that filtered between the

closed drapes, her skin was flushed a delicate pink, the locks of her hair were like tongues of fire against the white sheets, and on her lips was the drowsy hint of a smile.

"So, now that we've both admitted the truth," he murmured, pushing a tendril of hair back from her cheek, "what shall we do about it?"

Chapter 21

 Denys knew he'd be sailing close to the wind with this moment, but she was silent so long, he feared he'd just crashed on the rocks.

Still, there was no drawing back. "My opinion is we should marry," he said, striving to seem matter-of-fact about it all when he was actually nervous as hell. He rolled to his side, propped his weight on his elbow and his cheek in his hand. "It's the usual thing when people love each other."

Instead of answering, she sat up, pulling bed linens up from the side of the bed and wrapping them around her, covering herself. It seemed an odd thing for her to do after the passionate lovemaking in which they'd just engaged, and he felt his nervousness deepening.

"Do you remember my first day of rehearsal?" she

asked. "That night when you came by with sandwiches and I told you about the sort of dancing I used to do?"

"Of course."

"You asked me how I ended up in that situation. I didn't tell you everything."

"No?"

"No." She looked down at her hands in her lap. "There was a man I met there. He saw me dance. He wasn't the usual sort who came to the dockside taverns, so I noticed him right away. He was very elegant, very handsome, and very rich. His name was Robert Delacourt. A few nights later, he came back, and he asked me to have a drink with him. As you might guess, I did. I mean, he wasn't at all the sort of male attention I'd been accustomed to. I fell for him like a ton of bricks. We became lovers."

Denys had the feeling this was the man who'd been her only other lover, and he really wanted to stop this conversation, but he couldn't.

"I thought it was all very romantic. He was a railway tycoon. New money, you call it. I didn't care. I thought he was wonderful. He bought me gifts, flowers, dinners."

This was sounding far too familiar, far too much like his own seduction of her, and to the man he was now, it all seemed so shallow, and so unsavory. He drew a deep breath and let it out slowly. "Go on."

"We were together for several weeks, and then, one night, Robert told me he was having dinner with a very important man. A senator visiting from Washington.

Robert wanted me to come to dinner with them, explaining that he'd told the senator about me, and the senator very much wanted to meet me."

Denys frowned. It sounded innocuous enough, and yet he felt uneasy. Perhaps he just had a suspicious mind, but when he looked into her eyes, the awful suspicion he'd begun to harbor was confirmed, for though Lola was looking directly at him, he knew she wasn't seeing him.

"The senator was a very powerful man in Washington, Robert said, a man who could help him put a railroad deal through out west. We were to have dinner with him at the Oak Room. The Oak Room! I was so excited, I was giddy. I was so stupid."

She laughed a little, laughing at herself, and Denys's heart constricted in his chest.

"I thought he wanted me there to be the woman on his arm when he made this important deal. His helpmate, you know, or maybe even his future wife. But that wasn't it at all. He introduced me to the senator in a private dining room, and then, he just . . . left. I asked the senator when Robert would be coming back, and he said Robert wouldn't be back. I was his now, he said, and that he would be taking care of me from now on. It was as if I had just been traded."

As he had the night she'd told him about her days in burlesque and what had happened to her as a girl, he felt anger rising on her behalf, but again, he kept it in check. "What did you do?" he asked, and pressed a kiss to her forehead. "Did you bash him with an Erie?"

Her lips twitched just a little. "They don't have cast-iron skillets in the Oak Room. At least not on the tables."

"Ah. Champagne bottle, then?"

She frowned, looking confounded by his reaction. "You seem quite sure I rejected him."

"I am sure."

"But how can you be?"

"Because of what you said that day in my office. Don't you remember?" he went on as she continued to stare at him in bewilderment. "After I kissed you, and you became so angry with me—"

"Justifiably so," she cut in. "Given what *you* said."

He nodded, conceding that point. "Granted, but when you lost your temper, and fired off your guns at me, you told me you'd only been with two men in your life."

"I said that?"

"Yes. Don't you remember?"

She shook her head. "I was so angry with you that day, I don't remember what I said, to be honest. But given I did say that, how do you know I was telling the truth?"

"Because I just . . . do. I trust you. I believe you." He kissed her nose. "I love you. And," he rushed on before she could speak again, "I definitely know that one of those two men is me, quite obviously. The other, I now know, is this Delacourt bastard. Hence my conclusion regarding the senator. So, are you going to tell me what your response actually was to this odious man?"

"I tossed my wine in his face. Then I got up and left."

He laughed. "Perfect. Ripping perfect."

"It's not funny."

"You're right." He sobered at once, giving her a level, steady gaze. "I'm sorry, and don't think for one moment that I don't want to find this Robert Delacourt and call him to account, because I do. In fact, what I'd really take great pleasure in doing is thrashing him within an inch of his life. And the same applies to the man who tried to assault you when you were fifteen. And to that senator for thinking for one moment you were the sort of girl who would—"

"But that's just it, Denys," she interrupted. "I was that sort of girl. I told you, I used to take my clothes off in those taverns in Brooklyn. Robert saw me do it. The cowboys back in Kansas City used to come into the saloon just so they could watch me pull up the hem of my skirt and give them a peek at my ankles while I sang. I can't blame any of those men for thinking my virtue was for sale, and neither can you. You seduced me, too, if you recall. You made me your mistress. I'm—" She stopped, and bit her lip. "That's the sort of woman people think I am."

Given his own culpability, he couldn't really take issue with most of what she'd said, but he could take up the last bit. "You talk as if you're fated for that. You're not."

She looked down, her hair falling over her face. "Sometimes, I think I am," she whispered. "Men have wanted me since I was old enough to wear a corset, Denys. I've always known it, and I've never had any compunction about using it when I had to."

"Women have been doing that since Eve, my darling."

"Most women don't do it on a stage, but I did. Hell, I made a whole show out of it." She shrugged, plucking at the counterpane. "After that episode with the senator, I knew I had to leave New York. If I stayed, I was afraid of what Robert, or the senator, for that matter, might do. So I took what money I had, bought a steamship ticket, and went to Paris."

She gave a deep sigh. "Another ticket out of town and another fresh start. I'd read about the dancers in Paris, and I thought I could do that. French cabaret was an enormous step up for a girl like me. The only thing was, I'd never danced the cancan in my life." She shook her head, laughing a little as if in disbelief at her own brass.

"But it turned out you were right. You're good at it."

"Yes," she admitted. "I thought if this is the sort of woman that men *think* I am, well, then, why not exploit it? So I did. I changed my name to something I thought sounded deliberately seductive. I made a dance routine, I learned to sing in French, and do the cancan, and how to kick off a man's hat with my foot. I learned how to make anything I did—a crook of my finger or a wink of my eye or a shrug of my shoulders—seem like a promise to every man in that audience, but I knew it was a promise I'd never have to keep. And it worked. Men went wild over my act."

He cupped her face, tipped her head up. "You're not telling me anything I don't know."

"But that's just it, Denys. You told me you loved me, but you didn't. You were infatuated with an illusion, something I created, a fantasy. It wasn't me."

"At first, perhaps." He caressed her cheek with his thumb. "But I knew the first time we ever made love that what you did on stage was pure fiction."

"How did you know?"

He smiled. "Because until I showed you, you had no idea that a man could make you come with his mouth."

She blushed, her pale skin flooding with color from her face down to her throat and across her shoulders, down to the white sheet she was holding over her breasts. "Oh."

She was silent a moment, taking that in, then she said, "Your father knows about the senator."

"What?"

She nodded. "He came to my dressing room before the show last night and told me. Evidently, he's had Pinkerton men investigating me since I came back to London. He also told me he sold his half of the Imperial."

"Yes, I know about the Imperial. He sold it to the Earl of Barringer. They signed the papers yesterday."

"You know? But if you haven't seen your father, how did you find out?"

"I stayed at White's last night, and Barringer was there when I arrived. He told me the news. It wasn't really a surprise that my father would take that step."

She bit her lip. "I'm sorry, Denys."

"Don't be sorry on my account. And Barringer's not a bad chap. He won't approve of you, mind, for he's quite a stuffed shirt, but he can't out you."

"Forget about the Earl of Barringer. Denys . . ." She paused and gave a deep sigh. "I've quit the play. I'm leaving London, as soon as my maid has made the arrangements with Cook's."

Any step forward might have just been obliterated. He took a deep breath. "Why?"

"Denys, I told you, your father knows about my days in burlesque, about Robert, the senator . . . everything."

"I suppose he threw it in your face?" As he spoke, he felt a flash of anger, and he worked to force it down, reminding himself that no matter what happened today, he and the old man were headed for a reckoning. It was inevitable. "None of that matters, Lola. Not to me. Not at all."

"I wasn't the first girl Robert had used to put through a deal," she said as if she hadn't heard him. "He did it all the time, I found out afterward. I was just too infatuated to see what he was." She waved a hand impatiently. "I was a fool. The point is, your father assumed I had taken the senator up on his offer. If he tells anyone the story—"

Denys shook his head. "He won't."

"How can you be so sure?"

"Because he knows full well you could become his daughter-in-law, and he's not about to let that sort of story get about."

"But I'm not going to be his daughter-in-law, and we both know it, and so does he—and damn it, Denys, why are you smiling?"

"Because I'm glad."

"Glad?" She stared at him as if he had suddenly grown a second head. "Glad about what, for heaven's sake?"

"I'm glad you told me about all this. You've spiked the old boy's guns. Now, when he tells me all about your oh-so-sordid past, I shall take great delight in informing him that I already know all about it. But first, is there anything you haven't told me? Any other chaps out there I need to know about? Any other men you've coshed on the head, or run off with to New York?"

"No, Denys," she said meekly, but he knew she wasn't going to meekly march into a church with him. Her next words proved it. "Will you please stop ignoring the vital point? Robert thought that I was something to be used, something to be passed around and ultimately tossed aside, like so much trash. In a less crude sort of way, your people think the same about me. They think I'm trash."

"But I don't think you're trash. Do you think you are?"

"No, and we both know I don't much care what other people think of me, but to your family, to the society you want me to live in, I will always be trash. Marrying you won't change their opinion of me."

"I'm not at all sure about that, but even if you're right, do you really think your alternative is any better?" he asked her. "Another name, another ticket out of town, another fresh start . . . what's the point? How long and how far can you run from yourself?"

Her face twisted. "What else is there for a girl like me and a man like you?"

Abruptly, he rolled off the bed. "I have presented you with an alternative," he said as he began to dress. "Twice now, as a matter of fact. But you don't seem to fancy it."

"Because it isn't a viable alternative."

"Yes, it is. It's just not a perfect one, wrapped up with a ribbon and a bow."

"You think I care about that? Denys, here in England, marriage is permanent, until death do us part. My mother was able to change her mind, get her marriage annulled. But here, it's different. Your sort gets married, there's no hushing it up."

"True." He donned his shirt and tucked it into his trousers, then he reached for his socks and pulled them on.

"Marrying me would be forever. No way you could annul it later, even given my notorious past."

"That is also true." He slipped on his shoes and glanced around. "Where the devil is my collar?"

"Your father has already sold the Imperial. He'll do more than that if you marry me. He'll disinherit you."

"Ah," he said, spying his collar at the foot of the bed. He scooped it up, along with his cuff links, collar studs, and necktie, then he moved to stand in front of the mirror above her dressing table and continued to dress.

"What if he does, Denys?" she asked after a few moments.

He paused in the act of tying his tie and met her gaze in the mirror, pretending not to understand her question. "Worried I can't support you?"

"That's not it. I could support us if it came to it."

"I'd prefer that you didn't. The *ton* rather frowns on that sort of thing." He finished tying his tie and began fastening his collar studs. "Is that your real concern? Giving up acting? Because if it is, feel free to keep doing it. I shan't care."

"That's not it either!" she cried. "I love acting, I do, but if I married you, of course I'd have to give it up. I may not know much about viscountesses, but I'm fully aware they can't be actresses, too!"

He smiled to himself, noting the shift in her words, the use of the word "if." Another step forward, he thought, pleased and also a bit relieved she might be willing to give up the stage at some point. He was proud of what she'd accomplished for herself, especially last night, and if she wanted to continue to act, he'd support her decision, but though he was willing to fight that particular battle with the *ton* on her behalf, he couldn't say he'd relish the prospect. There would be plenty of other battles for them to fight as it was. "Then what is the problem?" he asked, turning toward her. "I love you. You say you love me. Are you really refusing me because you're afraid society won't accept us?"

She didn't answer, and he went on, "At Covent Garden, the things you told me indicated that you were concerned about what they'd think of me, and you were concerned about my future happiness, and while I think all of that is true, I also think that's not the whole story. Why don't you tell me the rest? Why are you really so afraid?"

She still didn't answer, and he decided to let it go. He had a plan, and he had a great deal more to do in order to carry it out. He picked up his waistcoat, buttoned it, and reached for his jacket.

"I have to go," he said gently. She nodded, but she didn't reply and she didn't look up, and he wondered if perhaps he ought to hold off, give her more time. But then, her voice came to him from across the room, soft and hushed. "Don't you know the reason?"

His hand tightened around the jacket in his hand. "I could hazard a guess," he murmured, studying her bent head and her tumbled hair. "I could say it's because everyone you've ever loved has abandoned or discarded you."

A faint sob told him he was on the right track. "I could go a bit further," he went on as he crossed to the bed, "and say that you're terrified I'll do the same." He cupped her cheek and lifted her face. "That I'll grow tired of you, and fall out of love with you, and take a mistress."

A tear fell down her cheek, and he brushed it away with his thumb. "I shan't," he said, and let her go. "You'll have to take my word for that, of course, but . . ." He shrugged and slipped on his jacket. "There it is. I'm asking you to trust me."

"It's not about trust. It's about the way the world works."

"You really think my family won't accept you if we marry?"

"I know they won't. Your father . . ." She swallowed hard, and Denys braced himself for more obstacles. "Denys, he called me a whore."

Rage exploded inside him even though he didn't move, and it was several moments before he could control it enough to speak. "He never will again. That I promise you. I will make certain he understands that if he utters one more derogatory word about you, he will have crossed the Rubicon."

"Oh, no," she moaned. "I never should have told you. I won't let you do this. I won't let you choose me over your family."

"I already did. I made my choice that afternoon in St. John's Wood, when I walked across that sidewalk and stepped into that cab. I chose you."

She shook her head, refusing to believe, and he decided it was time to roll the dice and let the chips fall where they would. "Let's put your lack of faith in my family to the test, shall we? I'm having a private dinner with them this evening, here at the Savoy. Consider this your formal invitation to join us."

She stared at him, eyes widening in panic. "I can't do that!"

"Yes, you can. It's very simple. You put on a pretty gown, you come downstairs, and you tell the maître d'hôtel you are with Lord Somerton's party. I'll be sure he knows to expect you. He will escort you to the door, he'll announce you, and you'll walk in. All very simple."

"And then all hell breaks loose," she mumbled. "Your father will never allow me to sit at your table."

"It's not up to him to allow it or not. I am the host, so his only choice is to stay or go. If he doesn't wish for our company, he's free to stand up and walk out."

"Denys—"

He sank down on the edge of the bed, and when she tried to turn away, he grabbed her arms. "You said you love me. Did you mean it? If you did, then prove it. Come down and face them. Run that gauntlet."

"I don't think I can."

"Yes, you can, because you are braver than you think."

"I'm not brave at all."

"But you are. Good God, you are, and you don't even see it. You fought off a man who wanted to assault you. You threw wine in a senator's face. You went halfway around the world to become a French cancan dancer when you didn't know French or the cancan. You decided to become an actress when you didn't know how to act. And after a humiliating failure, you walked out on stage last night to face an audience that fully expected you to fail again, and you proved all of them wrong about you. And you don't think you're brave enough to take on my family? Darling, give yourself a little credit."

"But it wouldn't just be your family. It would be the world. Your world, Denys."

"That's true, and it won't be all beer and skittles for you if you marry me, I grant you, even if we manage to win over my family. It will take courage and fortitude and a very strong will to face down the *ton*. Many of them will be cold, hostile, even vicious. They will say unbelievably cruel things about you and to you."

"And to you!"

"Yes," he admitted. "And it may very well last the rest of our lives. But I'm asking you to do it anyway. And you won't be alone, for I will be by your side every step of the way. On the other hand . . ." He paused and stood up. "You could take the easy way out. You could buy a steamship ticket and go somewhere else and change your name and repeat the pattern of your life. It's your choice, my love."

He raked a hand through her hair, pulled her head back, and bent down to kiss her. "Dinner is at quarter past eight," he said. Then he let her go, turned away, and walked to the door. Opening it, he paused and looked back at her over one shoulder. "If you're coming, don't be late. Among my set, being late for dinner is just not done. If you're not coming . . ." He took a deep breath. "Then God help me."

With that, he walked out and closed the door behind him, but before heading down the corridor to the lift, he paused to say a little prayer, for he knew that right now, he needed all the help he could get.

LOLA SAT ON the bed, staring at the doorway. He'd barely departed, but already, she knew Denys was right.

She had a very clear choice to make: another ticket out of town and another fresh start, or a whole new life that would be unlike anything she'd ever experienced before.

Being Denys's viscountess would be the hardest thing she'd ever taken on, much harder than learning the cancan or training as an actress—harder, even, than taking off her clothes for randy sailors. She'd be facing an audience harsher than any London critics had ever been, and she'd be more exposed than she'd ever been in any dockside tavern. And she'd never, ever, be able to run away.

And with that thought, as quick as the flare of a match or the snap of one's fingers, her choice was made.

She didn't want to run. She wanted to stay. Because she wanted to believe that happy endings did exist. And because she hated walking away from a challenge just because it scared her. But most of all, she wanted to stay because Denys loved her, and she loved him. She'd always loved him. And she was not going to run away from that. Not this time. Hell, no.

She'd go to this dinner party, and she'd walk the *ton*'s gauntlet, and she'd live with him and be his wife, and if his family didn't accept them, and society scorned them, that would have to be their loss.

She shoved aside the sheets and stood up, but she'd barely taken one step before a whole new question ran through her mind, a question that was of such importance, it stopped her in her tracks. Tonight might very well be the most important night of her life, and that forced her to face the same awful, agonizing question that had plagued women in this sort of situation throughout history.

What, in heaven's name, was she going to wear?

THE CRUCIAL QUESTION of Lola's ensemble for the evening was decided at last, due mainly to the excellent taste and critical honesty of her lady's maid, and at precisely ten minutes past eight, Lola was presenting herself to the Savoy's maître d'hôtel dressed in a brilliant, head-turning Worth gown of shimmering, moss green silk. White gloves sheathed her from her fingertips to her elbows, and peridot and diamond jewels sparkled in her hair, at her ears, and around her neck.

The maître d'hôtel, however, was not particularly impressed by Worth, or by jewels, or by any actress who might be wearing them.

"Good evening, Miss Valentine." The maître d'hôtel greeted her. His tone was polite enough, and he bowed his head a fraction, but contrary to what Denys had led her to expect, the man didn't move to escort her anywhere.

She tried again. "I am with Lord Somerton's party."

"Quite so." There was now a distinct hint of distaste in the man's voice, and he still didn't move. Lola waited, wondering what she was supposed to do now, and as the silence lengthened, she began to see a definite smirk lift the corners of the man's mouth, reminding her that if she continued to take this path, this daring attempt to rise above her station, she would face many more smirking faces, high and low. This, she appreciated, was just the beginning.

But Lola had no intention of being cowed by a mere maître d'hôtel. The best way to proceed, she decided, was to pretend she was on a stage, and she was playing the part of a viscountess. What would a viscountess do when faced with this sort of behavior from a mere servant?

Despite the nervous apprehension in her stomach, she managed to lift her brows just enough to seem intrigued by this lack of cooperation rather than threatened. "Shall I arrange for Lord Somerton to escort me in to dinner?" she asked, smiling a little. "Or shall I allow you the honor of doing so?"

Reminded that the viscount was on her side, the maître d'hôtel's manner became slightly less superior. "This way, madam."

He led her down a long corridor of private reception and dining rooms to one at the very end of the corridor. It was an opulent room of gold and white, where candlelight from crystal chandeliers cast a warm glow over perhaps two dozen elegantly dressed ladies and gentlemen, while footmen in Savoy livery moved among them with trays of sherry. On the far wall, a set of tall doors had been flung back, revealing a long dining table of white linen, gleaming silver, and sparkling crystal.

She'd been in surroundings like this before, attended

parties every bit as elegant as this, but never had she been among the aristocracy in such a setting. Suddenly, she wasn't just nervous and apprehensive. She was terrified.

"Miss Lola Valentine."

The maître d'hôtel's voice seemed to thunder through the room, and all the elegant ladies and gentlemen milling about seemed to go still. Conversation faded to silence, and Lola began to scan the room in a desperate search for Denys's face, but she got as far as Conyers and stopped, frozen in place by his cold, hostile gaze.

You are braver than you think.

Lola squared her shoulders, jutted up her chin, and returned his cold look with one of completely feigned indifference. He started toward her, but then, another man came into her line of vision, blocking the earl from her view.

Denys.

Despite all her pretenses, Lola couldn't help a sigh of relief, but it ended in a gulp of dismay, because instead of coming toward her, he held out his hand.

Panicked, she didn't move, for she could feel every eye in the room on her, and she was sure that with one exception, the scrutiny was not welcoming. This wasn't like that day at the flower show, for this time, she could easily escape. All she had to do was turn and walk out. There was nothing to stop her, nothing but Denys, waiting for her at the other end of the room.

Keeping her gaze on his face, on the tender smile that curved his mouth and the steady warmth in his brown eyes, she took a breath and started forward, one step, then another, walking society's gauntlet.

Even with her gaze fixed on Denys, it was a long journey to that side of the room, and with every step, she could feel society's disapproving scrutiny. But at last she reached Denys's side.

"You came," he said, and laughed a little. "I'm glad."

"Did you really think I wouldn't?"

"I can never predict what you're going to do, Lola," he confessed as he took her hand and bowed over it. "I do believe that's part of your charm."

She smiled at that, but when she moved to pull her hand away, he didn't let her go. Instead, he gripped her fingers hard in his and dropped to one knee.

"What are you doing?" She cast a frantic sideways glance at the earl, noted the purple flush of his face, and looked at Denys again, dismayed. Proposing to her in front of his entire family was like waving a flag in the face of a bull. "Stand up," she whispered. "For God's sake, stand up."

He ignored her plea. "Miss Charlotte Valinsky," he said, loudly enough for everyone to hear, "will you marry me?"

There were several shocked gasps, and somewhere behind her, a wail was heard. Lola could only assume that was Denys's mother.

Heat flooded her face, and she took another quick glance around, but though all the faces seemed a blur, the hot breath of hostility seemed palpable. "Oh, Denys," she berated him softly. "What have you done?"

He gazed up at her, that tender smile still curving his mouth. "Do you intend to give me an answer, or do you intend to keep me in suspense?"

She opened her mouth, but before she could reply, another voice entered the conversation.

"I have had enough of this!" The earl's voice was low, but in the quiet room, its icy disdain seemed as loud as a dynamite explosion. He set his sherry on a footman's tray and strode over to them. "Denys, stand up, for God's sake, and stop making a fool out of yourself."

Denys ignored him. He kept his gaze on her. "Answer my question, Lola."

"If you marry this woman, I'll disown you," Conyers told him. "You will be dead to me."

Denys turned his head to look at his father, but he didn't rise. "If that's so, I'm sorry for it, for your opinion and your affection are very dear to me. But some things—" He broke off and looked at Lola again, squeezing her hand tight. "Some things are even more important than the esteem and affection of my family. This is one of those things. Well, Lola?" he prompted, holding her gaze with his. "Will you?"

"Without my support for this marriage, you'll be cast out of good society," his father went on. "Beyond the pale, shunned by everyone."

"He's right, Denys," she choked. "You know he's right. Maybe you should think it over. Everyone will forsake you if you marry me. Your family, all your friends—"

"I won't," another male voice rang out, and Lola turned to find Jack coming toward them through the crowd. He paused beside Denys and looked at her. "I never forsake my friends, Lola. I won't forsake either of you."

"Neither will I." Another male voice had Lola looking past Jack's shoulder to find James also coming forward. "Miss Valentine," he greeted her with a bow before moving to stand on Denys's other side. "It's lovely to see you again."

"Lovely?" Jack echoed with a scoffing sound. "It's more than that. It's absolutely ripping." He grabbed her hand out of Denys's grip and bent to kiss it. "Shocking the aristocracy all out of countenance again, aren't we, Lola?" he added with a wink. "That's twice in less than a month. What will people say?"

She glanced from one man to the other, so stunned by their stalwart support that she didn't know what to reply. She supposed she ought to assume a dignified, ladylike demeanor, just to demonstrate to Denys's family that she wasn't the guttersnipe they thought her to be.

"Gentlemen," she began, but her voice wavered at once, her throat clogged up, and any pretense of dignity was lost when she gave a most unladylike sob.

Jack, thankfully, stepped into the breach. He looked down at Denys, who was still on one knee and waiting for an answer. "Do you need a bit of help with this proposal, old chap? You don't seem to be getting on very well on your own."

"I have the situation well in hand, Jack. Thank you."

He once again grasped Lola's hand, but before he could continue, Jack spoke again.

"Of course, of course, but in cases such as this, a man needs all the help he can get. Speaking of help," he added, glancing left and right, "where the devil are Nick and Stuart? They were milling about beside me a few minutes ago."

"I don't know about Stuart, but I'm right behind you."

Lola looked past Jack's shoulder, and when she saw Nick coming forward, she wasn't quite so shocked as she'd been to see Jack and James. But what did shock her was the beautiful, black-haired woman on Nick's arm, the same woman Lola had seen with Denys at the opera. Nick's wife.

They eased between Conyers and his son, and given Nick's higher rank, the earl was forced to give way. He stepped back, leaving Nick and his wife to become part of Lola's growing circle of support, and her shock began to fade, replaced by something deeper and far more profound.

Hope.

"Miss Valentine," Nick said with a bow, "you must forgive me for interrupting this romantic moment, but I simply cannot wait a moment longer before I introduce you to my wife, Lady Trubridge."

Of all Denys's acquaintances, Lady Trubridge would be the most damaged if scandal of any sort were attached to her name, for she was one of the powerful ladies in British society. But Lady Trubridge didn't seem to care about the risk to her social position.

"Miss Valentine," she said gravely, and Lola watched in amazement as one of the most influential women in London bowed to her.

"I am very pleased to make your acquaintance," she went on, her voice cutting through the hushed room like the elegant slice of a duelist's sword. "And I should like you to know that I would never forsake Denys." She met Lola's gaze. "Or any other friend."

"None of us would."

By now, Lola was beyond being surprised, so the Duke of Margrave's entrance into the conversation did not rattle her. She looked up, laughing a little as she watched Stuart come forward, moving past Conyers. On Stuart's arm was a tall, slim redhead Lola knew must be his duchess, and together, they moved to her other side, joining the growing, protective wall that surrounded Denys and her.

But the circle was evidently not complete, for Jack glanced around, and when she followed his gaze, Lola spied the stunning blonde who had been on Jack's arm at the flower show. She was standing beside Lady Conyers, but she wasn't moving forward, and Lola's rising hopes stilled, caught in the scrutiny of a pair of stunning blue eyes.

"Linnet?" Jack said. "You're the last, my love."

The woman glanced around, noting the faces looking at her, and then she heaved a sigh. "All right, all right," she said in the unmistakable accent of Knickerbocker New York as she came toward their group. "You win, all of you. I'll accept her. But—"

She halted beside her husband, those magnificent cornflower blue eyes giving Lola a look of unmistakable warning as she took Jack's arm. "But if you so much as wink at my husband, Miss Valentine," she murmured in a low voice, "I'll claw your eyes out."

Jack laughed, flashing Lola a grin. "My lioness," he explained, "is the jealous type."

"Lady Featherstone," Lola said, feeling horribly awkward as she proffered a bow, for it was painfully obvious the other woman knew Jack had once held a torch for her.

"Oh, for heaven's sake," the countess grumbled, and thrust out her hand in the uniquely American fashion. "You'd better get used to calling me Linnet, or we'll never become friends."

Lola looked down at Lady Featherstone's gloved hand, held out to her in friendship, and the countess's slim, bejeweled fingers began to blur before her eyes. Blinking hard, she took that hand in her own and shook it with heartfelt gratitude.

"Linnet," she managed. "It's a pleasure to meet you. All of you," she added. "I'm . . . I'm overwhelmed. I truly am. I—" Her voice broke as she glanced around, looking into the faces of the people who had just put their own social position in jeopardy, and though she wanted to say more, she just couldn't manage it.

Denys came to her rescue. "Now that the introductions have been made," he said, his fingers again capturing hers, "can we return to the matter at hand? I am still down on one knee here, Lola, in case you've forgotten."

She studied him, down on his knee, proposing to her in front of some of the most influential people of British society, and joy rose within her, so much joy, she thought her heart would burst in her chest. "You did this," she choked. "All of this."

"I did."

"Oh, Denys," Lady Conyers wailed from across the room. "How could you?"

She burst into tears, but Denys ignored her.

"I had to show you that you are not alone in this, my darling. Others may cast us out or refuse to receive us, but my friends—our friends—won't."

But Lola could hear his mother sobbing quietly nearby. "Are you sure?" she choked. "Are you absolutely sure? I couldn't bear it if you ever came to regret marrying me."

"I'll never regret it." He paused, taking her other hand. "I love you, Charlotte Valinsky. So, are you going to marry me, or not?"

There it went, the last shred of her control. Tears welled up, and to her mortification, she started to cry.

Denys's brows drew together in a little frown of doubt. "Was that a yes?" he asked. "I'm not quite sure—"

"Yes!" she sobbed. "Yes. I'll marry you, Denys. I'll marry you."

"Finally," he said with relief, and rose. "You made me wait long enough, Lola, really."

"This cannot stand," the earl said. "I'll disinherit you. You'll no longer be involved in any investments of our family. You won't have a farthing to support this woman."

"But I will, Father." His fingers entwined with hers as he turned to look at his father. "I have the brewery with Nick, and I have Arcady. You've no stake in either of those. They are solely mine. Oh, yes, and the Imperial, of course."

"I sold my share of the Imperial to Lord Barringer yesterday."

"So you did. But Barringer sold his share to me this afternoon."

"To you?"

"Yes. I made the purchase out of my private funds. For his part, Barringer was quite pleased to make a profit of two thousand pounds and walk away, especially when I told him Lola would never sell him her share, no matter how much he offered. I hope you don't mind that I spoke for you, darling," he added to her, "but I decided to take the chance that as partners go, you'd prefer me to Barringer."

"I don't mind," she murmured. "So we'll still manage it together?"

"Of course." He lifted her hand and pressed a kiss to her glove. "We're partners, remember?"

Conyers muttered an oath. "You are determined to do this, then?" he asked.

"I am, Father."

"I cannot talk you out of it?"

"No."

The earl turned to her, his eyes raking over her. "And you, young woman, have no intention of making him see sense?"

"No, my lord," she answered, and felt Denys squeeze her hand tight.

"I give it up," the earl muttered, lifting his hands in a gesture of exasperated defeat. "Do as you will, both of you, and on your heads be it."

"Do you accept us, then, Father?" Denys asked, as his father turned away. "Will you give us your blessing?"

"Blessing?" The earl stopped. Squaring his shoulders, he turned and looked at them.

"No," he said. "I cannot do so, for I see no blessing in this union. But—" he added, and Lola caught her breath. "I know when I've lost. And if I don't accept this woman, society never will, and if that happens, heaven only knows what the fate of your children will be. Your sons might not be admitted to Oxford." He shuddered as if that was a fate worse than death. "Your daughters might have to marry commoners."

The earl looked at Lola, and though his gaze was still filled with resentment, it did not seem to hold quite the same degree of contempt that it had in her dressing room last night. "God knows you're not the woman I would have chosen for my son, and despite what's happened here tonight, the rest of society will not be welcoming you with open arms."

"Quite right, Conyers," Lady Trubridge said, walking around her husband to take the earl's arm. "But I assure you, I shall be giving the girl a proper and gradual introduction to society once she and Somerton are married, and though it won't be easy, we shall all do what we can. Now," she added, delicately pulling the earl away, "I believe they will begin serving dinner in a moment, so perhaps we should adjourn to the other room?"

She began leading the earl toward the door, beckoning others to follow, but the earl didn't seem quite ready to depart. He paused, giving Lola one last belligerent glare over his shoulder. "You'll give up the acting, miss," he told her. "And do try and produce at least one son so that my imbecile of a nephew doesn't end up with my title."

With that, he walked into the dining room, Lady Trubridge on his arm. The others followed in their wake—Denys's mother with Nick, dabbing her eyes with her handkerchief, Denys's friends and their wives, and ten or twelve other people Lola didn't know at all. But as they went, each person gave her a nod of acknowledgment, telling her that among those in this room at least, she and Denys had support.

Denys's sister came last. "Welcome to the family," she said, giving Lola a smacking kiss on the cheek. "You've no idea what you've let yourself in for."

Lola smiled, liking the girl's sass. "Oh, but I think I do. I've already gone three rounds with your father."

"Papa?" She made a sound of derision. "He's nothing. Wait until you meet Grandmamma."

"Susan," Denys said warningly.

The girl laughed, stood up on her toes, and kissed

her brother's cheek. "Taking on the whole *ton*, Denys? My God, you're brave. Do you have any single friends like you?"

"I'm still single," James pointed out.

"Dearest Pongo," the girl said with obvious affection as she put her arm through his. "You know I adore you," she added as they turned away and started toward the dining room, "but I could never *marry* you. You're like a brother to me."

"Right," he answered hastily. "Of course."

Denys and Lola both laughed, watching them go.

"Poor James," she murmured. "Will he ever find love?"

"Don't worry about Pongo," Denys told her. "He's in love every week."

"Your sister is right about you, you know," Lola murmured as she turned toward him, still feeling rather stunned by all that had just occurred. "You are the bravest man I have ever known."

"My darling," he said, and pulled her into his arms. "I told you before, you're the brave one. And you proved me right, by God. Coming down to face them the way you did."

"I had to do it. You see . . ." She paused to take a deep breath. "When you left this morning, I took a long, hard look at my life, and I knew leaving wasn't the answer. Because I love you."

"And I love you. And love," he told her, bending his head, "is always enough."

He started to kiss her, but then he stopped, his lips an

inch from hers. "By the way, I now expect you to fully admit that I was right and you were wrong."

"About what?"

His arms tightened around her. "Happy endings do sometimes happen."

"I can't deny it." She laughed and wrapped her arms around his neck. "After all, you are definitely my knight in shining armor."

"Damned straight," he murmured, and bent his head toward hers. "And you shall be my viscountess, my wife, the mother of my children, and the love of my life until the end of my days."

"And society?"

"If society doesn't like it, society can lump it."

"Now that," she said, and kissed him, "is the best happy ending I've ever heard."

Acknowledgments

Some books need lots of research. Fortunately, an author can always find generous, enthusiastic people willing to help. For this book, I had two experienced actresses to help me with all things theater.

First, my thanks to professional actress Traci Lyn Thomas, who answered all my pesky little questions about auditions, rehearsals, and performance, and who explained to me in depth just what the differences are between producers, backers, and directors.

My thanks also to local artist and actress Bonnie Peacher for reading the final manuscript and verifying that I got the acting vibe right.

My heartfelt gratitude to both of you.